# Coming Home

## The Baycliff Valley Series: Book Two

H K Brown

# Content warning

*Coming Home* is a closed-door, second-chance, age-gap romance. It is friends to lovers with a surprise pregnancy. *Coming Home* will push boundaries while fading to black when it threatens to get spicy. It's perfect for those who want the emotional roller coaster while limiting the steam.

Please note that *Coming Home* contains content that may be sensitive to some readers. Some scenes include the mention of foster care, parental neglect and abuse, abandonment, the death of parents, and a panic attack.

*Happy reading*

# Prologue

I step past the threshold of the Smirking Tree Saloon in downtown Oklahoma City. This modernized country and Western bar is a favorite amongst my friends. It has a bucking bronco and live country music—and lacks the tacky bits. The last Western bar I went to had saddle seats and horns everywhere. There, the servers wore skintight, open-front plaid shirts, booty shorts, and boots; the servers here are in tasteful clothes—jeans, a bar-branded T-shirt, and a half apron.

I catch sight of my best friend, Megan, across the dance floor. She stands out in any crowd at five foot nine, with long, silky black hair, a slender body with curves in all the right places, and an eye color that changes with her mood.

Megan's ever-changing eye color has become her signature in our line of work of high-fashion modeling.

"Kayla!" Meg shouts, as she heads my way. "Let's get our dance on. I can't stay long."

I look over my shoulder at Mike—my other best friend, longtime crush, and sister's ex—and Leah, my sister, who I've dragged out with me tonight. In most cases, I'd never imagine being with someone my sister dated, but Mike and Leah went out twice—they never even kissed. It was just too weird for them, but they did create a long-lasting friendship. Plus, I think Leah knows how I feel—maybe. I haven't told her, but she does keep trying to push us together.

My plan for tonight was to help pull Leah out of her head, seeing as the anniversary of her mistaken-identity case—the one that resulted in her falling down the stairs—is coming up soon. On the walk over here, I ran across the one man who could possibly pull her out of this funk—Cam—so when I decide to join Meg rather than Leah, I don't feel too bad about abandoning her. She won't be bored for long—she just doesn't know it yet.

I shrug. "Lead the way," I reply.

Leah waves me off as Meg takes my hand and tugs me away. She and Mike head off in the other direction. By the time we get onto the dance floor and start swaying our hips to the music, Meg draws me in enough to be heard and starts in on me.

"Have you told Mike how you feel yet?"

"No, and I don't think I'm going to. I told you: I can't chance losing him over a stupid crush that I can't shake. Besides, I'm moving soon, remember? I'm finally going to put him behind me and move on. Isn't that why we decided I'd accept the new contract?"

About a month ago, Patty, my current agent, was contacted by an agency in New York about buying out my contract. At first, I wanted nothing to do with it, but seeing as I can't shake this crush, I accepted. Mike is the man of my dreams, but he barely notices me. I need to take this time and get over him. Living a life without everyone I know nearby is going to be hard, but coming home when my contract is up and being able to finally move on will be worth it.

"It is, but I think we were too hasty when we talked about it," she pleads. "Don't you want to know how he feels before you go? Think, Kay. If you leave and never tell him, when you come home, you could find him with someone else. How would that make you feel?"

My heart stops. Coming home to find Mike with another woman would be torture. I don't know if I'd be able to stick around and watch him love someone else while he still holds my heart.

But that's what I'm working on.

"I'm leaving to get over him. If it works, it shouldn't bother me."

She stops dancing and grabs both of my arms, causing me to look at her. "You're just scared, Kay. Nothing in life is easy. The worst he can say is that he's not interested, but what if . . . what if he *is*? The two of you are meant to be." She raises her brow in challenge. "Don't live with regrets."

"I already regret not telling him. How exactly do you tell one of your closest friends that you're secretly in love with them without blowing up the friendship?"

Mike walks over, joining us on the dance floor, halting our conversation. When he smiles at me, it does things to my stomach that I'd rather not admit. I know what I need to do now. How I'll do it, that's another question.

Three songs in and we're having a blast. Mike isn't much of a dancer, but when he lets loose, I get lost at the sight. He really is stunning when he isn't being so guarded.

Since the band left the stage, the bar is playing a bunch of different singers playing over the loudspeakers. "Wanted" by Hunter Hayes comes on, and I know immediately that I need to sit this one out. This song speaks so loudly of what Mike and I have that I need to step away. I can't let these feelings show until I know how he feels.

But Mike has other plans.

He pulls my back to his front and starts swaying as he leans his head into the crook of my neck. Moments like this are when I can truly forget that we're just friends. These are the times when I feel like there could be more. He's not like this with others . . . just me.

When I open my eyes, I know I've been caught enjoying the moment a little too much. Meg smiles knowingly but I can't help getting lost in the feeling of his arms wrapped around me and his body pressed up against mine. It feels like coming home.

Meg touches my arm, causing me to stop and look at her. "I gotta get. Sadie's home on break. I promised I'd only be gone a few hours." Sadie is her baby sister, the one she's had to raise on her own since her parents split. Her grandparents did the best they could, but by the time Meg turned eighteen, one had passed and the other was in a nursing home, leaving her the sole caregiver.

"Give her my love, will you?" I leave Mike's embrace long enough to lean in and kiss her cheek. I feel bad for her and the lack of a life outside of her sister, but I'd have done the same thing if the roles were reversed with Leah and me.

"Will do—and remember what I said. No regrets." She pulls back and looks up at Mike. "Take care of her, will ya?"

"Always." Mike leans down and kisses her cheek before moving back behind me.

"Love ya, girl."

"Love you too," she echoes. "I'll be up late tonight. Let me know how it goes."

I nod, confirming that I heard her.

Once she's gone, Mike and I dance for a while longer before I need a rest. We make our way to the table that Leah now shares with Cam, the first responder who found her after her fall last year—also the one man who can pull her out of her funk. Then, they hit it off right away and, now can possibly make something of this if they let themselves.

I plop down next to Leah, stretching out a bit, then lean back into Mike's embrace as he sits behind me. I love how he holds me. I'd be happy in his arms for the rest of my life if he let me. As I cuddle in further, Mike kisses the top of my head and puts his arm around me, hugging me to him. I better enjoy this while I can—there's no telling how he'll react when I tell him.

*If* I tell him.

"Hot Cop's back, huh? We good here?" I ask.

"Yeah, he's back," Leah huffs.

The four of us chat a bit before I zone out, conversation around me carrying on. Will I be able to get Mike alone tonight? As much as I love my sister, I wish she wasn't with us right now. I really need to tell him before I chicken out.

"Last call!" the server hollers.

We take that as our cue to leave. Leah decides to catch a ride with Cam, and Mike agrees to walk with me along the canal route home, granting me the time I've been wishing for.

Bricktown Canal is one of my favorite places in OKC, especially at night, if someone is with me. The businesses along the canal are full of people all day long, but at night, all the lights are on and the walk is quiet. The glow bounces off the water and gives the night a romantic feel. This is the perfect opportunity to tell Mike—I just hope I can do it.

"You're quiet tonight," he says, nudging me.

"I'm sorry. I just have a lot on my mind."

He wraps an arm around my shoulder and pulls me to his side, "I don't think I've ever known you to be this quiet before. Care to share?"

"No, thanks though." I know I need to talk to him; I just can't get myself to do it. Normally, I talk a mile a minute around him. I love talking to Mike, but tonight, I can't get myself to relax.

Just past our go-to coffee shop, I stop walking and turn to him, looking him head-on. *Take the bull by the horns, Kayla*, I hear Meg say. I shake my hands out and bounce my shoulders a little as I try to work the nerves from my body.

Mike rubs his hands up and down my arms before bending just enough to look me square in the eyes. "Kay, what's going on? You look like you're gearing up for a fight."

"Aw, the heck with it." I grab his face in my hands and lock our lips before I can second-guess myself. Not how I planned this, but it'll have to do. I can't get the words out.

The moment his lips touch mine, a current of energy flows through me, making me feel like I'm floating. I can't help but let loose a little moan. His whole body tenses briefly before he growls and pulls me into him, pressing us together as he deepens our kiss, taking my breath away. When his mouth opens over mine the slightest bit, giving me the first taste of the man I love, I'm lost.

How have I lived all my life without this?

He pulls back an inch and I can taste a hint of beer and mint left behind on my lips. I bite my lower lip and wait for his response, but when it doesn't come, I glance up at him, lifting my head a fraction. Hope flows through my body as I beg him with my eyes to let this moment be something he won't regret. The moment our eyes lock, Mike's hand on my lower back tightens and the other finds its way to the base of my neck. I wrap my arms behind him, pulling us closer together, drawing a growl from his chest. He lowers his head to nibble on my ear before kissing me just behind it.

When he stands to his full height, I'm ready to fall over, but the moment his eyes lower to my lips once more, I know I'll find the strength to stand if he kisses me again. I can hardly believe this is happening! Mike's hand in my hair tightens, bringing me to him once more. I could get lost in his kiss but the need for air is too strong to ignore. I pull back and look deeply into his eyes, trying to gauge his thoughts, but am interrupted by some loud people passing by.

Mike lets me go and takes a step back as I turn just enough to notice three rowdy men passing us.

"Kayla, is that you?" one asks.

Frustrated, I sigh and notice that he's someone I met a few weeks back at one of my photo shoots. His eyes move from me to Mike, who's now pacing while running a hand through his hair a few feet away.

"Tad, right?" I put a hand on my hip, hoping that he'll get the idea that I'm not pleased with his interruption and go away.

"Yeah, I thought I recognized you. How've you been?"

"Fine, but hey, I'm kind of in the middle of something here." *Or I was, before you interrupted.*

"Oh . . . yeah. Sorry about that." He looks at his friends, then back at me. "Would you maybe want to get drinks with me sometime?"

Who does that? I know he knows what Mike and I were just up to, and he still has the gall to ask me?

"No, thanks. I'm not interested."

He looks over my shoulder in Mike's direction and nods. "Sure, sure. Sorry to bother you. Nice seeing you again."

"You, too, Tad."

I watch them walk away, then turn back to Mike. Even in the dark, this man is a thing of beauty. He and I are opposite on so many levels, except our height. Mike is six foot three, with jet-black hair, slicked back and shorter on the sides. He has bottle-green eyes and caramel-colored skin and is a wall of muscles due to his days as an MMA heavyweight champ. His skin is covered in art that I'd love to learn one day. In contrast, I'm just over six feet tall with sandy blonde hair, Tiffany-blue eyes, and a frame like a number-two pencil. If I'm in the sun too long, I burn—I'm talking lobster red. The one thing I have going for me is my practiced confidence. It comes in handy in my line of work.

Mike runs his hands through his hair again. His nervous tic—this is not a good sign.

I take a step in his direction.

"No. Don't. What I did back there . . ." Mike starts.

"Don't say it. I don't regret a thing. I'm the one who kissed you, remember?" I'm also the one whose heart is ready to break. "Mike."

He stops me, and I brace myself for what's bound to come.

"Don't say it, Kay. Please," he begs.

How does he know what I was going to say? But the look in his eyes tells me that he knows. Even though I don't regret what happened, he does, and he doesn't quite know how to handle it yet.

While he paces, trying to gather his thoughts, I walk over to the canal and take a seat on a nearby bench, putting my head in my hands. If only Tad hadn't come when he did, things could be so different. Who am I kidding? Mike would still be Mike. He loves me like a friend, but never more. Sure, he kissed me—what hot-blooded man wouldn't if a woman threw herself at him like I did? At times, I've questioned in what way he likes me. Though this failed attempt at a kiss lets me know I fit squarely in the friend zone.

He walks over after a minute to join me, and before he has a chance to let me down, I start. "I'm sorry. I shouldn't have thrown myself at you like that. I know you don't think of me that way, but I had to be sure before I leave."

Mike places a hand on my knee, and I stay still not to spook him. "I'm not sorry that you kissed me, Kay. I enjoyed it."

Shocked, I turn ever so slightly to give him my full attention.

"If things were different, I'd be overjoyed right now, but I can't let myself go there. Your life is just starting out. I've got eight years on you, beautiful. You deserve so much better than the likes of me."

Eight years isn't that much older. He's thirty-two—it's not like he's old enough to be my dad or anything.

"Mike—" I start, but he stops me, *again*.

"My mind is made up. I want better for you in life than being with someone like me. You're the one thing that I won't allow myself to corrupt."

Mike grew up in a group home after his mom allowed her boy toy of the month to beat him. He had to fight for everything he had. After retiring from the MMA due to a knee injury, he got a job at Uncle Joe's—my uncle's restaurant—and has worked there ever since.

"Kay, you, Damon, Leah, and Joe are the only people in my life that I know won't leave me. If I give us a go and screw it up, I'd have nobody. I'd be alone in this world again. I can't do that. I'm sorry."

"I get it."

Losing my parents at an early age due to a horrific accident, I can understand the importance of having a few people that you'd go down for. I'd rather have him in my life as a friend than lose him altogether. Picturing life without Mike in it—him no longer holding me, kissing my head the way he does—brings tears to my eyes. How will I ever be able to move on from this man? He has my heart and I doubt I'll ever get it back.

Moving to New York just became a must. It can't come soon enough.

# Chapter One

I TUCK MY BAG in the locker and put my phone back to my ear. It's been two months since I confessed my feelings to Michael. A lot can happen in that amount of time—and my stay here in Oklahoma is ticking away. Before I know it, I'll be a New Yorker. My agent loves to remind me of that. I've been on call with her for the last fifteen minutes. I listen to her prater away, her words sounding more like those of a momma hen than an agent.

"Yes, Patty," I reply. "I'm sure I can leave in January. No, I won't need more time than that. It should be plenty of time to get things squared away." I open the door to the locker room and start making my way down the long hall toward the front.

"Okay then, I'll take your word for it." I hear her door open and Tab, her secretary, tells her that her next appointment is there. There are some muffled words and then she's back. "Just so you know, I'm still contractually obligated to work you until October, so you need to stay in tip-top shape. Remember your schedule."

I roll my eyes. The schedule is so ingrained in me by now that I could follow it in my sleep. "Yes, Patty, I know. Gym first thing in the morning, no sugar whatsoever, no . . ." I carry on repeating her strict diet plan—that I rarely stick to—and down-to-the-wire schedule for me during the day before saying goodbye. Had I known that Patty was more of a strict meddler than a regular agent, I would've never signed with her straight out of high school. She's gone as far as ordering some of her girls to get a tummy tuck or boob job. Thus far, she hasn't done anything of the sort with me, but she has no issue telling me how she feels if I put on so much as half a pound.

That's why today's outing has me hitting the gym extra hard. Patty would *not* approve. An extra mile should cover the movie popcorn I'll be indulging in tonight. I get on the treadmill, put in an earbud, and start slowly while working my way up to a steady run. I lose myself in a new audiobook while I glance at the weather on the TV ahead.

*Bill moves with determination as he crosses the bar to Genevieve, the love of his life, the one woman who can make everything come to a crashing halt. Sidestepping all others in his way, he's determined to make her his in all the ways that matter. Finally,* he thinks, *as he reaches her side.* "You are a hard woman to track down."

*She smiles and looks up at him through her lashes.* "What are you going to do about it now that you've found me?"

"*I'm going to make you mine, just like I should have done all those months ago.*" *He looks deep in her eyes, loops a hand around the back of her neck, and—*

"Looking good, girl."

I startle and nearly lose my footing. Seeing that it's Gunnar, I swat his arm. "You scared the heck out of me." I pause my book, pull out my earbud, and take my speed down to a slow jog. "You're here early."

Gunnar and I went out on a date nearly a year ago after he'd crushed on me for two. There was no spark, and no matter how much he hates it, he admitted it himself. We're good friends now, and he's my favorite running buddy.

"I wanted to see you." He winks, then matches my speed on his treadmill and starts again. "Are you still planning on moving away?"

"Yeah. I'll be signing my contract with them next year." I look down at the pedometer and see that I've been running longer than I thought. That's what a good book will do—I lost track of time.

"Are you sure you need to move? I'm gonna miss you."

"What am I, chopped liver?" Megan asks as she hops onto a treadmill on the other side of me. She and I normally work out together, as long as our schedule allows. "She's leaving me too."

I flinch. "I'm not leaving either of you. It's just that I'm trying to get my life together, that's all. I'll be back before you know it." I slow to a walk and dry myself off with my towel. "I'll miss everyone, but it's for the best. Besides, there's this thing called a plane, you know, and if you can't do that, we can always video call."

Gunnar smiles at that. "You would take the call?"

"Of course I would. You're like the annoying little brother I never had." I smirk, then stop my treadmill and walk over to the weight machines.

By the time I'm done, my legs and arms are burning. Thank God I'm off today. I wish I could take the day off from the gym too. That'll never happen. I grab my things and head in the direction of the showers. As I'm walking past the men's locker room, the door opens and out walks Michael and Damon, nearly bumping into me.

Mike smiles and takes me in. "Work hard today?"

"I did," I reply as I let Xena—the gym's manager—pass. "Patty made sure to remind me of my obligations to my form. An extra hard workout this morning and a water diet all day means you guys better be ready to deliver a big bucket of popcorn tonight."

Damon leans against the doorjamb and smiles.

"I see nothing wrong with your form," Michael says under his breath, looking me up and down. "You shouldn't have to starve yourself so you can have some popcorn."

"I'm not starving myself. I did just say I'm going to eat a big bucket of popcorn tonight, didn't I?" I raise my brow in a challenge as Damon smirks. I love sassing Michael.

A man trying to leave the locker room clears his throat behind the guys, and Damon steps to the side, but Michael steps forward, crowding me. *How is this not being interested?* He's so close, I can smell the mint of his toothpaste.

"Maybe we should have dinner and a movie," Michael says. "Sound good to you, D?"

Damon laughs behind him. "If Megan's on board, it sounds like a date to me."

"No date," Michael retorts. "Just four friends out for a night on the town." He takes a step back, clearing that heavy look from his eyes.

Damon pats him on the shoulder, laughing as he steps around him and heads toward the gym. "If you say so, man . . . if you say so."

Damon now gone, I'm left alone with Michael, feeling like a caged cat. I want to climb him like a tree and seal my lips to his, but I know that won't happen again.

My shoulders drop and I feel deflated at that realization. This is why I need to leave. Staying here, having these kinds of run-ins, does me no good. It'll drive me crazy if I let it.

I step around Mike, patting his arm and heading toward the showers. "See you tonight." Without so much as looking his way for a reaction, I head to the locker room, shutting him out and fighting to steady my racing heart.

I grab a handful of popcorn and shovel it into my mouth. The guys made good on their promise—I'm in heaven right now. I couldn't care less that they chose a scary movie this time—their turn because the last time was mine and Megan's.

All day, I've tried to get Mike out of my mind, but it hasn't worked. No matter how hard I try to mute my feelings for Michael, while I'm here, that just isn't happening. He's too good to me, too affectionate. It's been the norm for our friendship, so it would be weird to change now. People would know something was up.

I tried dating someone last month but found myself comparing him to Mike the whole time. What is wrong with me? He was a perfectly normal, nice guy, but he wasn't Mike. How will I ever be able to move on when this is what I have to compare it to?

"You good?" Michael asks.

"Mmm," I hum.

Meg leans in to steal Damon's nachos. Those two dated some time ago, and at the time, he wasn't ready to settle down. He was honest with her and called things quits while he focused on building his business. She focused on Sadie.

Before coming here, we stopped by his office, where he had an arm around her the whole time. Because he works with a bunch of big, burly men every day, I guess it makes sense. He doesn't want to share—D's playing for keeps.

I snuggle in a little further and grab a handful of popcorn from our shared bucket, bumping knuckles with Michael as I do. The current shoots through my hand, and I pull back before I can think better of it.

Megan grabs my other hand and squeezes before she leans in to me. I do the same. "Come with me?"

"Sure."

We stand and head to the restroom.

She opens every stall to make sure that we're alone. "He's smooth, you know."

"Which one?" I chuckle.

"Damon!" She throws her hands up in defeat. "He knows what he's doing. Why can't he just accept that this little flirtation we have can't go anywhere?"

I put my hands on either side of her arms and look into her eyes. "What'd he do?"

"What hasn't he done? He's driving me crazy!" I chuckle, which only makes her shake me off and start pacing the bathroom floor.

"Come on, Megie. You know he's head over heels for you."

Her eyes get big and she stops walking. "He is *not*. Damon's just a big flirt is all. Why do you think I can't be with him? I can't go there again, Kay. I will *not* let him hurt me again."

I turn and wash my hands from all the greasy popcorn. "Then tell him. Let him know that you can't go there right now. Be honest with him. But know that you run the risk of him moving on."

A woman walks in and spots Megan as she starts pacing again. The woman stops and looks between us, then turns back around, leaving us in peace.

"I can tell him. But . . ." Megan shakes her head. "No. I'll tell him I can't go there again. I can't let myself want more from him than he's willing to give. It was hard enough the first time."

Before I have the chance to say anything in response, she turns to the door, whips it open, and storms back toward the theater.

As I sit down, Michael puts his arm on the back of my chair. I lean in closer but not into him. It's already hard enough. I need to try to keep my wits about me—that is until a dang clown starts running down the street after a kid and then someone jumps up behind him, and . . . never mind. Michael's chest is so much more interesting than what's on the big screen. I muffle the scream I nearly let out in his embrace. Mike laughs but wraps his arm around me nevertheless, running his hand through my hair. I am *not* a fan of scary movies, but I can get on board with this.

A minute or two later, he pats me on my back. "It's okay now. You can look."

I don't know why the guys insist on watching horror movies with us when they know we get scared so easily. I'm sure it has to do with the fact that we cuddle in, but then again, if Michael wants nothing to do with me that way, then why? Why do everything a boyfriend would do with me except having the title and the privilege to kiss me whenever he wants? Ugh, it's so confusing.

I plop the drink back in the cupholder and put my head on Meg's shoulder. She pats my cheek and stays there with me for the rest of the movie.

After it lets out, the four of us take a walk down the canal, enjoying the night's breeze. This really is a beautiful place.

"I sure am going to miss all this."

"Then why go?" Damon asks. "I know how much you love it here, plus you have all of us. Why leave? The new contract can't be *that* good, can it?"

"It's something I need to do," I say, being as honest as I can with them without putting the blame elsewhere. "I know I'm young, but I want to find a man to settle down with, buy a home, and start a family eventually. Being here is fun, but everyone sees me as fun Kayla, Leah's little sister, or thinks that I'm too young to be taken seriously. Guys my age want the one thing I'm not interested in sharing. I know I have the image of a party-girl model who likes to have fun. I've been linked to dating around, but you guys know me. Sure, I dated a lot in school, but I think most of us did. I just want to pull my life together, I guess. Out there, nobody knows me. I can be who I want to be and not have anyone thinking otherwise." Plus, I need to let my heart move on. I don't say that out loud, though. If Michael wanted a chance with me, I'd stay in a heartbeat. I could change here, no problem. Moving away just gives me the distance I crave.

"It sounds like you've thought it through," Damon replies. "I hope you find what you're looking for."

We end up taking a water taxi, then walking some more before getting a late dinner on a balcony overlooking the canal. Grilled chicken salad is on the menu since I splurged at the theater, but the minute I see Michael's steak, I wish I could have a bite. He looks at me in question, and I shake it off and point to my salad. Yum. Nothing like rabbit food to please the boss. Thankfully, it's not too bad.

"So," Meg starts, "it won't be long before our Vegas trip will be upon us." Every October for the last four years, the four of us have made this trip together. It's been fun.

"It will," Damon replies. "This one's on me."

"I can't ask you to do that," I state. Vegas isn't the cheapest trip. I'd feel bad if he paid.

"You're not asking," he replies. "The business is doing well, and I want to treat my *friends*. So let me."

Mike nods in thanks. "I'm happy for you, man.

"Thanks, brother." Mike and Damon aren't biological brothers, but they might as well be. Both grew up in foster care and group homes. They were together so long that they became inseparable, just like any brother can be.

"Since you're splurging, does that mean we can finally stay at the Bellagio?" Megan teases.

"As you wish," he replies.

A warm shade of pink rises on Megan's cheeks. She looks back down at her plate. "I was teasing, Dame."

"I'm not. If that's what your heart desires, I'll make it happen." He clears his throat when Megan looks up into his eyes as if she has stars in them. Then, looking over at Mike as if he's not affected by her, he asks, "Can you pass the butter, please?"

Michael smiles and does as he asks.

Looking at the shock on Meg's face, I can only smile. Oh yeah, Damon is definitely playing for keeps.

# Chapter Two

I LOOK OVER AT Janet and smile. She and Uncle Joe have been dating for some time now. I love knowing that now that Leah and I won't be around as much, he'll at least have her. The two of us are in the kitchen gathering more beer and snacks while Leah plays referee. Tonight, we are having family game night—Cam and Mike included. Just before we got up to come in here, Mike called Uncle Joe old—well, "old man," to be exact—in teasing. Ever since then, Uncle Joe has been

on one, trying to prove that he can still hold his own.

"I swear that man can't face the fact that he's no spring chicken anymore," Janet teases.

"I heard that." Uncle Joe's voice carries in from the dining room. "You're supposed to be on my side, woman."

She looks over to me and winks as we load our arms and head back to the others. "I'm always on your side, Joey baby." She leans down giving him a quick kiss. "That doesn't mean that I can't admit that were both getting older."

He smiles at her mischievously and pops her on the butt. These two are so in love with one another, they have to constantly be touching. I'm beyond thrilled for them. To have Janet here with us fills a bit of a void that I've had all my life. Every girl needs her mom, and even though Janet isn't mine, she has stepped into the role nicely.

"Alright, you two," I say, passing Mike a beer, then handing a couple to Leah and Cam. "None of that lovey dovey stuff in front of the kids."

I sit down at the table and grab my cards—all I need is two sevens and then I can phase. Phase 10 is one of my favorite games. It's always fun, considering how competitive we all are.

"What kids?" Uncle Joe asks challengingly.

Janet shakes her head and hands him some snack mix.

I look over at Leah, who is laying back on Cam, not a care in the world if he can see her cards. Then I turn toward Mike. He, much like me, is focused on the game at hand. I feel out of sorts tonight. Sitting here watching everyone in love hurts. After this is over, I think a nice long soak in the tub and a face mask are in order. I need time to decompress. I haven't had much time to myself lately, and since I leave for a week to go to New York with Mike in the morning, I don't have much time for that. If any thing, going to New York with him will be more tortuous than it is sitting around this table watching everyone else fall in love.

I chance one more look at Mike and huff, the sit up to take my turn. I pick up a seven and discard a four. Only one more card and I can phase.

"What are y'all up to after this?" Janet asks.

"I'm going back out to the farm with Cam," Leah says, smiling my way.

"I'm going home to soak in the tub for a while, then I might turn in early," I add.

Uncle Joe looks over at me. "I figured you'd be staying with Mike since y'all fly out in the morning. You can always stay in your old room so that you're not alone. I'm sure he wouldn't mind picking you up here."

The thought of staying in my old room is depressing. "Thanks, but no. I'd like to have a quiet night in. I'll be fine."

"Alright, but the offer still stands," he replies.

I draw a wild card and lay down my phase, winning the game—my first time in nearly a year. I get up and do a quick victory dance before saying my goodbyes. While Mike is in the restroom, I sneak out. I know him well enough to know that he'll try to walk me home, and I really just want to be alone right now.

It's hotter than H-E-double-hockey-sticks out here.

This late in August, the heat of the day has every Okie wondering why we stay and don't make our way to a tropical location for a while. By eight in the evening, it has cooled just enough that people are finally out walking around or cutting their lawns. Even though the heat is still unbearable, it's better than the hundred-plus-degree humi heat of the day. At least the sun has started to go down.

I stop in the coffee shop—it stays open late due to the prime touristy location—and take a deep breath as the cool air hits my skin. I grab a cool strawberry refresher, then head back out.

I can't help but take in the canal as the glow of the lights bounce off the water. I'm really going to miss all of this when I move. It'll be hard enough leaving, but thinking about leaving Leah has me second-guessing. I don't know how I'm supposed to leave her, especially now that her stalker has taken things to the next level. He or she has made themselves a little more known as of late, leaving little trinkets and such lying around for us to find. With everything going on, the guys don't seem to be too far from us at any given time—always our protectors. Though since the stalker isn't after me, I have a bit more freedom than Leah does.

My phone starts ringing as I cross the street to my apartment.

"Hello?" I answer. I smile at an older lady and her daughter as they step off the curb, and I wait for them to pass before I step up.

"Hey, beautiful," Michael replies. "Have you made it home yet?"

"Walking in now. You can quit worrying." I walk up the stairs briskly, ready for the air conditioning. I make it to my landing in no time and slip the key from my pocket. I look around just to make sure nobody is standing in the stairwell that shouldn't be and let myself in. "I'm inside and locking the door behind me." I toss my keys on the counter and step out of my shoes.

"I'll always worry about you, Kay. Did you check the windows and make sure they're locked?"

I want to laugh at his protective streak, but considering that Leah has someone after her right now, I don't."No,

Dad, I haven't. I just got in. Doing that now." I walk into Leah's room and get started. Knowing that I'll be alone tonight, I want to make sure the apartment is all locked up.

"I'll wait."

"I'm a big girl. I got this."

I hear a beep on my phone and pull it away to see Mike requesting to switch the callto video. I swap over and find him leaving Uncle Joe's. I smile, then turn the camera so he can see the house rather than me.

"I'm sure you do, but I need to make sure too. Do a walk -through while I'm with you. I want to see all is well before I get off the phone."

I do as he says, but the more I move around, the more nervous I get until I regret not letting him come with me.

"You're freaking me out a little. Do you really think it's not safe for me to be here?" I grab the bat from beside Leah's bed and move around her room, showing Mike every nook and cranny.

"I don't know, Kay, but since you snuck out like that, the least I can do is check the house with you." He sounds a bit frustrated.

Maybe I shouldn't have been so childish. There *is* someone stalking my sister, after all.

Ten minutes later, I get the all clear. All windows and doors are locked up and nothing seems to be out of place. But now I'm a bit of a wreck. I walk into my room and look around, not sure of what to do next.

Michael stops walking and takes a moment before speaking. "Are you okay? Your hand seems to be shaking."

"I'm fine, just a little paranoid after all that. Maybe I should go stay with Meg." Even I can hear the tremble in my voice. I'm not fooling anyone. If I have to go through all of that just to make sure I'm safe, am I really?

"I can come and sleep on the couch again. Sadie's in town and you know how Meg is when she's here."

"No visitors," we both say at the same time.

I set the phone down on my dresser and pull out a shirt I stole from Michael a while back. It's one of my favorite things to sleep in. Stepping back so that he can't see me, I change out of my clothes and into his shirt—*my* shirt now—then make my way to the bathroom to wash my face, phone in hand again.

"I don't want you to have to come all this way just for me." Even though I say the right words, everything in me is screaming for him to come stay. "I'll have to get used to being on my own soon enough. Once I move, I can't just have you hop on a plane every time I get scared." The thought terrifies me. I don't remember a time when Michael wasn't there for me. It's not something I'm looking forward to, but I know for me to move on, it's something I have to learn to accept.

*But do I have to accept it right now?*

"You're not asking. I'm telling. I'm on my way."

I pull my soapy face back from the sink, squinting an eye to look at the screen. Sure enough, he's walking past the coffee shop now.

"Michael, I told you I need to learn to be on my own," I say defiantly. As much as I want him here, I also know that I need to try to close that door. He doesn't want this. I have to put some distance between us.

He looks at the screen for a second, then back at the sidewalk in front of him. "You will—when you move. But right now, I'm on my way." He unlocks and opens the door to my apartment building and starts up the stairs. "Soon, we'll go and find you an apartment in New York. I'll check out their security and leave my number in case anything happens. You'll be fine. I'm sure of it. Now come let me in, will you?"

I dry off my face and head toward the door, my heart humming in delight that he came. Knowing that Mike's on the other side, I don't bother looking through the peephole. I fling it open and fight the urge to throw myself at him.

When he sees me, he takes me in from head to toe, causing the corner of his mouth to twitch a tiny fraction. "That's where my shirt went. I've been looking for it."

I chuckle. "It's mine now. You left it here about a month ago and it's so comfortable, I couldn't stand to give it back." I step aside and let him in, locking up behind him.

Mike goes to the fridge and grabs a couple of waters—one for him and one for me—before moving to the living room to set up the hide-a-bed. I watch him move around the place like he owns it and notice something—I'm not nervous anymore. He makes me feel safe. When Michael walked in, all my fear of being alone went out the window.

"Let's get some sleep, shall we? Not all of us can nap on planes."

One flight and two days later, I look up at a four-story brick building—which is not much different from my place in Oklahoma—and feel like this could be it. Michael and I have looked at more than a dozen apartments that either are too small—like closet small—or have poor security. This one looks promising, though.

"Shall we?" He waves me in once the door is buzzed open.

"We shall." I duck and brush past him on the way in. I step into a nice-looking foyer. On the wall to the right, I see a line of mailboxes and a desk with a lady sitting behind it in a security shirt.

"That's a plus," Mike says.

"No kidding." It's nothing fancy, but the security is a nice touch. "They said the second-floor staircase is on the left." I walk past the bench and potted plants and find the stairs.

A man about my age takes the last step, smiles at me, and then makes his way out. There's an elevator, but seeing how I currently live in a three-story walk-up, I don't have a problem walking up one flight.

"Ms. Covington?" a young man asks as soon as we make it to the second-floor landing.

"Yes. That's me. You must be Jackson." The building super. The manager had something to do today so Jackson is showing us an apartment that's currently available.

He opens the door and steps back out, letting Michael and me in to look around. The apartment kind of reminds me of the hotel we're staying in right now, except that it has a small living area and kitchen that our room doesn't have. Not what I'm used to, but it does have all the necessities and a small island. Luckily, this place comes furnished. I might need to stop and get a few things, like curtains and lamps, just to make it home for the time being, but it'll work—except for the awful maroon carpet, but I'll manage.

Mike saw all he needed and is now on his way downstairs to talk to the security lady. I take one more quick look at the bathroom then seek out Jackson. I find him just beyond the front door. "I'll take it."

Jackson looks up from the keys he's been fiddling with and smiles upon my approach. "I don't normally do this, so forgive my to-the-point ways. Utilities, internet, and basic cable are included in the rent. There's no phone service, and no pets allowed without a fee."

We go over where I can find the trash chute, then make our way to his place so I can fill out an application and leave my security deposit. By the time I find my way back to Michael, he's sitting on the bench, looking a little upset.

"Why would you go with him and not get me? Anything

could have happened. You don't even know the guy."

I put my hand on my hip. "Michael, this is a secure building. He'll be around me a lot, so if I couldn't trust him now, how can I live here? Everything is fine."

"So you rented this place, huh? It's really happening." He looks down at his feet for a moment before he stands up and puts an arm around my shoulder. "Okay, then. How about we check out your new zip code? We can get some lunch and maybe do a little shopping. I promised Leah a souvenir."

We exit the apartment building and go in search of something to eat, finding a little pizzeria around the corner. We get our order and find a small bistro table at the back of the shop. It's quiet this late in the afternoon, but I can only imagine that during lunch, this place is packed. And as a bonus—the pizza is amazing.

"Thank you for coming out here with me. You didn't have to."

He finishes the bite in his mouth before taking my hand in his and smiles. "I know I didn't, but I want to spend as much time with you as I can before you leave. I'm going to miss you, Kay."

"I'm going to miss you too, Micheal." *More than you'll ever know.*

Mike looks over my shoulder and nods. He looks con-flicted. "Seven years huh?"

I nod. "Once I sign that contract in January, I'm oblig-ated. Yes." Mike's hand tightens just the slightest. "I can always back out until then, but . . . once it's signed, I'm stuck." Hint, hint. Just say the words, Micheal. *If you ask me to stay, I would,* I think. I'd love no more than to give up this contract and stay back in Oklahoma with the man I love and the only family I have ever known.

Mike faces me once more. His mouth opens before he stops himself. He looks down at our hands before with-drawing his, then looks up, smiling in a friendly manner. "Well then, I guess we should toast to frequent flyer miles," he lifts his drink to cheers, "and to finding an apartment. I'm happy for you Kayla. You're really doing it."

I smile—even if I'm not feeling it—and clink my drink to his. There for a minute, I thought he would ask me to stay, not tell me that he's happy for me. I guess I should know better than to get my hopes up. It's a good thing that I put the deposit down on my new place. Waiting around for Micheal to change his mind is pointless.

# Chapter Three

Mike and I have been back home from New York for three weeks. Tonight, he's staying at our apartment. He came over for games and decided to stay the night rather than walk home. I had a nightmare and found myself crawling into bed—our pull-out couch rather—with him minutes ago, seeking comfort . . . instead of seeking out my sister for the same thing. He startled awake and began to jump out of bed, but when he saw the look on my face, he pulled me to his side and lay back down. Michael runs his hand over the top of my head as I lean into his touch. Finally, my heart rate steadies. I feel like purring—the amount of peace I get from this one touch is insane. It's like everything in me calms in his embrace.

"Do you want to talk about it?"

"I don't remember it, really," I say, and I don't. "I just woke up terrified and in tears. I couldn't stay in there. I had to find someone. I'm sorry I scared you. You were the first person I came across."

"It's fine, beautiful. I'm glad you did." He puts his lips to my forehead, kissing me. "I'm happy to help you calm down."

Michael holds me to his chest, running his hand up and down my back. He has always had a way of making me feel safe, but in his arms, I feel like I can let go, like nothing can ever scare me again. I pull my head back enough to look up at him through my lashes. Even though it's dark, the moon illuminating the room is enough for me to make out the tautness of his jaw.

"You're killing me, Kay," he growls.

His hand finds the back of my head and pulls me in for a brief kiss—this time, square on the lips. He withdraws from my mouth long enough to whisper my name. His hand tightens in my hair before his lips find mine once again. Before I can think about what this moment means for us, Michael tilts his head, pulling me closer still, and deepens the kiss, making my toes curl.

Holy heck, this is happening!

My eyes seal shut in hopes that if I'm dreaming, I never wake up.

My hand wraps around behind him, and I run my fingers along the short hairs at the base of his neck. Mike uses his other arm to tug me in close, so close I can feel the ridges of his muscles against my front. This is heaven—to be in his arms like this and have him let loose. I hope that it never ends and he can finally let me in.

A sound in the background has Michael pulling back abruptly. I whimper in protest.

He runs his hand through his hair, looking at me with wide eyes. "I'm sorry." He rolls over on his back and lets out a frustrated breath. I hold mine. "I didn't mean . . . Kay, this can never happen aga—"

No! You can't do this, not again. I want to argue—I mean he's the one that kissed me after all—but am stopped in my tracks.

"Oh my god! Who are you?" Leah says loudly from her room. "Mike, get in here! Someone broke in!"

My eyes shoot in the direction of her room. Before I can move, he's up and out of bed. Pointing for me to stay, he tosses his phone toward me and is on his way to see what's going on. I call the police and hurry to check on Leah. I run into her room, but before I can reach her, I spot her on the phone. I look up just as Mike is making his way out the window in nothing but his boxers. *Please be careful.*

I've always been so bad in these situations. Leah normally tells me what to do. I stand here and wait, not wanting to startle her. She still hasn't noticed me yet.

"But you're not. Cam, you're not here and I'm scared," she says with a shaky voice. She falls to the floor, barely able to catch her breath.

I'm on my way, tossing the phone aside in my rush. Leah is shaking and in some kind of trance or something. I try to get her attention but fail miserably.

"Leah, honey, please . . ." I plead. "Breathe, sis. I need you to try to breathe. I'm here."

I wipe at my tears frustratedly when there's a loud bang at the front door. I run to grab it, flinging it open, and am nearly knocked over by Cam as he barrels past me. His brother Tom is mere steps behind him, reaching out his hand to steady me.

"She's . . . she won't. . ." I try, but I can't get it out.

Tom pulls me in for a firm hug. "It's okay. Cam's here. She'll be fine, I promise. He won't let anything happen to her."

I look over his shoulder, hoping to spot Mike walking up, but he's not there. I really hope he's okay. Michael should've waited on the police. He doesn't need to be out there alone, chasing God knows who.

I pull back and walk toward Leah's room again, hugging myself as I do. I step past the doorway and see Cam sitting on the floor, cradling my sister to his chest while rubbing his hand up and down her back. The worry on his face is unlike anything I've ever seen before. My heart breaks. I wish I could have a love like that.

"Why isn't she pulling out of this?" I whisper.

Tom has me in his arms again, holding tight, and though he means well, all I want is to be back in Mike's strong arms. I want to help and yet all I can do is stand here helplessly, unable to look away.

"Come on, sweetheart, I need you to breathe. You're safe now," Cam says.

I wish I could believe that. I've never seen her so far gone before.

"Leah!" Cam fusses. "Leah, sweetheart, wake up."

I gasp when I see her fall limp in his arms. He pats her cheek, hoping to get a reaction.

Nothing.

I run over and kneel beside Cam, taking Leah's hand in mine.

The front door opens, and I look up as the EMTs and a couple of police officers come our way, following behind a worried-looking Tom. As much as I would like for that to be Mike, I'm grateful help is here for my sister. Tom stands beside the police filling them in, giving me time to check on Leah.

"She came to a moment ago," Cam says, "but these episodes really take it out of her."

I scoot over and watch them check her vitals. "She's going to be okay, right?"

Cam only has eyes for Leah, but one of the EMTs looks at me. "We can take her in for observation if you'd like, but I'm sure she'll be fine after she gets a good amount of rest."

"I'd like to take her home with me, if that's okay?" Cam says. "My sister's a paramedic and lives next door. If anything happens, she'll be my first call."

I nod.

"Sounds like she'll be in good hands then," the EMT states. He packs his stuff away before standing.

"Make sure she gets some water and Tylenol as soon as she wakes up. She might get a nasty headache." Waking the morning after an attack, Leah has always complained about her head hurting. So much so that we keep meds on hand now.

Cam stands, not releasing Leah for a second as he looks to Tom. Without a single word spoken, Tom leaves, heading down to get to the truck, I imagine. The officers are now looking over Leah's room.

I lean in and kiss her head. "Will you let her know that I love her and will be checking in first thing?"

"I will. You can always come with us, if you'd like."

I'd love to be there for her, but I'd be more of a burden than help. Plus, I need to make sure that Mike's okay after all this. I have a feeling that in one way or another, he's going to blame himself. "Thank you, but I'll stay here. I need to let Uncle Joe know what happened and check on Mike. Besides, she has you now. Take care of her, will you?"

Cam nods and heads toward the door. As I watch them leave the building, all I can wonder is what would have happened had I gone to Leah's room rather than Mike's bed. Would this have happened still, or would I have spooked the intruder and made it worse?

So much for nightmares—this is my life.

I set my bag down on the edge of the bed and look back over my shoulder toward Mike. With the break-in there is no way I'm staying in that apartment. When I said that I would bunk with Megan or Uncle Joe, Mike was not having it. He insisted that I come here, to his apartment, and he hasn't let me out of his sight since. His protective personality has ramped up even more.

"If you're going to stand there, the least you can do is let me change the bandages on your feet. You're going to bleed through. You're not staying off them like you were told."

When Mike was crawling out the window after the intruder, he stepped on glass with both feet. He made it back to the apartment building as the EMT was ready to leave. When I saw the pained look on his face as he walked up the stairs, I asked the EMT to look him over.

Michael ignored the EMT's suggestion of us taking him to the emergency room in favor of them bandaging him up and agreeing to take over-the-counter meds for pain and staying off his feet for a few days. Since everyone left, he has yet to sit down.

"I'm fine."

Not letting him talk me out of helping him, I walk over, grabbing his hand and the grocery bag that I picked up from the local pharmacy on the way over to his place. Once we make it to the bathroom, I have him hop up onto the counter.

"You don't need to do this." Even through his protest, he does as I ask.

I grab two hand towels from the linen closet behind the door and kneel in front of him, taking his slippers off. I look up at him from my kneeling position and catch him staring back at me. "I know I don't, but I want to. Just let me take care of you."

He doesn't argue, only sits there as I put on some gloves and begin to remove the dirty bandages around his feet. He winces when I pull his foot up, face level so I can see.

"Sorry. I just want to make sure that they didn't miss any glass."

"It's fine," he grumbles.

I clean the area with rubbing alcohol as I was instructed to, blowing on it to help lessen the burn. Michael's toes curl as I do. I look up at him and see his eyes darken, intently focused on me. Feeling empowered, I carry on. I reach into the bag and grab the triple-antibiotic ointment and apply it before wrapping his foot up and moving to the next. Once I'm done, I stand and allow him to put some of his weight on me as I help him to his room. I sit him on the edge of his bed, and after he scoots up to the back, I put a few pillows under his feet.

"How's that?" I ask.

"You don't need to do this, Kay. I'll be fine."

"You keep saying that, but you risked your life to take care of us. Let me care for you. It's the least I can do."

I fluff the pillows and grab the blanket, pulling it up and over him. I run back out to the fridge and grab a water, then the Tylenol from the cabinet along the way. When I make it to his room, I sit on the edge of the bed near his waist and hand him a couple pills and the now-opened water. After he takes them, I reach past him to grab the remote.

Michael grabs my arm, stopping me inches from him. I look into his stormy eyes, then close my own, letting out the breath I've held on to since we first touched.

"Michael," I whisper.

"Kayla," he says as his lips graze mine.

Before we can take it any further, I hear the door just beyond his open and shut.

I pull back abruptly and stand—thank God for interruptions. I could have just made another mistake. I can't handle him rejecting me again. This has got to stop.

I refuse to look at him as I take a deep breath and tell him the truth. "Michael, I can't do this anymore. You know how

I feel about you. It's not fair of you to keep kissing me, only to tell me sorry afterwards. You said it can't happen again—I will respect that—but you need to respect me and the fact that I can't just be someone you fool around with and then set aside. This is me walking away. If you ever kiss me again, you need to be ready to have a relationship with me. If you can't do that, then please, no matter how hard it is, walk away." I take a steady breath before continuing. "My heart can't handle this back-and-forth."

With that said, I make my way out of his bedroom. Damon is standing just beyond, in the kitchen. He gives me a questioning look before looking further in the room in Mike's direction.

I shake my head. "My place was broken into tonight. Mike jumped out after them and got glass in both feet. He's supposed to rest for a few days."

I walk past Damon and head in the direction of what will be my room for a while, in hopes that I can build a small wall around my heart. If I don't protect it, I have a feeling I'll never make it out of here unscathed.

# Chapter Four

I PULL BACK THE curtain to look out at the sound of a horn honking. "Hurry up, Meg. The guys are here."

Stepping back from the window, I go in search of my shoes. Today, we're leaving for our annual Vegas trip. I'm equal parts thrilled and worried. Mike and I have been friendly since I moved into his apartment just over a month ago, but nothing like our normal, touchy-feely ease. He and Damon I stay until I leave for New York. Though the tension is real, I agreed without argument. I can't stand the thought of being at my place anymore. I sleep at Meg's as much as I can. On occasion, Mike and I stay with Can and Leah for game nights too. Being with others helps—if I'm left alone in Mike's presence, it doesn't make staying away very easy.

"Ready!" Megan replies from the other room. Megan runs into the living area, hand waving in the air. "I found them." Her keys dangle from her hand.

"I don't know why you won't hang them near the door like most everyone I know."

She glances my way briefly. "I'm not like everyone else. That's why I'm your favorite."

"You're in the top five," I tease.

"You're evil," she retorts, tossing a pillow at me, followed by her chuckle.

I bat it away and move to slip on my sandals, then grab my bag and meet Meg near the door. She looks in the mirror to make sure she looks just right. I can't help the slow smile that forms on my face. Damon is wearing her down, and I'm here for it.

"You ready?"

"I am if you are," she replies.

We grab our bags and head out, locking up behind us. Stepping out onto the front porch, we're met by the guys, freshly showered and looking good. Mike is in dark blue jeans and a white form-fitted T-shirt, tattoos on display.

Damon is his exact opposite in all black, not a single tattoo showing.

D steps forward and grabs our bags from us, handing mine over to Mike.

"Thank you," we say in unison.

Damon winks at Megan and then heads to the waiting Tahoe. He opens the back door for us before walking to the back. I catch Megan checking him out, so I nudge her side and smirk. Damon is a good-looking man, that's for sure. He's taller than all of us at six foot six, with a slender build. Don't get me wrong, the man is a wall of muscle, but while Mike shows his off in his size, Damon doesn't. At one point in life, Damon lived the same fighter lifestyle Mike did, but that didn't stick. He's more of a techie than anything. His dark hair, dark eyes, and matching complexion give him a mysterious look that has attracted more than his fair share of women. I don't blame Meg for being cautious.

I hop in and scoot to the passenger side across the bench seat, followed closely by Meg. I look out the window and catch a glimpse of Michael. Megan knows what happened between us the night of Leah's attack and the guilt I've felt following.

"Are you going to be okay?"

"I'll be fine. You know me. I can smile through anything."

She starts to say something, but then the front doors open and we're cut off when the guys join us in the cab.

"Do you think we'll be able to make the Maroon 5 concert while we're there?" Meg asks.

I couldn't be more grateful that she changed the subject. More pity is *all* I need right now.

"There's something about Adam Levine that I can't get enough of," she continues.

"Hey, now," Damon says. "What about me?"

"You know you're hot, but I'm single. I can look."

My eyes roll. These two. I wish they'd get on the same page already. Now that his business is flourishing and Sadie is off to school, nothing is in their way.

"You don't have to be," D retorts.

I space out, looking out the window as those two gab on about this and that. Being so close to Mike for nearly a week is going to be hard. At least living with him, I can hide in my room or go and stay elsewhere, but I can't do that when we're supposed to be on a vacation together. All I can do is hope that this trip goes off without a hitch.

"Let's go, girls," Damon says as he parks. "We have a plane to catch."

Catching the early bird to Vegas is a lot less stressful than it would be if we took a later flight. Not too many people like to wake up at the crack of dawn. By the time we get inside, check our bags, and make it through security, our flight is nearly ready to board. I wish that every time I have or will travel could be this easy, but most of the time, it's not. When I reach the attendant, I haven't even looked at my ticket.

"First-class passenger," she states. "You don't have to wait in line next time. You have priority boarding."

When Damon said he was paying this time, I didn't expect first-class treatment. "Thank you," I reply. Turning back, I watch the others as they check-in.

"Dude, you didn't have to do that," Mike says. "I could have flown economy."

Megan bumps Mike out of the way and lets her scan her ticket, then takes my arm and leads us to our seats. "Thanks, handsome. A girl can get used to this."

I take my seat near the window and look back at Megan as Damon puts a hand on her arm, stopping her. "Can I talk to you?"

She looks over at me as if to gauge my response.

"Go, have fun. I'll be fine."

"Are you sure? He can wait a few hours longer if you need me."

I smile and tilt my head toward D. "I'm sure." I take my book out of my bag, then hand Damon my carry-on. He tucks it away for me before moving across the aisle with Meg. Mike takes a seat next to me, bringing his glorious smell with him. I lean more toward the window than needed and work to get comfortable, subtly putting a bit of room between the two of us. That is not an easy task, as the size of him takes up more than his fair share of room. His arm skims mine as he settles in, causing tingles throughout my body. It takes me a minute, but I finally relax. I open my book and stare at the words rather than read them as I count down the minutes until we land.

I'm jostled, causing me to startle. I open my eyes and realize I've fallen asleep along the way. No longer lying against the window, my head is comfortably planted on Mike.

I sit up quickly, wincing at the pain as I kink my neck.

"You okay?" Michael asks.

"I'm fine," I lie.

While stretching, I notice from my window that we've landed. I hear a throat clear from behind me and turn to find Megan, just beyond Mike, waiting in the aisle for me.

"Go ahead, ladies. We'll meet you by the restrooms with your carry-ons," Damon states.

I step over Mike's enormous legs and take Meg's hand. "Come on." She begins pulling me down the aisle like she can't get off this plane fast enough. "They'll be right behind us."

As soon as we step into the terminal, we find the nearest bathroom.

"How'd it go with D? Do I hear wedding bells?"

She raises her brow and moves to the sink. "Um . . . no. Dame just made sure that I knew how seriously he's taking things. You know how you told me to have a talk with him?"

I nod, looking at her through the mirror.

"Well, I did. I told him that if he and I ever get back together, that will be it for me. I'll be all in, and if he ever leaves me again, it would be through death do us part."

My eyes go wide in shock. I put my hand on her shoulder and turn her to face me. "Did you . . . uh?"

"God no, Kayla." She chuckles. "It wasn't a threat. I just wanted him to know that if we ever get back together, he better see us walking down the aisle rather than it being a short thing again. I loved the man once and it nearly killed me to let him go. I won't do that again."

"I get it." I pull out my lipstick and step up to the mirror to freshen up while she continues.

"He told me that he can see it. Dame's been working hard to give me the life he only dreamed of as a kid. He's scared that he might fail me, but he wants to try." She hops up to sit on the counter." I'm in trouble, Kay. That man is going to be the death of me."

"*Or*," I close my lipstick, put it back in my bag, and look at Megan, "it could be the beginning of something beautiful. He's met his match in you, Megie. I'm so happy for the two of you." I'm thrilled, but as my eyes begin to burn, I know that happiness for her brings sadness for me. I might not get my own happily ever after, and as much as I want that for those I love, I also want it for me.

Megan hops off the counter and pulls me into a hug. "I'm sorry, sis. That man's an idiot if he doesn't want you." She pushes me back so she can see me. "You take your moment to break, but then put that armor back on. You deserve so much better. That much, he got right." She takes a deep breath and motions for me to do the same.

I take a steady breath, square my shoulders, and find my center before looking at myself in the mirror. "You are strong . . . You are beautiful . . . You are deserving." It's something I say when I feel like I need a pep talk. I do this a few more times, then look back at Megan and smile. "All's good. You ready for this?"

Though my heart still hurts, the pep talk works and my armor is back in place—for now, anyway. My outside might show confidence, but my inside is broken.

"There she is." Meg smiles. "Beautiful and confident. Now, let's paint this town red."

I link my arm in hers and head toward the door. If Mike wanted me, like really gave us a chance, I'd break down all these walls and jump into his arms.

Not all dreams come true.

We meet the guys outside the bathroom and then head out to grab our bags. Once outside, we find the waiting limo and load in. Meg isn't the spoiled-princess type, but she's being treated like a queen by the man she loves. I can only imagine the flutters her heart feels right now. She and I sit arm in arm, but she only has eyes for him.

"I can hardly believe he got us a limo," she says in a whisper.

"You deserve it," I say, nudging her.

She smiles brightly. "So do you."

My smile falters, but as quickly as it fell, I put it right back in place. I can't let my feelings get in the way of what could very well be our last trip to Vegas. Once I'm gone and trying to get Michael out of my system, there's no telling how things will go. It's time to enjoy it as if I might not get another chance.

We pull up in front of the Bellagio. I wasn't expecting D to come through on his promise. He must have spent a fortune on this trip. I wonder what kind of client he got that would allow him to afford all this.

We check in and make our way to our room—or suite, rather. It's amazing. There are two bedrooms—one king and a double queen—each with their own bathroom. Upon entering, there's a large living room—dining room combo with a wet bar off to the far right. On the way here, Damon ordered lunch to be waiting for us, and it smells amazing.

"Let's grab some food and get changed. We have Maroon 5 tickets for tonight," Damon says, interrupting my perusal.

"You got us tickets?" Meg asks, astonished. "For tonight?"

"Of course I did. I know I give you grief about your love for Adam, but I couldn't let you come to Vegas and miss your favorite band. Plus, I don't want to waste one minute of our time here."

I swear if she doesn't make things with him official, she'll regret it in time.

"Thank you, Dame." She walks over to him and pulls him down to kiss his cheek. "I really appreciate it. Everything. It's all just so much, but . . . I notice."

Damon winks and then kisses her head. "Anything for you." He stands to full height and puts his hand on the small of her back, leading her toward the table. "Let's eat. I want to make sure you're well fed before we go barhopping tonight. If you hang all over me, I don't want it to be from the booze."

I chuckle. Last year, Meg got drunk. We rarely ever do—a beer or three is our norm. She was attached to him like a koala after she had her sixth. He hasn't let her live it down yet, and I doubt he ever will.

"Barhopping? I thought you said you grew out of your old ways," Meg says. At one point in time, Damon was pretty much a lush. He and Mike could drink all night, then wake up and go to work without any signs of a hangover. Though they didn't do it too often, I can imagine that in their younger years, they might have. I haven't seen either one of them hit it hard in years now.

"Barhopping can be fun, even if you don't get drunk. I promise, my old ways are behind me. There is a three-drink limit for me nowadays."

"Come on, y'all. The food is getting cold," Mike interrupts.

We make our way over to the table, where I sit with my back to the window and grab a burger. Meg, being the traitor she is, leaves room for Mike next to me. He takes the seat and steals one of my fries. Normally, I'd react by stealing one of his in return or swatting his hand away, but this time, I decide not to. I take a bite of my burger instead, letting it slide.

"So," Damon starts, "you two have been dancing around this for some time now. Are you guys really going to let this . . . whatever this is," he motions with his hands between Mike and me, "slip between your fingers?"

"I don't know what you mean. There's nothing going on," I say. I stuff a fry into my mouth, ready to move on from the topic of Mike and I.

"You know what I mean," D retorts. "You and Mike are miserable. You hardly talk anymore."

I look to Meg for help.

She nods and turns toward Damon. "Drop it, D," she states.

I dig into my food, barely looking up. If I could shrink myself and crawl under my plate, I would. If only *Honey, We Shrunk Ourselves* was a thing. I'd give just about anything to have one of those tasers right now.

"You okay?" Mike asks. He takes a sip of whiskey and raises a brow. I guess his three-drink max is starting early.

"I'm fine," I reply, bringing my burger back to my mouth. Maybe if I keep it full, I won't have to speak anymore. I hope this isn't any indication of how this whole trip will go.

At this point, I'd rather have stayed home than feel like I'm being interrogated.

# Chapter Five

Megan and I have been getting ready for a night out in Vegas with the guys for the last hour. Finally, we're ready to go. We step out to the common area and find them ready and waiting. Mike is still nursing his whiskey from dinner and watching some kind of game on the TV with Damon, who is hydrating for our night out. As they hear the door click shut behind us, they stand and make their way over.

Feeling Mike's eyes on me, I want to hide. I glance his way, and sure enough, he is looking me over like a hungry predator. I'm wearing a little, shimmery, white backless dress that hits midthigh. The look is completed with black hoop earrings, a high pony, and my killer red lip stain. I'm keeping it simple but Vegas ready.

Damon nudges his side and Mike shakes off his look, smiling softly.

"Looking good, ladies," he says.

"I agree," Damon adds, taking Megan's hand in his. "Absolutely stunning."

Mike extends his arm for me to take, but Megan slips in and motions for him to join Damon instead. Since we got here a few days ago, Mike has been sending mixed signals again. It's not only confusing for me, but for Megan and Damon too. Mike joins D—little things like this make me grateful to have Meg here with me. As much as I want to throw myself at him, he said we can't happen, and I have to respect that.

We walk ahead of them on the way out of our suite.

"He sure can't keep his eyes off you," she says. "I can only imagine if I let him get his hands on you." She chuckles. "I mean, if that's what you want, don't let me stop you. But, you know, at least make him—"

I shoulder-bump her nervously, laughing. "You're terrible. You know we're not like that. He doesn't want to be with me."

"Oh, he wants you alright. He hasn't stopped checking you out yet. He's just an idiot and won't let himself be happy."

She's right about one thing—Mike's eyes haven't left me since I stepped out that door. If he really won't let himself have me, then why does he keep acting like he wants me?

When we reach the elevator, I push the down button and change the subject.

"What about you?" I ask. "Don't let me get in the way of what you can have with D. I see the way he's checking you out."

Megan is in a scarlet-red, skintight dress that falls to her knees,with a slit up to her thigh. Her skin is simply glowing. No makeup is needed—just a shimmery gloss on  her lips.

"You're my girl. Dame understands. He might not like sharing me right now while he's trying to make a move, but  he also knows I'm not going to let you drown."

I hate that what's going on between me and Mike is affecting their start. I know one thing for sure—I can't let this come between Megan and her future. I turn and link my arm with Mike's. Despite everything that's going on, I know he'd never intentionally hurt me. I'll be fine.

We start out at a club, then another bar a couple hours later. As the night progresses, the two of us finally let go of the tension that's been hanging between us. He's even been acting like he used to with me—loving and kind. I nearly

forget about the last few months. It's like nothing ever happened between us. I've missed this side  of Mike.

The four of us decide to forgo the limo on the way back
to the hotel and walk the Strip. Damon and Megan lean in
on each other as the fountain goes off in the background. It
really is romantic.

Michael pulls me to a stop at the fountain's edge and
gets  down on one knee.

I step back, feeling my mouth drop. I'm not sure what
to make of this. Does he think this is funny? Surely he's
joking, but why? It's mean, if you ask me. He knows how I
feel about him.

Mike takes my hand in his and looks up at me.

He's not going to propose. Is he?

"Kayla," he starts. "I know this is the last thing you'd
probably think of me doing right now." He looks past me
at Megan and Damon and smiles.

I turn to see the look of shock on D's face and tears in
Meg's eyes.

"Kayla, will you be my wife? Tonight."

It is at that moment that my life takes another turn—this
one, I can get on board with.

Megan grabs my makeup bag off the countertop and makes me sit down on the bed, my hair already in curlers. Three things are rolling around in my mind as she starts making me look like a bride.

One—I can't believe I said yes.

Two—I can't believe I'm doing this without my family.

Three—am I *nuts*?

Michael and I haven't even dated. We haven't so much as been a couple until this moment, and it wasn't that long ago that he told me he didn't want a future with me.

*What am I doing?*

"Your thoughts are so loud they're giving me a headache," Meg says. "If you don't want to go through with it, we'll stop. God only knows how you're feeling right now. He should woo you before he asks you to marry him. Heck, he didn't even have a ring." Megan tips my chin so she can look at me head-on.

I smile softly. "I don't care about a ring, Megie. You know that. Maybe this is his way of ensuring I won't just up and leave him. You know he has abandonment issues because of his mom." Michael's mom is nothing to write home about. From my understanding, she never beat him, but she also never stopped the flavor of the month from touching him either. She was so strung out all the time that she couldn't give him the life he deserved, and when the government stepped in, things weren't much better. The only good thing that came out of his situation was his bond with Damon.

"You might be right," she says. "But still, he better be over all this running-away-from-his-feelings stuff now. If he doesn't treat you like the queen you are, I'll have an issue."

There's a knock at the door, followed by Damon sticking his head inside. My stomach dips. What if Michael sent him to tell me he's not going through with the wedding after all?

He smiles my way, putting me at ease, then steps in, kisses Megan on the cheek, and sits down beside me. "Mike is at the chapel already. I thought I'd come back and escort the bride."

"Thank you," I reply. I can't help but wonder how Damon feels about this. "Do you think I'm making a mistake?"

Damon's face always says what his words don't. "I'm not

going to lie to you—Mike proposing shocked me. I didn't think he'd ever do it. I'm happy he did, though. He's loved you for a long time. Mike has just been stuck in his head for so long that he hasn't let himself have you." He hands Megan my eye shadow palette and then continues. "Growing up the way we did doesn't make it easy to commit to someone." I feel Meg flinch at those words. "You need to see if from our side. We were kids and we were abandoned by everyone who said that they loved us, cast aside to live like juvies. That can do damage to someone. I won't say it'll be easy, but the love the two of you share will help you through. So can therapy. When we get back, you should suggest he gets it and support him through it."

Megan finishes up my look and pulls some jewelry out of her bag as Damon pulls me in for a quick hug.

"Thanks, D," I say.

He pats me on the back and steps back. Meg rushes over to us, putting her diamond teardrop jewelry on me—much more bridal than the edgy black look I had on—then steps back to assess my look. I already had on a white dress, though it's not bridal. It'll have to do.

"Perfect," she says.

Damon smiles. "As good as a Vegas bride can be on a moment's notice. You look beautiful. Mike's a lucky man."

Meg and I take his offered arms and make our way to the chapel at the other end of the Strip, where Michael is waiting. I wish I could tell my family, but I don't want to be yelled at if I call them and tell them what's going on. Megan and Damon will have to do. Maybe one day we can remarry and have my family around—or at the very least, a reception where they can celebrate with us.

We pull up out front of the chapel and my nerves amp up big time. Am I doing the right thing? Should I ask Mike to wait? What if he's changed his mind while we were apart? A riot of questions roll around in my mind. I try to quiet the nerves, but Meg is too good of a friend to not pick up on them.

She puts her hand on my knee, calming me slightly. "I will have the driver take us back to the hotel right now if that's what you want. There is nothing that says you can't wait and have a real wedding back home. Just say the word."

I put my hand on hers and smile. Megan is the best friend anyone could wish for. "Thank you, but no. I'm sure we'll be planning a family-sized wedding in no time. I want to show Michael that I'm committed to him. To show him that I'm not going anywhere." I close my eyes and take a deep breath to find my center. I open them and nod. "Let's do this."

We step past the threshold of the chapel and find Mike propped up against the wall across the way. One look at him and it's like a flurry of butterflies take flight in my stomach. As he glances up from his phone, I know the moment he spots me. His lips curl into a slight smile as his gaze slowly travels up my body. A warmth spreads through me, unlike anything I've ever felt before. When our eyes finally meet, the roguish grin on his face is unmistakable.

He walks my way, extending a hand out to me. "You look amazing."

"Thank you. With such short notice, I had to use what I had." He and I find a spot on the wall and wait our turn, as there's a couple ahead of us. Megan buys me a veil and bouquet, wanting to make sure I feel every bit a bride.

As the happy couple ahead of us steps out of the room, they meet at the door and share a passionate kiss before paying the cashier and leaving in a fit of laughter.

Mike walks in ahead of us and down to the altar.

I step back against the wall behind me and take a deep breath. It's Michael—the same man you have known and loved for a long time.

The music starts, and Megan steps through the door next. A minute or two later, the bridal march begins.

Damon comes to my side, offering his arm. "Every bride

deserves to have someone walk them down the aisle, even in a Vegas wedding. Shall we?" he asks.

"We shall." I square my shoulders and link arms with him. I'm a pile of emotions, but knowing Mike is waiting on me, I paste on a smile.

We walk through the double doors toward the love of my life. He wouldn't have asked me to marry him if he didn't want this, I'm sure of it. I lock eyes with Michael as I walk down the aisle toward him, and he gives me one of his megawatt smiles. I know without a doubt that I'd have said yes no matter how he proposed. He is it for me—the only man I want to give my life to. All my unsettled nerves are gone the moment Mike takes my hand in his.

The Elvis impersonator has us recite our vows and pronounces us husband and wife. No sooner than the words are out of his mouth, I'm being pulled into the fiercest kiss of my life and tugged out the door. Megan laughs as she runs after us.

All I can think is, *Here's to our happily ever after.*

Stretching out my aching muscles, I stifle a yawn. Yesterday was a big day for me. I married the man of my *dreams*. He's still asleep in the bed next to me, softly snoring. Meg took his old bed so that we could share the king. I turn and face Michael, who looks like a dream come true. When he begins to stir, I tuck in closer. It's still hard to believe that I'm a married woman now. A thrill runs through my body at the thought. I just spent the night in the arms of the man I love. I'm floating on cloud nine and couldn't wipe the smile off my face if I tried. *Is this real?* I trace my finger over the defined lines of his abs, smiling as I feel the quiver of his stomach under my touch. I could do this all day and never grow tired of it.

His arm tightens around me, pulling me in further. "Morning beautiful," he grumbles in his sleep-worn voice.

"Good morning, Mr. Buchannan," I sigh.

Mike opens his eyes and looks over at me with a smile. He pulls me in closer, and I happily oblige, cementing my body to his. His eyes grow big briefly before they close. He takes a moment, releases me, opens his eyes, and lifts the cover to look. It's then that he growls and hops out of bed in search of his clothes.

This is not the reaction I expected.

"What have I done?" He pulls on his boxer briefs and runs his hand through his hair, pacing back and forth.

I sit up and grab his shirt from the floor, pulling it on and buttoning it partly.

"What the hell happened? Why would you let it go this far?"

I flinch as if he slapped me. "You're the one that asked for this, not me. I thought you wanted us." Standing from the bed, I let the blankets hit the floor before sidestepping them. As I draw near, he walks across the room away from me.

"I told you that this would never happen. Now I wake up in bed next to you, no clothes in sight. How is that respecting my wishes, Kayla?"

I take a step back and rest on the edge of the bed for support. "I never made another move after you said that. Michael, *you're* the one who took a knee and asked me to marry you. This can't be on me when all I did is what any wife would do on her wedding night."

Seeing his eyes grow to the size of a saucer would almost be comical if it weren't at my expense.

"This isn't funny, Kayla."

I grab my phone and pull up the pictures of last night before handing it to Michael. "You don't remember any of this? Asking me to marry you, meeting me at the chapel, saying 'I do,' the kissing . . . or anything else?"

He looks them over, growing greener by the minute, then stops and tosses my phone on the bed. "I'd been drinking. You don't sleep with someone who's had a little too much, let alone marry them. Why would you do that? It's wrong, Kayla! I never would have thought that you, of all people, would take advantage like that." He runs a hand through his hair frustratedly. "It's like I don't even know you."

The pain in his eyes hurts my heart, but how dare he?

"We had a three-drink rule." Surely, I would have noticed if he were drunk. Right? "I would've never agreed to any of that if I had any indication that you were impaired in any way. You know me better than that." I shake my head in disbelief. "You are my husband! I slept with you because it was our wedding night. That is what newlyweds do, Michael! Not once did I take advantage." I swallow the tears that threaten to fall as I look over at Mike. "I gave you everything out of the love I have for you." The fact that we're spending our first morning as a married couple arguing like this guts me.

"I never said three drinks like y'all did. Plus, y'all know that sometimes I might not seem drunk, even if I am."

I try to think back to our three-drink conversation, but right now, I can't even think about anything other than this man in front of me. "So then, marrying me is a 'stupid, drunken decision,' is it?"

He can't even look at me. Instead, he nods. "Yes."

The tears I've been fighting finally fall. Everything in me wants to fall to the ground and beg him to see me, to forgive me, but for what? I married him thinking that he loved me . . . rushed, yes, but Mike never does anything he doesn't want to do. Instead, I wipe the tears and nod. "I'm sorry you feel that way. I will try and fix this. Just give me some time."

Mike bends and gathers his things from the floor. Once he has enough, he walks to the door, his back still to me. "I'm sorry that I ever let loose last night. I thought I had *friends* I could trust. I guess I was wrong."

As the door clicks shut behind him, my knees buckle under the weight of my heavy shoulders, and I fall to the ground. Burying my face in my hands, I let the tears flow. How will I ever be able to look at him again?

I'm in love with a man who wants nothing to do with me.

# Chapter Six

I pour myself a mug of steaming hot coffee and take my first sip of the day, then grab a fruit-and-grain bar from the counter and take it back to my room. Today marks three weeks since Mike and I married in a quicky Vegas wedding. Things around here haven't been the best since. Michael has said that he's sorry a lot, but I've never been able to fully hear him out. It's always hurt too much. I don't trust him like I once did. The things he said to me, I just can't forget. Now that I don't have work and Leah has been taking care of Cam—he had some sort of accident while on vacation with her—I have been moping around the house a lot. I've gone out once or twice—running to my lawyers to have the divorce papers drawn up and to the store to get heartbreak food—otherwise I'm in my room.

I know I need to get out of my head, but I can't seem to shake the memories. Before Vegas, I knew where I stood with Mike, and I was working on building that wall to keep him out. Then he obliterated it when he confessed his love to me the night we said 'I do.'

I feel bad for Damon—poor guy doesn't know how to act. With me staying in my room so much, we are rarely together, but there are moments that we cross paths. In moments like that, I never know if I should act as if nothing happened and try to be friendly or act as if I don't know him anymore. Either way, it sucks.

There's a knock at my door. I stand to open it. It's Michael.

"Can we talk?" He looks down toward his feet, then back at me.

"Sure." I open the door wide and motion for him to join me. He takes a seat at the foot of my bed while I sit at the head, tuck my phone under my pillow, and bring my coffee back to my mouth. I nod, and he starts.

"I'm sorry for the way I handled things and for the strain it has put on us the last while. I'm sure you're tired of hearing me say it—I know I've told you a dozen times or more, but I really am. Is there any way I can fix this?"

"Fix what exactly?"

He reaches out to put his hand on my foot, but I tug back, putting it up under my leg.

"If you'll give me the chance, I can get us out from under this mess of a marriage and things can go back to normal. No more regrets. You can stay here, and we'll move on. We can go back to being friends. It'll be like nothing ever happened."

You'd think those words would gut me, but they sting a little less the more he says them. It's like I'm getting used to it or something.

"That's the thing, Michael. You regret it happening. You can't stand being with me. But when I said I do, I gave you *everything*. You, sir, have my heart. Even if I wish I could take it back, I don't work like that. I can't stay under this roof with you any longer than I have to. It hurts too much. Unless you want to go to therapy and give this a try, I need to go. If for nothing else, to move on from this."

"I'm sorry. Is there anything I can say to make this better?"

I set my coffee down on the side table and look across the way at him. "You've broken my heart, Michael. When you break someone like that, sorry means nothing. Show me that you mean it—that I can trust you again."

"What if I don't know how?"

"I don't know what to tell you." I lie down and cover back up. "Can you shut the door on your way out? I'd like a nap before I have to go pack." As I hear him stand and the door shut firmly behind him, I grab my phone and look at our wedding pictures once again—something I've done on more than one occasion. *Will we ever be that happy again?*

I let the tears fall and lull me into a restless slumber.

I grab some clothes from the closet at what has been my home since the week I turned eighteen. Living with my sister has been amazing, but now that she's officially moving in with Cam, I'm vacating so she can sell the place. Since we have a cold spell moving in this weekend, today worked best. Leah offered to let me stay, but this really isn't my home anymore. Before I know it, I'll be off to New York, making a new life for myself.

I just want to move and get out of here already, but I promised Leah that I'd be home for the holidays, and I'll stick to that no matter if it kills me. With November starting next week, I don't have much time left. I'm glad I stayed, though, because if not for that, I would've left shortly after coming back from Vegas. Then, I wouldn't have been here when Cam called Uncle Joe over video chat—I had stopped in to pick up some of his fried green tomatoes when the call came through.

He asked us both for our blessing. Cam plans on popping the question this weekend. The cool part is that he asked us if we'd like to be a part of it. I can hardly wait! I'll stand there and smile as if I haven't had my heart shattered into a million pieces. That's what you do for someone you love.

The move from our place to a storage unit shouldn't be too hard. We have a lot of gym friends that plan on helping. No matter how abashed Mike is right now, he's still making sure that I'm taken care of. That's the thing about Michael—we can drive each other up the wall, but I know that he'd never hurt me. Well, physically, anyway. He's already destroyed me emotionally, but I have to accept my part in that too. This morning, after I let myself break, I went to my lawyer for another meeting over the divorce. Now that I have the papers in my possession, I can give them to Micheal to sign. I haven't had the chance to tell him yet, but I'm sure he'll be happy to hear the news.

I grab my flat iron and pack it in one of the few boxes that I'm bringing with me to Mike's, then to New York. The rest will stay in storage for when I return. It's mostly stuff from my parents, furniture, and a few odds and ends that I won't need for now. I move to the kitchen and gather my special coffee cups. There aren't many dishes that belong to me, but what I do have is kind of special. Most of it I made. I love arts and crafts. I just don't do them often—but when I get the chance, I take it.

After packing up all I want to take with me, I move back to my room and make sure that I've got everything I need. By the time Gunnar and Damon move my stuff, I'm ready to crash. Mike has avoided me like the plague since he got here. It sucks that Leah has already called us out for fighting, but I can only do what I can.

After Gunnar puts the last box in my U-Haul, he grabs the keys from me. "I'll drive." He runs off to the front of the truck.

I pull Leah in for a hug as her crew starts loading up. "I'm going to miss you."

"Same, but remember you have a room with us whenever you want to visit. Just let me know and I'll make sure the bed is made up for you." She pulls me in once more, then looks over my shoulder at Mike. "You can come out too. Don't feel like you're trapped where you are. I can see something's going on between the two of you."

I nod. "Thanks, but I need to stay in the city. For now. I might take you up on that another time."

Uncle Joe walks our way and pulls us both in for a hug. "My babies, all grown up."

"We've been grown up for a while now, Uncle Joe," Leah chastises.

"Sure, but now you two are leaving the nest."

"I haven't lived at home since I turned eighteen." I laugh.

"No. I guess you haven't, but now you'll be more than a block away. It's a bit different."

Leah and I smile at one another and pull him back in, kissing each of his cheeks. This is something we used to do when we were little.

He chuckles. "Oh, girls. Never grow up." Uncle Joe walks off and joins the guys near my U-Haul, probably giving Gunnar instructions on how to properly haul my things.

Cam joins us, cast on one arm, and snakes the other around Leah's waist. "Sorry, sweetheart, but we need to head out. I forgot to grab my medicine when we left."

Leah turns to look at him, kissing his chin in reply. "I'll be right there."

He smiles at me and takes off back to their truck.

"Don't be a stranger," Leah says. "Just because I'm leaving the city doesn't mean that I don't have room for you in my life. Remember—*the Covington sisters for life.*"

I smile, loving how she said it in the singsong way that we always did growing up. "The Covington sisters for life," I reply.

It's nice to know that no matter what life throws at me, I will always have her.

I hop in the passenger side of the U-Haul and put in my earbuds. When we make it to my storage unit, the guys heft in most of the items, only letting me carry light boxes. We're done in no time and on our way to drop the truck off and head back to Mike and Damon's for a night in. I'm so tired that when we make it back, I take the divorce papers out of my bag, throw them on the dresser, and head to the bathroom for a nice, long soak in the tub.

I turn on the water, add a lavender bath bomb, and then strip down and hop in. This is heaven on sore muscles. It's so relaxing that I don't realize when I fall asleep.

"Earth to Kayla," Megan says from the doorway.

I jolt, causing water to slosh over the side. Calming a moment later, I notice that the water has gone cold and begin to stand.

"Good lord, warn me next time before you decide to give me full frontal," Megan teases.

"Oh, shut it. It's not anything new for you." Between the gym and our quick changes for work, Meg and I have become more than comfortable with the nude body. After I dry off, I grab my robe from the back of the door and slip it on. It's not until that moment that I spot what Meg has in her hands—the divorce papers. I take a step her way and try to grab them. "Come on, Meg, hand them here, will you?"

"Why didn't you tell me that you were getting these?" she asks as she pulls them back.

"Because they don't concern you."

She nods and hands them back. "I'm sorry, sis. When are you giving them to him?"

I fold them back up and walk out to my room, going in search of some sleep shorts and a tank top. "I had planned on doing it tonight. He's been all about getting this marriage taken care of, so I figure the sooner, the better."

"You're probably right. I can ask Dame to join me in picking up dinner while you do, if you want."

"Thanks, that'd be nice." I drop my robe and throw on my clothes. "I didn't know you were coming over tonight. I'm glad you're here though."

She steps in and gives me a quick hug. "I'm only ever a call away. Plus, I got bored. I thought a game and dinner sounded fun. Come on, let me get D and you go give Mike the gift he's been asking for."

My gut sinks when she says it like that, but I know she's right. This is something he's been all but begging for.

I take a moment and gather myself before walking out in search of Mike. Once I hear the front door shut, I make my way to the living room.

"Hey. You look comfy," he says as I walk in.

"I am." I sit down on the chair across the way.

He takes the remote and turns off the TV when he sees me looking at him rather than the show.

"Can we talk for a minute?"

"Sure. What's up?"

I reach out and pass him the papers that I'm sure he'll be happy to see. "I had my lawyer draw these up. I'm not asking for anything. I'm sure you'll want to look them over, but I've already signed them. When you're ready, it's marked where you need to sign."

He flips through the papers, then looks over at me.

"You're still going, huh?"

I nod. "I am."

"So it doesn't matter if I sign these or not. I'm still losing you."

I turn my head a little, trying to get a read on him. The way he's acting now makes no sense to me. I thought that this is what he wanted.

"You said no to therapy and to trying. Losing me seems inevitable at this point."

He thumbs the papers in front of him and looks like he has a lot on his mind. "It's not like you'd stay for me even if I wanted you to," he sighs.

"I already told you I would stay if you and I could make it work. You are really beginning to confuse me; you need to go to therapy, Michael. Work through your trust and commitment issues."

"I'll have my lawyer look these over and I'll get back to you." He stands and takes the papers with him.

Standing from the chair, I walk to the kitchen, grab a cup of coffee, and head back to my room. I sit at the head of the bed, looking at our wedding pictures yet again. "Ugh," I say in frustration. *Why do I keep doing this to myself?*

I power off my phone and toss it on the bedside table, then put my cup next to it. *This is so depressing.* I lie down in bed and cry myself to sleep. I can hardly wait to get out of here.

# Chapter Seven

We're all supposed to get together later this evening for game night, but I can't seem to pull myself off the floor of my bathroom. The way I'm feeling, I could almost swear that I hit the bottle a little too hard last night, but I haven't drunk anything since Vegas. I grab my phone from the counter and pull up my doctor's number and hit dial.

"Dr. Jordan's office," a woman answers. "This is Mary speaking. How can I help you?"

"Hi Mary, this is Kayla Covington. I'd like to see if I can be squeezed in for an appointment with Dr. Jordan."

I hear her clicking away on her keyboard. "What kind of appointment are we scheduling today?"

"I think I might have some kind of stomach bug; I'd like to see if she can give me something to help me stop vomiting." I sit up and hug the toilet as my stomach starts rolling again. Thankfully, it's a false alarm.

"There are several nasty bugs going around right now. Dr. Jordan is booked solid. Let's see if I can find anything soon . . . Do you have a temperature?"

"No."

"I'm sorry, Ms. Covington, we're booked out until December sixteenth. I can set you up with that appointment and put you on the call list in case anything comes up between now and then. Or you can come to the walk-in clinic from seven to nine in the morning. It will be her last until after Thanksgiving."

"Do you have any openings with her PA?" I ask. If I can avoid the clinic, I want to.

"Not until December. I'm sorry. With the holidays upon us, it's nearly impossible to get in. Covid, the flu, and strep going are all going around, so we can only take people with temperatures at a moment's notice. If you'd like, I can ask her to send you in some nausea medication to get you through Thanksgiving."

"That's fine. I'll come to the clinic in the morning, thank you."

"Okay, I suggest you get here twenty minutes early and wear a mask."

"Thank you. Will do."

Mary and I hang up. I hop in the shower, hoping it will make me feel a little bit human again.

Megan sits on the edge of my bed and looks over at me. Tonight's game night was cancelled due to me not feeling well and the restaurant being shorthanded. Normally, Leah, Uncle Joe, and Mike would be making a fuss over me while I'm sick, but both Mike and Uncle Joe are working, and Leah is stuck out at the farm.

"What are you doing here? I'm sick. You shouldn't be around me." I know I sound like I'm fussing, but I'm not. I really am grateful that Meg came, but I don't need her getting sick because of me.

"You've got to try and eat something, Kayla," she fusses.

"I can't. It'll come right back up." I scoot up to a sitting position with my back against the headboard.

"At least drink the broth. You need some nutrients." She raises a brow in challenge.

I know that she's not going to quit until I do, so I take the cup from her and give it a go. As I sip on the warm broth, I spot the bag she set on the bed. "What's in there?"

"I stopped off at the drugstore and got a stomach bug kit." She chuckles. "Sorry, the lady at the counter call it that and it kind of stuck." She opens the bag and shows me what she grabbed—Pedialyte, Tums, ginger drops, peppermint, and some Sprite. "How long have you been sick?"

I shrug. "A few days maybe."

"You don't think you could be . . . you know."

"Could be what?" I yawn.

She finishes loading the stuff back in the bag and sets it aside before looking back at me. "I just wonder if . . . well." She looks down at my blanket and starts picking at a loose string. "Do you think you could be pregnant?"

I wish I hadn't just taken a sip of the broth. In shock, I choke on the broth, it burning the heck out of my nose and throat. Megan stands and comes to pat me on the back and takes the cup from my hands.

When I'm finally able to get air back in my lungs, I look her way, giving her what Leah calls the stink eye. "Why on earth would you say a thing like that?"

She sits back down, hands raised as if she's not wanting any trouble. "I don't think I've ever seen you this sick before other than back in high school. You're always so healthy. Plus, you did just get married a month ago. If Mike really was drunk, I'm sure he wasn't as careful as he should have been."

I think back to our wedding night and try not to get swept away in the way Michael made me feel. That night, I felt  like I was the only woman for him, the one he would cherish for the rest of his life. It was glorious—

"Kay," Meg says, nudging me. "Did you hear me?"

"Huh?" I question. "Sorry, I spaced out for a minute."

"I could tell. Your cheeks are as red as a tomato," she teases.

"Come on, Meg, don't give me grief. What'd you say?"

"I asked if you have any other symptoms?"

I look at her furrowed brows. "You'll have to help me out more than that. I've never been pregnant before. What other symptoms?"

She shrugs her shoulders and takes out her phone. After typing something, she looks my way. "According to this, there are a several." She looks back down at her phone and starts naming them off: "Spotting." Check. "Nausea." Check. "Fatigue." Check. "Mood swings." Check.

The list goes on. By the time she finishes reading the list, I am a mess. I can no longer hold back tears.

"Oh honey, come here," Meg says. She tosses her phone to the side and pulls me in. "I didn't mean to upset you. Are you okay?"

"I'm not sure," I cry. "What am I going to do, Meg? Mike doesn't want me, let alone a baby."

She pats me on the back and makes me rise to look at her. "First, let's get that kind of thinking out of your head. Let's find out if you are before you start worrying. Mike may be an idiot, but I don't think that he's cruel enough to walk out on you while you're carrying his child."

"I won't trap him, Meg. He has made it perfectly clear that he doesn't want me. Things are already tense between us. I won't hold him in this marriage, no matter if there's a baby or not."

"I know you won't, but I think you should at least give him the chance to know. Maybe it's best to keep it between us until you do. No sense in tempting fate."

Megan gets a call, and when she sees that it's work, she takes it. After a minute, she hangs up and sits back next to me. "I have to run—the proofs that are due tomorrow need to be reshot. I'll be back later. If you think you can manage, run down to the store and grab a test. When I get back, you can take it and get a little piece of mind."

"Oh God, work. What am I going to do about work? I can't sign a new contract if I'm pregnant."

"Kayla," she says sternly. "We'll take this one day at a time. First, let's find out if you're pregnant, then we'll go from there."

I nod and she gives me a quick hug before heading out.

I lie back in the bed and cover my face with a pillow and scream. How has my life gotten so out of control? I toss the pillow aside, followed by the blanket, get up, and get dressed. There is only one way to know if I am pregnant or not.

"Let's go buy a test."

I pace back and forth in my bathroom, my phone on the counter beside me. When I got back with the test, I couldn't wait any longer. I ripped open the box and peed on the little stick. Meg called me a moment ago, asking if I had the chance to grab one and telling me she was on the way back.

"Hello, Earth to Kayla," Megan says, pulling me from my thoughts. "It's time."

I try to swallow my nerves. "I'm here, sorry." My legs wobble a bit as I stand in front of the counter, my heart pounding so hard it feels like it'll beat out of my chest.

This moment will change everything. All the signs are there—I haven't had a regular period since before Vegas, my moods are everywhere, and I've been so sick lately. Let's not even mention how bad the smell of cooked eggs hit me the other morning.

I reach for the test, but my hand is shaking so bad, I pull back, bringing it to my chest. "I don't know if I can do this," I whisper.

Tears prick the corners of my eyes as the magnitude of this situation sets in. The thought of looking at the results sends a wave of panic through me.

"Meg," I choke out, "he doesn't even love me." A wailing cry sound comes from inside me as the thought of him reminding me of that plays out. "And if I'm carrying his child, he won't love them either. I can't do this."

Unable to stand any longer, I find the nearby wall, sinking to the ground with my back against it. I pull my knees to my chest, lay my head down, and let it all out.

In the background, I can hear Meg. "Kayla, talk to me, hun." Her voice sounds panicked.

I let out another sob. How has my life gotten so messed up? I'd love to have a family, but I have never dreamed of having one with a man who wants no part of being with me. My heart hurts so much right now. Living here is already hard, but if I'm pregnant, I can only imagine how bad it will get. I know he'll never touch me, but his words cut deeper than a knife.

"I'm here," Meg says just before I hear a pounding at the door from the other room. "Someone let me in! I'm coming, Kayla. I'll be there in a minute."

The pounding gets louder. No matter how much I know I should get up and get the door, I feel stuck. I can't catch my breath.

I hear what sounds like a door opening, followed by Damon's voice. "Megan? Is everything okay? Are you okay?"

"I'm good, but if you don't get out of my way, you won't be. Let me in—Kayla needs me. Move. Now!"

"What's wrong with Kay?" he asks. His voice comes out jumbled, as if he's running.

"Damon," she starts as I hear the door to my room open. "Kayla will be fine once I get to her. Don't worry." The door closes and then she is entering my bathroom. She tosses her stuff down and then sits next to me, pulling me into her.

"I'm sorry," I cry. "I feel so weak. I should be able to look but I just can't."

"You don't need to apologize to me for anything. You should've never tried to take it alone. Had I not suggested you go and buy it, this would've never happened."

"It's not your fault."

"It's as much on me as it is you." Now that I'm a tad bit calmer, she nudges my chin so that I'm looking at her. "Do you think we can look at it now?" She stands and extends her hand out to me. "You are not alone in this. I'm right here with you."

I take three calming breaths and stand. Holding her hand, we move to the sink and look. "What does that mean?"

"How am I supposed to know? I've never had the need to take one before." She bends and grabs the box out of the can and begins to look it over. "Well, there is a second line, but it's very faint. Maybe it's too soon to tell? It's only been a month, right? Maybe we should wait another week or two."

I take the box from her and am equally confused. "Do you think we waited too long to look at it? Maybe the line could have faded or . . . maybe it popped up in time."

"Maybe?"

I toss it and the box in the trash and sit on the toilet lid. "I can ask Dr. Jordan to test me when I see her. If not, we can wait until after Thanksgiving to do it again. It's only a few weeks away." I think I need to wrap my brain around the thought before I test again.

"No beer or wine in the meantime, just in case. Maybe you can pick up some prenatal vitamins at the pharmacy. I mean, all signs point to you being pregnant, so act like it until you hear otherwise."

Meg and I decide to call in an order for dinner and cuddle in for a movie marathon. I'm grateful to have a friend like her. I have no clue how I would have made it otherwise. I know I have Leah, but with all that she has going on, I can't imagine telling her about Mike and me right now. My husband may not love me, but my family—Meg—included would go down fighting for me. That has to be enough.

# Chapter Eight

IF TODAY WEREN'T FRIENDSGIVING followed by Thanksgiving at Cam and Leah's, I might just stay in bed. I missed the walk-in clinic with Dr. Jordan and was unable to grab that December sixteenth appointment. Instead, I got one on the twenty-seventh, a few days before I'm scheduled to leave Oklahoma City. Thankfully, she called in some Zofran for me. The first few doses didn't do much, but now that I have a stronger dosage, it has helped me some. Between that and the vitamins I picked up, I feel a little better. There is still some nausea and vomiting, but the baby book I downloaded says that's normal. Like Meg says, "Act like I am until I know otherwise." Until I know for sure, that is just what I'll do.

I step into the shower, wishing myself to feel somewhat human again. Now that I'm not drinking nearly as much coffee, I'm dragging.

Once I'm out, I grab a cute pair of skinny jeans and throw on my knee-high black boots, then find my mustard-yellow crop top and black leather biker jacket. Normally, I'd go for cute, but right now, I need armor. I'm really not in the mood to be harassed today. This is my "don't mess with me" outfit. Twenty minutes later, my face is on and my hair is done. I'm ready to face the day.

I step out to find an empty kitchen but smell the turkey, so I put on oven mitts and open the door to check on it. It's nearly done, the juice oozing out as I prod at it. My mouth waters just thinking about having a leftover turkey sandwich tomorrow. I haven't been eating much—nothing smells or sounds good—but this has my stomach growling. I close the oven door, toss the mitts on the island, and turn to leave the kitchen. Now that it's almost done, I need to set the table and start the side dishes.

Mike steps in my way, blocking my path. "You can't ignore me forever," he states.

I've been so depressed over what's going on with him that I've barely come out of my room. It's not like I've been intentionally avoiding him, but no matter how many times I tell him, he doesn't believe me.

"I haven't been feeling well, Mike. I told you this before. Let it go."

Mike folds his arms across his chest, drawing my eyes to the firm muscles on display. I can't help but look. If only things were different. Mike is a good-looking man, and he is still my husband.

When he catches me looking, he smiles and steps in my direction.

I hold out my hand, bracing it against his rock-hard chest. "Don't. Can we just get through today? Please." I'm so over this back-and-forth. All I want to do is enjoy what bit of time I have left before the move.

"Are you really going to hold this against me forever? I miss my best friend."

"I'm your wife, Michael, not your friend. You might wish that night away, but to me, it was real. I gave myself to you in every way. I'm sorry. I just can't go from that to sitting on the couch and cuddling you when the visions of being with my husband play through my mind. It's selfish of you to even ask." I can't take this anymore. I don't know whether to cry or punch him. He's just so frustrating. I move to step out of his path, but he reaches out, putting a hand on my arm.

He seems to deflate when I won't back down but doesn't release me. "I'm sorry. I really am. I hope you know that."

Until he signs the papers, I can't be what he wants. Maybe, not even then.

"I've heard you a million times." I look down at his hand on my arm and then back at him. "Let go, Michael."

He takes his hand off me and steps back.

"If you have ever cared about me, please stop reminding me of how much of a mistake I am. You might not love me, but it's the love I have for you that hurts me every day. Sign the papers and quit being so cruel."

I step out of the kitchen and head to the bathroom, shutting the door behind me. Mike's okay with holding me, protecting me, loving me as a best friend, but not okay with being married to me. How does one go from making love to their husband to cuddling with the same man in a platonic-friend kind of way? I just don't get it.

Instead of dwelling and making myself feel worse, I splash some water on my face. I have to put my game face on, no matter how bad I feel. It's not you—it's him. There is nothing wrong with you, I hear Meg say in my head. She's had to remind me of that more than a few times. I stand up straight, look in the mirror, and square my shoulders. I close my eyes and find my center, take three deep breaths, then open my eyes once more. *You are strong . . . You are beautiful . . . You are deserving,* I chant. I say it a few more times until I feel myself standing taller and know I can face the day.

Now that Mike's in the kitchen cooking, I decide the living area looks cozy and head that way.

Ten minutes later, Damon joins us, freshly showered with a big smile on his face.

"Looking good, D," I say.

"Thanks, Kay. Happy Thanksgiving," he replies. "You look gorgeous."

"Thank you, kind sir." I stand and do an over-exaggerated bow. "A lady doth try."

He shakes his head but smiles, nonetheless. "Meg will be here in a minute. I'm going to run down to the garage and help her up. You want to come?"

"I appreciate the offer," I smile, "but I'll stay out of your way. Go get your girl."

He nods and heads toward the door. Damon is supposed to be moving into his new house soon. I can only imagine what it'll be like around here once he's gone.

I step into the kitchen and help move things along. I'm taking the rolls from the oven while Mike carves the turkey, as Damon and Megan walk into the apartment, arms loaded with dessert. Sadie steps in behind them and then the intercom rings on the wall. Mike steps over and buzzes them in. Minutes later, Gunnar, Pop, and Xena all walk in, arms full of side items.

When the food is finally on the table, Damon gathers everyone around to say grace over the meal. "Alright, ladies, get your plates," he states.

Not one to argue, I grab Sadie and Megan and head that way, followed closely by Xena, Pop's daughter. I try to get a small portion of most everything. It all looks so good, except the corn casserole—normally my favorite, but this year, it makes my stomach roll. I take a seat at the table, plate and drink in hand, and start picking at my meal. It all looked good a minute ago, but now it just looks blah, even the turkey.

"You better eat up, girlie," Pop—the owner of our gym, also like an adopted father to Mike—says, "These guys will eat it for you if you don't." He's not wrong either. I've had Gunnar eat off my plate more than a few times.

Gunnar sits down next to me, catching stink eye from Mike, who looks like he was about to take that seat. "How's it going, gorgeous? Are you still leaving us?"

I take a sip of my cranberry mocktail and nod. "I'm fine. I'll be out of here just before New Year's. How are you? Find a new workout buddy yet?"

"Nobody can replace you," he says with a wink.

Meg nudges my side as she leans in.

Gunnar smiles and pivots to talk to Pop.

I turn Meg's way and raise a brow. "What was that for? You have bony elbows."

"Quit fussing. It's Thanksgiving." She nods her head toward Damon on the other side of Sadie, and I nod in understanding. "Do you care if I ask him to stay with me and Sadie rather than going out to Leah's with y'all?"

Even though I hate the idea, I can't fault her for wanting what she wants. I shake my head a bit and smile so she knows that I'll be fine. "We can take Sadie if you want some alone time." I wink.

"No, thanks. It's not like we're a couple yet. He hasn't asked me again, but . . ."

"When he does, you will be," I finish for her. "I thought you were going to tell him you were ready."

"I was, but I decided I'd rather wait on him. He likes making moves; me, not so much. I don't want to take that away from him." She smiles brightly, then stands and takes her plate, reaching out for mine.

Damon appears behind her, putting a hand on her arm to gain her attention. "Why don't you ladies visit for a while? Gunnar and I can handle the cleanup." She starts to argue, but he cuts her off. "Megan," he starts, "in less than two months, Kay is leaving. Let me do this. You can clean later. I know you're going to wish you had this time when she's gone."

I hand him my plate in thanks.

She leans in, kissing him on the cheek and earning a few catcalls from the group of rowdy men. "Thank you, Dame." She turns back to me, grabs my arm, then leads me to the living room.

We sit and talk and laugh for what seems like hours. Time with her is always fun.

"Ready to go?" Mike asks.

I look at the clock on the wall and see that it's time to head out. "Did the turkey and pie get done?" Leah said that the one bird Uncle Joe is bringing might not be enough, even though she's making two hams. I think it's overkill, but she wants today to be perfect, considering it's her first holiday on the Cameron farm.

"Yeah. I have the roaster and pie plate by the door." I nod and stand. "Let me run to the restroom and grab a coat. I'll be ready in five."

He walks off while I give Megan a hug. She holds me tight for a minute and speaks low so only I can hear her. "I put a pregnancy test under your bathroom sink."

"Thanks," I reply. I planned to get one the other day, but that never happened. With a final goodbye to Meg, I make my way to my room, do my business, and shove some TUMS in my bag.

The ride down the elevator with Mike is silent. By the time we get to the truck, I pull out my phone, put in my earbuds, and turn on my audiobook. I lean against the door and close my eyes for the ride.

Minutes later, we're pulling down the rock drive of the Cameron farm. I still can hardly believe that Leah's getting married so soon. That's insane to think. I wish I could tell her about Mike and me, not to take the spotlight from her but so that I could talk with her about everything. If I did, though, she would be mad at Mike, and then she'd get

Uncle Joe involved, and Michael's fear of losing us would come true. Even though I'm hurting right now, I still don't want to hurt him.

Mike parks the truck in front of the garage. As I move to open the door, he stops me by, putting his hand on mine. "Can we talk? It'll only take a minute."

"Now's not the time. I need to get in there and help my sister."

I open the door the rest of the way, grab the pies, and step out, quickly making my way inside. Thankfully, nobody is in the half bath downstairs, so I deliver the pies to the table and then make a quick dash in and shut the door behind me. Once it's securely shut, I put my hands on the counter, bracing myself so I can focus on my breathing. After my heart rate is back to normal, I clean my face and remind myself, You are strong . . . You are beautiful . . . You are deserving. I cannot fall apart in front of my family.

"Joe's here," I hear Cam say as I open the door. "We better help him get the food in."

Instead of joining them, I walk upstairs in search of Leah. I find her in her bathroom getting ready, and I watch as she leans over the counter, fixing her eyes. She's in a pair of dark blue high-rise skinny jeans and a tucked-in white V-neck tee covered by a puffy fall-orange sweater.

Leah and I couldn't be more different in our looks. I take after our mom, while she looks more like our dad. She stands at five feet, four-and-a-half inches tall—if you don't add that half, she's spitfire enough to remind you. While I'm pencil thin, my sister was blessed with curves in all the right places and a little meat on her bones. My light complexion, hair, and eyes are contrasted by her olive tone, dark brown eyes, and nearly black hair. Leah is four years my senior, so she stepped into the motherly role after our mom passed and has been amazing in making sure I always can count on her. No matter what life throws my way, I always have her.

Keeping this thing between Mike and me from her is eating at me, but seeing how happy she is, I know it's the right thing to do. This can wait until I know if I'm pregnant or not and after her wedding. I sure am going to miss her.

I shake my head and snap out of it. Today is about family. I'm not about to ruin that.

"Hey, sis," I say, standing to my full height and walking into the bathroom. "You about ready? Uncle Joe just pulled up and has a car full. The guys went to help unload."

"Yeah. Let me grab my shoes," she replies. We walk into her room, I stand by the door and wait while she steps into her boots, before heading on down.

As we hit the bottom step, she comes to a stop, taking it all in for a moment. Considering how full this house is and how empty our holidays normally are, I can only imagine how she feels right now.

I pat her on the shoulder and lean in. "This is amazing, isn't it? I'm glad you found a man who's willing to let your crazy family be a part of his. I don't know what I'd do without you in my life."

I'm grateful to have my sister and Uncle Joe, but after I move, I won't be able to say the same for Mike. It hurts like heck to even think it, but with the way things are, I know it's only a matter of time before I lose him for good.

Leah turns and pulls me in for a hug. "You'll never have to know. I'm getting married and gaining a new family, but that doesn't mean anything will happen to us. You're always welcome here, Kay."

I wipe at the tears that threaten to mess up my makeup.

Cam pulls Leah into him from behind. She turns in his arms and gives him a tight hug.

I look over the top of them to find Mike staring at me. My stomach does a flip. I can't breathe. I need a moment to pull myself together. I look back to Cam and Leah, who are still in an embrace. "Alright, you two. I'm going to go freshen up real quick." I turn and walk back upstairs, finding my way to the main bath. I sit on the edge of the tub as I try to reign in my emotions once more.

A knock at the door comes a few moments later, startling me. Before I have a chance to gather myself, Janet walks in. "Oh, sorry, I was looking for you, but I didn't mean . . ."

"It's okay. I'm glad you're here. I could use a friend."

I know that if I ask her not to say anything, she won't.

"Can I tell you something?"

"Anything, sugar," she replies, sitting next to me on the tub's edge.

"Uncle Joe can't know. Nobody can, really."

"You have my word. I won't say a thing."

Sitting right here on the edge of the tub, I spill everything—from the moment I told Mike how I felt to the moment he broke my heart. I want to tell her about the maybe baby, but until I know for sure, I'd rather keep that to me and Meg. The less people who know before telling Mike, the better. By the time I let it all out, the pressure on my chest has lessened, but the shock on Janet's face is more than I accounted for. When she engulfs me in a warm embrace, I know that I have someone I can trust to have my back no matter what. If only I could still count on Michael—my closest friend—but after everything, he isn't the man I thought I once knew. That hurts more than our failed attempt at marriage.

# Chapter Nine

Mike and I walk through the threshold of the apartment after an eventful Thanksgiving dinner. All night, he acted as if we were the same as we used to be, with an added seductive look on occasion. Granted, we were around family that doesn't know what's going on, but it still drove me crazy. The least he could do was lay off a bit. Leah must have seen him at one point, because she made mention of him finally asking me out. I laughed it off like I used to. The longer it went on, the more pain I felt.

On the ride home, he didn't say one word to me. I'm ready to burst.

I turn to face him as soon as I get near the table. "I can't do this anymore, Michael. You either want me or you don't, but you can't stare at me from across the room as if you desire me. It's wrong on so many levels. Plus, trying to talk to me about this every day has to stop. If you can't chill out, I'm going to get my own place until I move. You have made it clear that you don't want me, so let's leave it at that."

"I'm sorry," he starts.

I toss my keys down on the table and take out my earrings. I'm so over hearing those words—at this point, I feel like they're empty. "I've heard those two words come out of your mouth more in the last month than I'd like to hear in a lifetime. It's enough." I throw my hands up in the air and go to the fridge to grab a water before walking back through on the way to my room.

"We have to talk, Kayla."

"We will, but not right now. I can't handle it anymore. Do me a favor—don't bring up this monstrosity of a marriage at all until Leah's wedding is over. Give me this time with my sister. Even if I can't be happy about our wedding, at least let me be happy for her."

He takes the water from my hand when I struggle to open it. Mike opens it without any issue, then brings it to his mouth, taking a gulp before handing it back. "Okay, I won't bring anything up until after the wedding. But we *will* be talking, Kayla. You have to hear me out."

I swear, he is so frustrating.

I turn and walk to my room, shutting the door a little louder than I probably should behind me. I strip down to my underclothes, grab my pajamas, and go in search of the pregnancy test. I just want to know. No more waiting.

I open the box and set everything out before I text Meg.

**Me:** *No more waiting. I need to know if I'm pregnant or not. Wish me luck.*

Three little dots appear on the screen before I set my phone down. I wait nervously for her reply. She doesn't keep me waiting for long.

**Megan:** *Give me ten, I'm on my way.*

**Me:** *No. You stay there with Sadie and Damon. Enjoy your family Thanksgiving. I just wanted to let you know that after tonight, I can't wait any longer.*

**Megan:** *Do you think it will work? I heard that you need to test in the morning, after you wake up.*

**Me:** *I don't know, but I sure hope it does. If not, I'll be making a trip to the pharmacy tomorrow.*

**Megan:** *Let me know as soon as you do. I'm only a phone call away.*

I take a steady breath and go to do my business—but drop the stick in the toilet.

“Ugh. Seriously! Can I not catch a break?” I fish it out with the toilet wand, throw it out, then move to wash my hands.

**Me:** *I dropped the dang stick in the toilet.*
**Megan:** *Really? Dang, that sucks.*

Tell me about it. I've been waiting this whole time and now that I'm finally ready to know, this happens.

**Megan:** *You probably should have waited until morning anyway. I'll be over first thing tomorrow with a few more tests. Or do you think you can get in with your doctor, maybe?*
**Me:** *I have an appointment already for the end of next month. I tried to get in sooner, but she's booked.*
**Megan:** *Can you not go to the clinic?*
**Me:** *I can, but if I am pregnant, should I? Mary said that Covid, the flu, and strep are going around right now. Wouldn't getting sick hurt the baby?*
**Megan:** *I don't know, Kay.*
**Me:** *I don't either but I'd rather not chance it.*

**Megan:** *Let's take this one step at a time. I'll grab some more tests in the morning, then we'll go from there.*

**Me:** *Okay, deal. Thank you for having my back.*
**Megan:** *Always.*

I put my phone down and turn on the shower. My muscles ache and I am ready to let the hot spray soak them. All I can do at this point is wait.

Megan walks in with a brown bag in her hand. Both guys are off to work and I'm lying around feeling bad for myself.

"Come on, chica," Meg starts. "I hope you've got a full bladder and a Solo cup."

I walk to the kitchen and grab a disposable cup before running after her toward the bathroom. Megan shoos me into the restroom, only joining me when she hears the sink running. She opens the bag and empties its contents on the counter. A mountain of tests come pouring out. I look from them to her and back at them.

She smiles. "I cleared the shelf. I'm sure after this, we will know for sure if you are or not. No more uncertainty." Megan gets busy opening a test while I get to dipping the sticks in the cup. Once we are done, she sets the timer. We take a seat up against the far wall and wait. I bring my thumb to my mouth and begin to chew.

She swats it away, taking my hand in hers. "No matter what it says, I'm here. Leah and Joe will be, too, if you want them to be."

My eyes go wide. "You know how they would feel about this. I can't tell them until I have seen my doctor and Mike knows. Besides, Leah's wedding is in a week. Now is not the best time to tell them my news."

The timer goes off and she stands, pulling me up with her. We walk to the counter arm in arm and stand there and stare. Tears hit my cheek before I can stop them There is no way that two dozen tests can be wrong.

"I'm pregnant."

I frustratedly toss my phone onto the bed. I just spoke with Mary at my doctor's office, and she let me know that there is nothing she can do to get me seen any sooner. She offered to refer me to an OB, but according to my last period, I wouldn't be seen any sooner than the appointment I have with them. At this point, my options are to go to the clinic hours, call my local health department, go to an urgent care, or wait. With so many illnesses going around, the best option seems to be to wait.

I walk out to the living room where Mike is sitting, playing on his phone. I have been debating on telling him about the baby now or waiting until I have doctor's confirmation to show him. Finally mustering up the courage to tell him, I sit on the couch opposite him.

"Do you have a minute?" I ask.

He glances up from his phone, smiles, then looks back at his phone. "What's up?"

"Can we talk?"

"Shoot."

I wait a moment to see if he'll grant me his attention, but when he doesn't, I get up from the couch unnoticed and head back to my room. I have too much going on this week to deal with that. Mike deserves to know, but I also deserve to have his full attention when I tell him.

I pull out my phone and find my family group text.

**Me:** *Need any help with the wedding? I'm bored out of my mind sitting around here.*

**Leah:** *Always. Maddie said she and a few of the girls are coming out later. Want to come?*

Maddie is a cheerleader for our NBA team—OKC Thunder. Leah met her not that long ago when we got a VIP box for their wedding party. They hit it off right away. I have to say, the girl is cool—a good fit to our friend group, that's for sure.

**Me:** *Yes, please. I need to get out of the house.*

**Uncle Joe:** *I have to take a load out there in an hour. I can give you a ride if you want.*

**Me:** *Please. I'll see you soon.*

After I get changed, I head back out to the living area and wait for Uncle Joe.

Mike puts his phone down and looks over at me. "I thought that you wanted to talk. You don't have to leave."

"We can talk later. I'm going to go help Cam and Leah for a while." I slip on my coat and grab my keys and phone from the table.

"Are you sure?" Mike questions.

"Yeah, we can talk after the wedding. There's a lot to do. I really should be helping Leah get things done." After the way he blew me off earlier, I know that I'm chickening out, but—

There's a knock at the door. I step that way and open it.

"There she is." Uncle Joe smiles at me and pulls me in for a hug. He pulls back with a scowl on his face. "How is it possible that you've lost weight? You're already too thin as it is." He looks over my shoulder and fusses. "Michael, are you not making sure that my girl eats?"

I link my arm in his and begin to pull him out. "I'm a big girl, Uncle Joe. I make sure I eat on my own. I just so happen to have gotten sick; I'm feeling much better now. Don't worry, I'll be fine." I pull the door shut behind me as I finish that sentence and turn to lock the door.

"You've been sick? Why didn't you call me?"

I push the button to the elevator and turn back to face him as we wait. "This is why." I smile. "You'd worry yourself sick, not being able to be here to take care of me. You have a restaurant to run and a wedding to get ready for. You don't need to worry about me too."

"You're my kid—of course I'd worry, that's what

parents do."

After Mom and Dad passed, Uncle Joe adopted the two of us and raised us on his own, never once marrying. He may be rough around the edges, but he loves us with his whole heart.

The door to the elevator opens. We step into the center, where I take his arm and lean on his shoulder.

"You're the best dad any girl could ever ask for." I lean in and kiss his cheek. "But, Uncle Joe, you need to take care of yourself first. You've already raised us. It's time for you."

He kisses the top of my head. "No matter how old you girls get, I will always be there to take care of you. The two of you and Janet are my everything."

The door to the elevator opens as the burning in my eyes intensifies. The two of us step off into the lobby, where I'm able to regain my composure.

"You're getting soft in your old age," I tease. Uncle Joe is anything but—he's a big, buff, tattooed biker that my friends used to tease and call "mean ole Joe." To us, he'll always be a teddy bear.

"There's nothing soft about me." He beats his chest in teasing.

"Okay, let's go, tough guy." I laugh as we make it out to his waiting work truck. Since the restaurant caters weddings, he has one with the restaurant's logo plastered to the side, same as the box trailer that's pulled behind it. "Are the guys there to help unload all this?"

"Pat and Butch said that they'll help me with the tent. Cam is at physical therapy but said he'd help when they get back. The trailer is staying there with the tables and stuff in it until the wedding. I thought it might be easier since I'll be hauling food and cake the day of."

We load up and head out toward the Cameron farm. A day with my family is just what I need. Hopefully the Zofran keeps working. I can handle the nauseous feeling so long as I'm not hugging the toilet the whole time.

"How are things at Mike's?" Uncle Joe signals to get over, and we're on the interstate in no time.

"Fine. I have my own room and bathroom. That makes it bearable. I don't think I'd be able to manage if I didn't." I laugh.

Before he has the chance to respond, a work call comes over the speakers. Since he's in business mode, I take out my phone and turn on my audiobook while slipping in my earbuds. Minutes later, we're pulling down the white rock drive of the Cameron farm, heading to the back where Cam and Leah's house sits.

I hope a day away from the house, spent with my family, is good for Mike and me.

# Chapter Ten

Cam and Leah's wedding is a beautiful affair. I can hardly believe December is already upon us. The look on his face as she walks down the aisle to him nearly breaks me, but I manage to keep it together. I'm thrilled that she found a man like Cam. After they're announced mister and missus, the wedding party gets busy bringing in tables and moving chairs. But once the party is in full swing, I'm worn out.

I stand near the drink table and look out at the dance floor. Cam links his fingers together with Leah's, raising them above their heads. "My wife, y'all." Leah smiles as if he set the moon and stars above just for her. He brings his arm down, wrapping it behind her, and pulls her in for a kiss as they begin to sway. I've never seen anyone more in love than these two. *This* is what I want—I want a man who is willing to shout out just how much I mean to him.

I grab a water, then check with Marie—Cam's mom—and make sure all is well before making a plan to slip out soon. I want to stay long enough to see them cut the cake, so I busy myself with side work. Spotting Uncle Joe and Janet across the way, I start moving.

Michael steps into my path, and instead of avoiding him, I stop and smile. No need to make a scene.

"May I have this dance?" he asks, hand stretched out.

"Sure." I put my practiced smile on and take Mike's offered hand, following him to the dance floor.

Once there, the song changes to "Truly Madly Deeply" by Savage Garden. Being held in his arms, in this romantic setting, swaying to this song, and breathing in his cinnamon and citrus scent that reminds me of home is too much. I'm itching to leave. I look over his arm and see Leah and Cam in each other's arms, lips locked, and nearly burst into tears. I'm beyond happy for her, but I am in my own version of hell right now.

"Do you think that could have been us?" Mike whispers.

I look up at him in question.

"I mean, if we could be together, do you think we could have what they have?"

I pat his chest and huff. "Don't go catching feelings just because you're at a wedding."

Mike looks at me with sad eyes. "I just mean that if things were different, maybe we could've made it work."

I stop moving and look him dead-on. "Things aren't, so why even humor the thought? You've made it known that you don't want me, so quit playing with my feelings. Sign the papers and let me go. It's not like you want me anyway." Before I lose what control I have left, I step back from his embrace and turn toward the drink table, walking away.

I look over my shoulder and run right into Uncle Joe and Janet.

He reaches out and steadies me. "You okay, baby doll?"

"I am, I'm just thinking about sneaking out."

Janet smiles softly. She must have seen where I was coming from.

"I'm just feeling pretty run down and would like to go and relax a bit."

He takes the back of his hand and feels my forehead like he did when I was little. When he's certain I have no fever, he backs off. "Maybe a good night's sleep will help. You get some rest and call me if you need anything." He looks out at the dance floor, then back to me. "You okay to get home, or do you need a ride?"

"I can take her home," Mike says behind me. I tense as his voice sends chills down my spine. "We're going to the same place anyway."

"It's fine. You two should stay and celebrate. I can go grab Meg," I try.

Uncle Joe starts walking me toward the waiting Gator, Mike hot on our heels. "I'd feel better knowing you had Mike there taking care of you."

If I don't let him come, Uncle Joe will worry and spend more time checking his phone than he will enjoying the party. I climb into the Gator and try not to pull away when Mike sits next to me rather than the empty seat up front.

"Love you, kiddo. I'll check in tomorrow."

"Love you too. Tell Cam and Leah congratulations again for me." I hate sneaking out like this without saying good-bye, but she's in a good place and I don't want her worrying about me.

"Will do." He kisses me on the head, then looks to Mike and nods. "You take good care of her now."

"Always."

I look to Janet, who seems a bit conflicted, but I don't have a chance to address her as the driver takes off down the hill. Mike and I sit in silence while we make our way to his parked truck. I guess rather than going home to relax,

I'm going home to hear how much he's sorry once more. How many times can someone hear the same thing repeatedly before their heart combusts? I feel like I'm at my limit already. These next few weeks are going to drag on at this rate.

I step past Mike into the apartment, tossing my bag on the table. "Why? Why did you follow me? I would've been fine with Meg. I needed space from you, Michael. You're really starting to confuse me. One minute, you tell me how much you regret what happened between us, and the next, you're telling me that we could be like them. What the hell? This has got to stop. I can't do it anymore." I walk into the living room, plop down on the couch, and slip off my heels before I start removing my jewelry. What I really want is to take off this dress and remove the pound of makeup on my face, but that'll have to wait. If he wants to hash this out, I guess now is as good of time as any.

Mike walks in, taking his sweet time as he removes his blazer and tie.

It really is a crime that I can't enjoy this moment. He has no business leading me on. I shake myself out of it and look up at him. I can't get lost in thought right now.

"Well . . . are you going to answer me, or did you follow me home just to annoy me?"

He sits down next to me and tries to take my hand. I pull away, stand quickly, and move to sit in the chair on the other side of the coffee table. I can't think with him touching me.

"You don't need to touch me to talk to me," I state.

He flinches but recovers quickly. "I'm sorry for it all. I do love you, Kay, but I can't do this. Yes, I regret marrying you. I regret a lot of how I've handled it. But I can't help that I have moments of weakness where I can't control myself. I want you but I shouldn't. I'm no good for you. Do you not understand that?"

Talk about a gut punch.

"Michael, what I understand is that you are not the man that I thought I knew. The man I knew wouldn't keep this going—he wouldn't keep hurting me. You need help. I don't know what made you change, but I don't like it."

"What changed?" He stands and begins to pace. Now it's his turn to get loud. "What changed is the fact that I have the woman I have always wanted but have sworn never to be with. Like you said, I'm messed up. You can't go through what I did and be okay. You just can't. How could I put you through that? You deserve better."

Why can't he see that he's punishing himself for something he didn't do? He's keeping himself from being happy and hurting me in the process.

"Maybe I do . . . but Michael, I chose you. If you didn't want me, fine, I can get over that, but you're telling me that you do, and that hurts. You have taken care of me from the moment you met me. What happened to you in the past is in the past. It's not a reason to never allow yourself to have a life. Quit letting it ruin your now." Does this mean that there's hope for us when I tell him about the baby? No. I can't let myself think that way. He needs to get help before he can even think about being a dad. Dad . . . that sounds so—

"Leave my past out of this!" he booms. Mike runs his hand through his hair and starts pacing the room. "You don't know what it's like to have a mom tell you how big of a mistake you are every day of your life. How not growing up with a father affects you. How it feels to grow up in group homes, fighting for the tiniest bit of normalcy. You had love, Kayla. You know you can love another without hurting them. Everyone who's ever claimed to love me has hurt me the most. Why would I fight for that? What if I'm like them?" He steps toward the wall of windows overlooking the canal and sobers.

My heart breaks. Will we be continuing the Buchannan way if our little one doesn't have their dad in their life? As much as I want Mike present, I have to be prepared for him to say no.

"You have no clue what it's like." I see a tremble run through him. He seems to be in his head, as if he's reliving all those moments as a kid in a volatile household.

No matter how I feel right now, I don't want him to feel alone. I stand, wanting to show him that I care. Michael deserves to feel love, even if he can never reciprocate it. His back still to the room, I reach out and place my hand on his shoulder. He reacts, turning quickly. His elbow flies back midturn and connects with my cheek, causing me to stumble.

"Aaah!" I yell as I step back and fall over the stool, landing on my butt.

Mike shakes free of the haunted look and reaches out, attempting to get to me as a shirtless, pajama pant-clad Damon runs into the room. He puts himself between Mike and me.

"Kayla, are you okay? I heard the scream. What the heck happened?"

"I'm fine," I say. I reach my hand to my throbbing cheek as I move to sit up. That's going to leave a bruise for sure. I should've known better than to approach him from behind when he was triggered like that.

"What did you do?" Damon turns to Mike.

He looks down at me and appears confused. "I'm sorry . . . I didn't mean—"

"No more," Damon says. "I've been hearing you say sorry for months. You need to pull your head out your—"

"Enough!" I state as I attempt to stand. "We were arguing. I stepped up behind him. He didn't mean to hurt me. Leave him be. All is fine."

I straighten my dress and grab my belongings in an attempt to leave the room. I need ice and my bed. Our conversation can wait. Tonight is not the night to tell him about the baby.

"What the hell happened?" Damon asks Mike for a second time.

"She told you what happened."

"That's not what I mean and you know it. This isn't like you, man. I thought you were going to make things right with her, not make it worse."

Trying not to hear anymore, I loudly open and shut the cabinet. After grabbing a baggie and a dish towel, I move to the freezer.

"You can't mean that, man. Kayla is the best thing to have ever happened to you," Damon states.

So much for not hearing them.

"I still can't help but think that if I had never met Leah, my life would be so different. I'd never have so many regrets with Kayla, and she'd be better off."

"Not true. You'd be a lonely fool."

I put ice in the baggie and seal it, my eyes stinging and cheek throbbing.

"Maybe, but I can't help but wish I'd never met her."

My hand goes to my mouth to cover the gasp. If he wants that, then fine—I'll disappear. It's time to pack. I know better than to stay where I'm not wanted.

I make my way to my room and grab my phone, then do a quick search for a hotel near the airport and hit Dial.

"Garden Suites, this is Liberty. How may I help you?"

"I'm calling to see if you by chance have a room available for a few weeks' rental. I leave at the end of the month." If I'm still going. Will Mike even want me around when I tell him? Will I even be able to take the job now that I'm pregnant? I sit on the edge of the bed, holding the ice to my cheek, while she taps away on her keyboard. At least this will give me the space to figure things out.

"When would you be needing it?"

"Tonight, if possible."

"I'm booked up for the night."

"I just need a single, and as soon as you have one."

"I have a room that I can give you tomorrow."

Liberty and I go back and forth, but by the end of the call, I give her my card info and have a reservation for tomorrow. I can check in as soon as two o'clock. Now, all I have to do is pack up and get out of here without another fight.

I lie back, keeping the ice to my cheek, and take a steadying breath.

My mind rolls through the people I could call and talk to, but I think twice. I need to learn to do things by myself, and there's no better time to start than right now.

My hand finds my still-tiny belly. "It's just you and me now, baby." I pull up my pregnancy book on my phone and begin reading. If I'm going to do this alone, I better learn what I need to do.

# Chapter Eleven

I SIT AT THE table near the only window in my hotel room, phone in hand, on hold. It's been two weeks since I left Mike's. I've been avoiding *everyone*, giving myself time to grieve the loss of not only my marriage, but my best friend. Time is ticking, so I decided I need to get some things done. Three minutes ago, I called my new agent's office in New York to get answers. His secretary said he was on another call, so while I wait, I sit here thinking over my life choices.

"This is Oliver. How can I help you?"

"Hi Oliver, this is Kayla Covington. You're expecting me there just after the new year."

"Ms. Covington, it's nice to hear from you. What can I do for you?"

I nervously bounce my leg and prepare for the onslaught. If Patty were on the other line, I can only imagine the wors that'd come out of her mouth.

"I just recently found out that I'm pregnant."

There's a hesitation on the other side. "Do you have doctor conformation?"

"I don't."

"Then it's not an issue. When you get it confirmed, it will be. Since you're new, we have a three-month clause anyway. That time will let us know if we're a good fit or not. Clearly, if you're pregnant, we won't be. You gave us your word—give us those three months and then we'll give you your freedom." Oliver muffles the line for a moment as he talks to someone else. There's a knock at my door just as he gets back on. "We'll see you in January, Ms. Covington." Then the line goes dead.

Well, he sounds like a delight to work for. Hopefully, I just caught him at a bad time.

I open the door to find Janet standing there with a smoothie and muffin in hand.

"Come in." I move aside and wait for her to step inside while I look around her to make sure Uncle Joe isn't here too. Why is she here? I wonder.

We take a seat at the little dining table near the window.

"Thank you for breakfast. I didn't even know you were coming today. How'd you find me?" I haven't told anyone where I'm staying for this reason—I don't want anyone hunting me down. Plus, if Uncle Joe knew, he'd be here in a heartbeat, loading me up and bringing me home with him. This place isn't exactly nice.

She passes me my breakfast before settling in with her own. "I went to Mike's when the two of you didn't come to game night. I wanted to make sure that you were okay. When he wouldn't talk, I made Damon tell me where to find you. My question now is—why are you staying in this run-down hotel rather than with your husband? And why haven't you been talking to Joe and Leah?"

I tell her what went down the night of Leah's wedding, then explain that I needed a break from everything. I can't seem to bring myself to tell her about the baby just yet. At the rate things are going with Michael, I don't think she'd keep it to herself. I'm sure that she has my back, but everyone has a limit.

"This isn't like you, sugar. I know he's being a turd, but you're on borrowed time. You should be spending it with your family, not letting that boy run you off."

She's right, but seeing Mike everywhere makes things *so* much harder.

Janet reaches across the table, placing her hand on mine. "I told Joe and Leah that I forgot to tell them that you picked up a gig at the agency and were on assignment. That's why you missed game night, but you'll be back soon. Leah's expecting us at her house tomorrow. They put off decorating for Christmas until now, but she's hollering that it needs to get done."

"Why doesn't she just put the decorations up?"

"She might be with Cam, but she will always need her sister. I think this is her way of showing you just how much."

This would have been the first year since I was born that Leah and I didn't decorate for Christmas together. While I expected as much now that she has her own little family, it still stung, thinking I'd be forgotten. It's all happening so fast. I'm thrilled she thought to include me.

"Maybe." I haven't even bought a single gift this year. How can it be the middle of December, and I have nothing? This is not like me. By now, I would normally have been finished. "Are you busy today?"

"Sugar, I'm all yours. What do you have planned?"

"How does a trip to the mall sound?"

"It sounds like I wish I had your uncle to carry our bags." We share a laugh before she sobers. "Eat up and then we'll head out. I'm well overdue for some shop therapy."

By the time we make it to the mall, it's packed. Who knew that it'd be this busy during the middle of the workweek? Janet and I make our way to the second-story shops first. When I catch a whiff of the pretzel shop, I pull her with me. "Just one salted pretzel with cheese and a Coke ICEE and then we can get started."

"It's nine o'clock in the morning, Kayla." Janet might be fussing, but she's smiling and not stopping me from pulling her along.

"What does it matter when they smell so good? Besides, you know they'll be fresh this early. You can't honestly tell me that your mouth isn't watering right now."

She chuckles and gives in. "I guess today can be cheat day. I mean, I did already have a muffin."

"I have no idea why you're on a diet. You're gorgeous."

When we get to the counter, I place my order, then Janet follows up with hers next. I pay and then we step back and wait. When our pretzels are ready, we grab them and a table. We make small talk about what stores we want to hit before I settle in.

"You and Uncle Joe are coming up on two years now, aren't you?"

"Yeah, it's crazy to think. I never thought I'd be with another man so seriously after Rick died."

"How are you feeling? I know you struggled in the beginning. Are you coming around to the thought of possibly marrying one day?"

Janet is a widow. At the start of her and Uncle Joe's relationship, she was hesitant. She felt like she was cheating on her late husband. Two years, though, should show that Uncle Joe is committed to being there for her and taking it at her speed.

"I am. Losing Rick was one of the hardest things I have ever gone through. He was the love of my life. You know, much like your mom and Joe, Rick and I met when we were just kids. I can see now that someone can have more than one great love. Joe can never take Rick's place in my heart, just like I can't take your mom's." Mom and Uncle Joe were never a couple but that didn't stop them from loving one another. Before Mom met Dad, Uncle Joe thought they'd marry one day—until Mom came home from college pregnant and in love. "And that's okay, we both know that now. I'll always love Rick, but I have to let him go and live my life. I love Joe, and you girls, plus I know Rick would want me to be happy. Y'all are my family." She reaches out her hand and wipes the tear from my cheek. "I'll never replace your momma, but I love being here for you."

I put my hand over hers and lean into it. "I love you too. I appreciate that. I don't even remember Mom, only the stories. You are the only person I've ever had that came close to one." A part of me feels guilty for saying that, because if Mom could be here, she would, but having Janet love me the way a mom loves her kids . . . it lessens the pain of not having one. It'll be hard leaving her behind.

I'm sitting in the gift-filled backseat of Uncle Joe's car—I took an Uber to his place and caught a ride. He's driving Janet and me out to Leah's. Today, we'll be decorating for Christmas. About an hour ago, Uncle Joe told me to bring my gifts, as tonight will be for family and friends. There will be food, games, and a gift exchange. I can hardly believe Christmas is in a matter of ten days now—and then I move to New York the next day. I got the call that my apartment is ready when I am. No sense in waiting an extra week. I might as well go. It would be nice to go back and try to talk to Mike about the baby and the divorce, but I am tired of fighting, and I know the stress is not good for me right now. Putting some distance between us might be what we need. Besides, it would be nice to get some time to settle in before I have to start working. As much as I hate the thought of leaving, I decide it's time.

I take out my phone and check in with Meg.


**Me:** *Hey, girlie. You're coming tonight, right?*

**Meg:** *Yeah, I told you that I would.*

**Me:** *Awesome. We're almost there. When are you heading out?*

**Meg:** *Dame just got here. I'm riding with him. I think he said we're giving Mike a ride, so be ready for that. How are you feeling?*

**Me:** *I figured he'd be there. He normally is. I can't be mad at him for showing up. I just hope things aren't too weird.*

**Meg:** *Same. Hey, I gotta go. D is ready to get there and wants to chat. I'll see you soon.*

**Me:** *Ok. See you then.*

**Meg:** *<3*

I scroll through the messages I've been putting off answering for the last week and come to Mike's. When I left the house, I put a note on his bedroom door, telling him that I was okay, but I would be giving him what he wanted—space. Since then, I haven't looked at his any of his texts because I know it will either lead to a fight or me running back to him out of habit.

I needed some time. I scroll all the way down to the last text, ignoring the rest.

**Mike:** *I wish you'd quit ignoring me.*

So that he doesn't make today uncomfortable, I type out a response.

**Me:** *I was ignoring everyone, not just you. I needed to get my head on straight. We still need to talk before I leave, and you need to sign the papers.*
**Mike:** *Do you know how worried I've been? I didn't mean what I said, Kay. I'm sorry. Will you come home please?*
**Me:** *I'm fine where I am. Don't worry, I'm safe.*
**Mike:** *I can't help it. I really wish you'd come back. I miss you.*
**Me:** *You can't have it both ways. I'm going to go for now. I don't want to argue anymore. I'll see you at Leah's. Please don't make things weird.*

I silence my phone and drop it into my bag. I let him know that I was okay—that's all he gets from me. I lay my head back on the seat and close my eyes for the remainder of the drive. When we get there, Cam and Tom come out to help unload the gifts while Janet and I make our way inside to find Leah.

We find her standing at the kitchen sink, swaying her hips and simply glowing. Janet and I stop to take in the beauty that is my sister. Married life seems to agree with her. I'm going to miss her most of all when I leave. I'm so thankful that Janet found me and made me get out of that hotel. Had I let this time pass me by, I would've regretted it. I catch a tear that threatens to fall. I can't seem to stop crying lately. It's really getting on my nerves.

Janet takes my hand in hers and squeezes. "Come on, sugar. Let's make some memories."

We walk into the kitchen and surround Leah in a hug. I'll miss this. I didn't grow up with a mom, but I had Leah and, now, Janet. How will I get along without these two? Just as the tears begin to fall again, I feel the strong arms of Uncle Joe wrap the three of us up.

"My whole world in my arms. I could die a happy man." Janet tenses. "Don't go talking about dying," she scolds as he releases us. "I'm getting my second chance at love. I'm not ready for it to be taken away."

Leah pulls me aside as Uncle Joe assures Janet that he's not going anywhere. Leah tugs me into the garage and starts squealing about her upcoming honeymoon and just how dreamy married life is. It's sad that I have to put on my practiced smile with her. I can't handle hearing about how glorious married life is when mine is falling apart. No matter how much I want happiness for her, it hurts to hear. I'm pregnant and I can't tell a soul. I should be overjoyed, talking baby names and making future plans. Instead, I'm hiding away and trying to figure out how to do this alone.

"Kayla!" Leah warns.

She pushes me to the side just in time. The boxes we were standing in front of start to tumble, one falling right where I was standing.

Leah makes it to my side and puts a hand on either arm. "Are you okay?" She starts looking me over but is pulled away as Cam comes rushing in to look her over. Uncle Joe follows behind him. In a matter of a minute, the garage is full of people. If Leah's stalker wasn't still out there, I might think this was overkill.

"Hello?" Mike's voice carries into the garage from the house.

"In the garage!" Cam yells back.

Tom and Maddie start restacking the boxes as Uncle Joe is fussing over me, making sure I didn't get hurt. Cam wants the guys to do a sweep of the place just to ensure this really was an accident and not one set up by the stalker. I look up when I hear Megan's voice near the door. My eyes have a mind of their own apparently. They smooth right over her and zero in on the man just behind her.

Michael. My stomach flips and my heart speeds up at the sight of him. How will I ever get over him if this is how my body reacts at the sight of him?

I'm taken from my perusal as Megan pulls me in for a big hug.

"If you don't want to talk about going back to Mike's, avoid being alone with him," she says before pulling back. "My God, I've missed you."

"I've missed you too. We need to have a girls' night, you and I."

"Agreed. Come home with me?"

"I can do that. I'll have to go back and get some clothes first."

Megan grabs Damon's arm, bringing him to our conversation. "Kay's coming home with me tonight. Can you give her a ride back to her hotel to get her stuff before you take me home?"

"Sure can. Do you ladies want to come to the house for games tomorrow?"

"I better not," I reply. "I don't want things to get out of hand. Thanks for the offer though. Maybe we can go grab lunch before I leave."

"Let's get out of here," Cam interrupts. "Dad and Pat are coming in with the tree."

All is dropped for now as we follow the crowd, leaving the garage. We move to the kitchen, where I help Leah get some cocoa started. The other ladies bring in the decorations while the guys start sorting the lights, and a few of them put the tree where it goes. Leah walks out to the living area and puts on Christmas music, then pulls up an inviting fireplace scene on the TV. I stay back in the kitchen, finishing up the cocoa, trying not to make a mess as I take it all in. I hate that I'm going to miss out on so much. Flying home every so often when I'm not working won't be anything like hopping in the car and coming over because I miss them. It might only be a few months now, but I'm used to always being with them.

"There you are," Mike says, entering the kitchen. I turn to find him standing behind me. "What's up?" I ask.

"Leah sent me to get you. She wants you to put the angel on the tree this year."

"Oh, okay." I turn and put down my cup, then start walking alongside Mike toward the living area.

"You two have to kiss!" Tom hollers. We're just past the dining room in the living room walkway. "You're under the mistletoe."

I look up, and sure enough, we are. *Great! Just what I need.*

Mike leans in and I give him my cheek. When he starts to pull back, I pat him on the chest to make it seem playful. "Sorry, buddy, cheek only." I wink and head toward the tree. I plaster on the best smile I can.

This is going to be a long night.

# Chapter Twelve

I take a sip of water and look across the way at Meg. She keeps urging me to just shout it out—that's not how I envisioned telling the father of my child that I'm pregnant. But maybe this is how I should tell him. Game night, just the four of us, is interesting to say the least. Telling him now, with Damon and Megan here, would give both of us the support that we need. Mike has barely spoken a handful of words to me and seems to be on his best behavior—Damon by his side to ensure it. I've caught Michael looking at me from the corner of his eye more than a dozen times. Maybe this is the right time to tell him. I stare blankly at Mike; he sees me and returns it.

"That was fun," Meg chimes. "How about a new game?"

"Sure. What do you want to play?" Damon asks.

"Two truths and a lie," I state before I can stop myself. I blink and look out across the table at the others as if gauging their interest.

Megan smiles mischievously. "Good idea."

Damon raises a brow. "It sounds like the two of you are up to something."

"I'll start," Megan says. "My true eye color is blue. I'm a softy on the inside. I cannot stand seafood."

"Easy," I reply. "Your true eye color is green, not blue."

She nods and smiles. "Your turn."

I give her side-eye—she set me up and she knows it. I was hoping to warm up to this. If I don't get this out now, I won't say it at all. I take a deep breath and take Megan's offered hand. Damon looks at me with worried eyes and then down to our joined hands and nods. I look at Michael before I start.

"I'm legally married. I can hardly wait to leave for New York. I'm pregnant."

Michael visibly swallows. He looks down at his hands and grips the bottle hard enough to crumple it.

Damon looks between Megan and me and smiles softly when I nod.

"How?" Michael growls.

I ignore his rough behavior and start speaking low. "Michael." I reach out to take his hand in mine, but he yanks it back before I can.

"How, Kayla? First you marry me and then you get pregnant? I told you I didn't want to be with you, so you make sure to tie yourself to me for life?"

Damon stands and tries to get Mike to follow, but he refuses.

"I never would have thought you were as low as one of those fight bunnies. I guess I was wrong. You're worse." He stands so fast that his chair falls to the ground in a loud clatter.

Megan is at my side, pulling me into her embrace while Damon pushes at Mike's chest, yelling obscenities. I can't take my eyes off the train wreck that is happening in front of me. My heart breaks and I gladly accept Megan's shoulder to cry on. I guess I have my answer. He doesn't want either of us.

Tomorrow morning is Christmas—before I know it, I'll be hopping on a plane to New York. I cannot sit around and wait on him to throw more stress my way. I'll use this time—however long it takes Oliver to find new talent—to put some space between Mike and me. I think at this point, I need it as much as he does. If not more.

Who knows? Maybe I'll like New York enough to stay.

I open the door to find Damon standing there, hands in his pockets. "Merry Christmas." He kicks at the ground as if he's uncomfortable. I can't blame him. I left the apartment last night with Megan while he and Mike were in a yelling match.

"Merry Christmas to you too." I walk over to the bed and slip on my boots. I'm in my red leather pants, black knee-high boots, and my green ugly sweater complete with twinkling lights. Gotta love a good ugly sweater party. "Did you pick up Megan yet?" She and Sadie had Christmas last weekend so that Megan could spend the week with me, knowing that I'll be leaving tomorrow.

"No, we're going there next. She had to wrap your gift first. Are we still on for you coming back to our place after the party?" We planned on me checking out of here today and staying the night at their place, but that was before last night.

"I can, I just don't want it to cause any more drama

with Mike."

"He promised me to be on his best behavior. If he starts anything, I'll give Meg my keys so she can take you home with her." Megan hasn't had a car in years. She sold her old one to get her and Sadie in a home and hasn't ever replaced it.

"I'll grab my bag then."

Tonight is all about putting my game face on. I don't want to leave tomorrow, but after last night, I'm more convinced than ever that this is what's best for us right now. I wish I could tell my family about Mike and the baby, but until I've seen the doctor and have given Mike time to process, this is a secret I'll have to keep. Here goes nothing.

Today is a smaller gathering than the last—Cam, Leah, Uncle Joe, Janet, and the four of us—Mike included. Though he hasn't said much to me, I can feel his eyes on me. Cam and Leah had lunch with his family so that this could be more chill, in her words. I sit down at the dining table and take in the faces of my family. Life is so hard. I remember Uncle Joe telling me when I was younger to enjoy my childhood rather than trying to grow up so fast. I wish I had listened because right now, all I want is to crawl into his protective arms and let him shield me from harm's way.

Leah scoots in next to me and pulls me in for a hug. "You look so sad. Can't you just stay? You don't really have to go, do you?"

I glance at Mike across the way and then down at my food. "I am sad. I'm going to miss this, but . . . I need to do it. It's time for me to grow up."

Leah sits up and smiles. "Growing up is a trap, you know. We all love you just how you are."

"Not everyone," I mumble.

"What's that?" Leah asks.

"I said, I know. I love you all too." I push my food around on my plate, trying like hell to gain an appetite, but I don't.

"I propose a toast," Uncle Joe says. He holds up his beer and looks at all of us, a smile growing on his face as he looks around the room. His eyes land on me. "To my girls. No matter how far away they may be, they've been such a blessing in my life. I wish you two all the happiness in the world." He clears his throat, then hoists his beer once more. "And to frequent flyer miles—may they rack up quickly."

"Hear, hear," some cheer. Others laugh—either way, it was sweet of him to say.

I don't eat much of dinner. My stomach in knots as realization hits me hard—there is so much that I'll be leaving behind. By the time we get back to Mike's, I call it a night. Crawling into bed, I hug my pillow tight. Tears begin to fall, but I don't have much time to dwell as Megan walks in and lies next to me, replacing my pillow. As I fall asleep, I can't help but wonder if I'm making a mistake by leaving.

"Good morning, Mrs. Buchannan," Megan says as she rolls over to face me.

"I'm still a Covington. No sense in taking his name when he doesn't even want me."

"Oh, please. He's just being a jerk—he wants you, alright." She scoots up in bed and looks back at me.

"Are you sure you still want to go? You don't want to stay and fight for him?"

I battle within to hold back the tears as they begin to sting my eyes. "Megan, it's been months. Mike hasn't changed yet. He still doesn't want me—or our baby. All this back and forth is tearing us apart. I need to move on."

Even though I hate the thought of leaving, if I stay, our relationship will come to the surface and Mike will be collateral damage. If I leave now, we both have room to heal. I'm just removing myself from the situation.

She rolls to her side, bouncing the bed enough to make my stomach protest at its action. Thankfully, it's a little more settled than it has been, but that doesn't stop the upset.

"You know as well as I do that he loves you. If you don't fight for him, he'll let this end. Is that what you want?"

"It doesn't matter if he loves me or not. He won't let himself have me. I have to accept that."

There's a knock at the door before it's pushed open. The smell of blueberry pancakes and bacon rolls in behind Mike and Damon. They're carrying food trays filled with my favorite breakfast. Tears brim my eyes when Micheal won't even look at me. I'm sure this is Damon's doing, not his.

I sit up and make room for the guys at the foot of the bed. The four of us are quieter than I can ever remember being while we pick at our food. Before long, I excuse myself, throw on some joggers and a T-shirt, and start loading my bag for my flight. An hour later, we're on the way to the airport. Once I'm all checked in and ready to board, we start our goodbyes.

Damon pulls me in for a hug. "I want a call when you get there."

I nod.

"You take care out there, you hear me? I'll hop on a plane at the drop of a hat if you need me. All you have to do is call."

"Love you, too, D."

He steps back and lets Meg replace him.

"Are you sure about this? You don't have to go." She smiles softly.

"I do."

"I'm going to miss you," Meg says, trying to dry her eyes. She pulls me in for a big hug. I swear if she was any bigger, she'd crush a rib.

"Me too. Take care of these knuckleheads, will you?" I look at Damon, then back to her. "I know you wanted to wait on him to ask, but the girl can ask too."

She smiles brightly and looks toward Damon. "I forgot to tell you. I said yes. He and I are a couple now."

I pull her in for a rocking hug, squealing at her excitement, then look over at Damon, who smiles. "I'm thrilled for the two of you. No wedding unless I'm here, got it?"

Megan chuckles before turning and stepping into Damon's open arms.

"I'm glad she'll have you while I'm gone. You better take good care of her."

Damon kisses the side of her head, holding her close. "Forever."

"My turn." Mike steps forward, surprising me. The others step back, giving him room. "I wish you would stay."

"I think we both know that if I did, it would only get worse." I take his hand in mine and look deep into his bottle-green eyes. "I will always love you; it might not be what you want to hear, but I want you to know it anyway. We didn't work out, but you need to know that love doesn't equal pain. True love is forgiving and forever." I put his hand on my stomach, the first time other than Meg that anyone has touched it like this, and smile. "We created a life, Michael. One that will need us both to be strong. Get some help and become the best you possible—if not for me, then for this little one."

He squeezes my hand and, with his other, reaches up to move a piece of hair from my face, tucking it behind my ear. "For what it's worth, I'm sorry I was such a jerk. I let my past control me and I took it out on you." He smiles and nods toward our joined hands. "I called a therapist. Maybe he can help me get my head on straight. I know it's too late for us, but I want you to know I'm trying."

I remove our hands from my stomach and lean in for a quick hug. "I'm proud of you. If you need someone to talk to, don't hesitate to call."

"Do you mean that?" he asks in surprise.

"I do. I want the best for you. I know this will be hard, but it really is the right step in healing. Of course, I'll be there for you. Always."

He leans in and kisses my forehead like he used to, causing me to close my eyes. "I signed the papers." He looks down at his feet, shoulders slumped. "I wanted to hold on to you with all I have in me, but I know it's not healthy. I need to let go." He looks up at me, takes the papers out of his coat, and hands them to me. "Can I kiss my wife one last time before you file?"

I can't speak right now, I'm in shock, but I nod in acceptance.

Mike frames my face in his hands and leans in, taking

my breath away. He brands me as his, taking my heart with him in one soul-searing kiss right here in the middle of the airport. When he pulls back, he nudges my chin to look at him.

"I will always love you Kayla. You'll always be the keeper of my heart. I'm sorry I was horrible at showing you. This is on me." He kisses my nose softly. "Take care of you and our little one. If you need anything, I'm only a phone call away." Then he turns and walks down the corridor, leaving me more confused than before.

It's time. I wipe my eyes and fumble to grab my carry-on. Looking between Mike and the plane, as much as I want to run after him, I don't. He might feel this way now, but like he said, he's letting me go. I thought my heart hurt before, but this is what it feels like to be shattered.

I hope I'm not making the biggest mistake of my life by getting on this plane.

# Chapter Thirteen

I stand in front of my new apartment, dig the keys out of my purse, unlock the door, and take a single step in before dropping my bag to the ground. Standing to my full height, I take it in. The levity of the move hits me hard. This is the same apartment Mike and I saw, but for some reason, it feels emptier now, colder and darker, if that's even possible.

"Howdy. Are you the new neighbor?" someone asks in a Texan accent.

I'm startled and turn. I see a cute little woman, who can't be more than five-four, with red hair and bright green eyes, standing in the doorway across from mine. I bet she's due any day now. Her stomach is nearly as big as she is tall. She pushes off the doorjamb and takes a step toward me, hand extended.

"Hey, yeah, I am." I smile and meet her halfway. "Kayla Covington." I stick my hand out to shake hers.

She returns the shake with a firmer grip than I expect. "Shannon Carter, and this here," she rubs her belly and smiles, "is Elizabeth. She'll be here before you know it."

"Congratulations. I bet you can hardly wait." She nods her head in confirmation, then steps aside as one of the movers brings up a load of boxes. "I'm just across the hall if you need anything. Ben—the only other neighbor in our hall—and I have dinner together a lot. You're always welcome to join. It's hard being new to town. If we can help, don't hesitate to reach out."

"Thank you. I'd love that." She nods, then turns and steps past her threshold and shuts the door.

Thank God I have someone I might be able to get along with right next door.

I step out of my apartment and head down the stairs. The movers are bringing in the small truckload of boxes I had shipped, but I still have a few more bags that the Uber driver dropped off downstairs. Bending down to grab the bag, I nearly fall over from a bout of dizziness.

"Whoa," a man says, putting a hand on my waist to steady me. In his New York accent, he continues. "You okay there?"

I turn to see a handsome man near my age in a sharp-looking business suit. He's tall—six foot two-ish—with blond hair, hazel eyes, and the build of a runner. His smile lights up his whole face. I'm instantly drawn to him.

"Are you okay? You seem pretty out of it."

"Yeah. I'm okay. I just got dizzy is all." I try to move, but things start to spin again.

"Whoa," he says in a rush. He's by my side, helping me sit, in a flash. "Moving day can be rough. When's the last time you ate?"

"Just a little before I caught my flight." The trip took twice as long as it should have—one issue after another. We sat on the tarmac for two hours before taking off due to a "maintenance issue." Then when we got here to New York, we had to wait for an empty boarding bridge to let us off. I was never so happy to get off a plane as I was that one.

He looks at his watch, then narrows his eyes. "You realize that it's nearly six in the evening and you haven't eaten? Come on, we'll get you fed."

I'm worn out, and thanks to Michael's farewell, my stomach has been in such a frenzy I haven't eaten a thing. I didn't even realize how late it had gotten. "You don't have to do all that. You don't even know me," I argue.

He smiles brightly and shoulders his messenger bag. "I might not know you . . . yet, but I know you need help." He sticks out his hand and helps me stand. "Let's get you inside and I'll come back for these bags."

"If you give me a minute to gather myself, I'll be fine."

He smiles softly and follows me upstairs and into my apartment. "Why don't you order us some dinner? My treat. I'll go get your bags." Before I can argue, he hands over his phone, already open to a food app. "You can buy me dinner when you're settled. Tonight is my treat. I know how expensive moving day is—besides, it's my turn to buy." He sets down his bag, takes off his tie and blazer, and starts rolling up his sleeves on his way out.

"I don't even know what you like," I fuss.

"I'll eat anything except anchovies. Those are just creepy."

I'm a little taken aback at the comfortability I feel with this man. I don't even know his name and yet here I am, sitting on my couch with full access to his phone while he moves my things. I don't know whether to be thrilled or creeped out.

"Oh, hey, Shannon," I hear from the hallway. "Hey, Ben," she replies.

"I have our new neighbor ordering us dinner. It's my turn to buy if you have time to join us," Ben asks.

"Sure. I'd love that. Thank you."

I guess I'm getting to know my new neighbors tonight.

Shannon walks in, following a suitcase-wielding Ben. He puts them down in the corner, then walks back down for the last.

Shannon stops beside me. "Hi again. I hope you don't mind me joining. I can leave if you want."

"Oh, no, please stay. Is there anything you're craving? I haven't ordered yet."

"I'd love something cheesy, but I'm up for anything, really." She absently rubs her belly.

I put in my order and do the same for Ben, then pass the phone to Shannon, who adds hers. In a matter of minutes, Ben is plopping down on the couch next to me.

"There you go. Everything is up here now. So, Kayla, right? What's for dinner?" Ben asks.

"Yes, it's Kayla. And I ordered some cheeseburgers and fries." I return the smile. "Thanks for buying dinner and for moving my stuff up here."

"No worries. Us transplants need to look out for one another."

"Transplant?" I question. He doesn't sound like a transplant.

"Yup, southern Oklahoma. Near the Red River. I've just been here so long that my accent is  non-existent now."

"Oh, nice. We'd basically be neighbors back home. I'm an Okie myself." My phone pings on the table, and I stand to grab it. "Excuse me. That's probably my family checking to make sure I made it." The dizziness is less but still there. I grab my phone and take a seat back on the couch.

**Leah:** *Please tell me that you made it okay. You've been silent for some time.*

**Uncle Joe:** *Give her a little while. I'm sure she's moving her bags in. If we don't hear from her before bed, then we can worry.*

I send a quick response.

**Me:** *My plane landed. A neighbor of mine helped me move my stuff in. Love you and miss you already. I'll message later after things calm down around here a little.*

I check the next text thread, seeing that Megan and Damon have put me in a group, and send out a reply.

**Megan:** *Let me know when you land. Love you and miss the heck out of you already.*
**Damon:** *I shouldn't have let you talk me out of moving you there. Please tell me you have help moving your bags.*
**Me:** *The flight had a delay, but I made it. Sorry I didn't text sooner. My neighbor Ben saved the day and is buying me and our other neighbor dinner. I'll call you guys later. I have company right now.*

I silence my phone and return to the conversation around me. "Sorry about that. My family just wanted to make sure I made it."

"No problem," Shannon says. "We were just talking about going out this weekend. You're welcome to join us."

"I'd love that. Thank you."

I'm glad that I met these two. Feeling homesick is bound to happen, but with them nearby, maybe it won't be as bad as I thought.

I crack open my eyes to take in the surroundings of my new apartment that is now full of boxes. Since I left Oklahoma quicker than I had planned, today is full of phone calls—canceling with Dr. Jordan and finding a new PCP around here—then I have to run out to get some groceries and cleaning supplies, followed by some unpacking. What I really want to do is crawl back under the covers and hide out for a while.

Last night, I fell asleep looking at pictures of Mike and me at our wedding. Again. I really need to stop that. Not willing to let the depression set in, I throw back the covers and sit up, grabbing my phone along the way. Thank God I thought to turn it on silent last night. The number of messages I have is insane.

**Megan:** *How are you and baby this morning?*

**Damon:** *It's still weird to think that Kayla and Mike are having a baby.*

**Megan:** *It's not weird at all. We all know those two belong together. This little one will be a powerhouse for sure.*

**Mike:** *Do you guys mind? I'm trying to sleep. I had a long night.*

**Damon:** *You'd be able to sleep if you didn't just send your wife and kid halfway across the world.*

**Mike:** *Don't give me crap, man. You still live under my roof.*

I guess they decided to let it go after that because the messages stop. Now that I'm up and reading my messages, I chime in.

**Me:** *Sorry, guys, I just got up. It was a long, tiring day yesterday. I guess I'm a bit worn out. I'm doing okay, I guess. I miss being back home, but I think this will be good for me. Baby must be doing well. I'm not feeling sick this morning. I'll call later this evening if you guys are free. Video call?*

**Mike:** *I'm down. Call at 8:30. I'll be on my break then. I have to close tonight.*

**Megan:** *I should be home by then.*
**Damon:** *I'll be back by then too. Talk tonight.*

I close out the group chat and open the one with my family. Just like the other thread, there are several messages waiting on me.

**Leah:** *Morning, sis. I miss you already.*
**Uncle Joe:** *Me too. I miss both of you.*
**Leah:** *I literally live ten minutes out.*
**Uncle Joe:** *Ten minutes too far.*
**Janet:** *Let the kids grow up, babe.*

I chuckle at the thread; I can imagine Uncle Joe already—his grumpy scowl growing on his face as he reads that. I miss him too.

**Me:** *Morning, Love you all. I have a busy day ahead of me. I can call after dinner if you want.*
**Leah:** *You bet.*
**Me:** *Talk then.*

I set my phone down on the bedside table, get up, and head to find my bathroom box to locate a towel. Six boxes later, I have acquired said towel and am ready to let the water soak bone deep before I have no other choice than to get my life as a New Yorker get started. The shower is amazing—even better than the one at Mike's place. There is a shower wand, a rainfall head above, and jets on the wall, along with a bench seat. By the time I finish, I am beyond relaxed and ready for the day.

After some breakfast, I make my calls. It doesn't take me as long as I had thought it would to find a new PCP. On the third call, I get an appointment with Dr. Emmons next week. I'm just about to grab my keys and head out to find some food when my phone rings. It's Michael.

"Hello?"

"Hey," he says.

I walk to the couch and take a seat. At the sound of his dejected voice, I know that this might take some time. "How are you?"

"I had my first appointment with Richard—my therapist. I don't know if I can do it, Kay. Today was a get-to-know-you session, but sitting there on his couch, it just felt so clinical. I know I need to work on this, but bringing all that back up . . . it makes me feel like I'm going back in time. I can't quit thinking about it."

I wish I could reach through the phone and comfort him right now, but I can't. If only he had spoken to me like this while we were living together, maybe we could have fixed us. "Is there any way that you can call off tonight?"

"Maybe. Leah's still in town. I might be able to get her to cover for me. Why?"

"Take the day off and go to the gym and work this stress out of your body. That has always been your outlet, so use it. It'll help you." I lie back on the couch and look at the ceiling, pinching my nose. "I know it's going to be hell to bring it all back up, but it'll be worth it in the long run. Your life with your mom has haunted you for as long as I've known you. Don't let her win, Micheal. You are stronger than that."

He's quiet a moment before starting again. "Thanks, Kay. I'll call Leah after I hang up. After everything, I didn't think you'd take my call."

"I told you that I would." I sit back up and look at my phone to see the time. With all that I have to get done today, I have to get a move on. "I really am proud of you. You've taken a huge step in healing. You should be proud of yourself too."

"Yeah, maybe."

"You really should be. I'd love to keep talking, but I really have to get. I have to find a gym and some food before the end of the day." Then I think of all I've done already and remember to tell Mike. "I nearly forgot. I found a doctor. I go in next week to be seen. I'll let you know what she says when I leave."

"Oh, okay. Talk to you later. Thanks again, Kay," Mike rushes out, then the line goes dead.

I look at my phone for a long moment, wondering why he ended the call so abruptly, but shrug it off. There's no figuring him out anymore. I'm here to give us space and to do a job—and that starts now.

I stand and head to grab my keys. Last night, I set the divorce papers on the table near the door so that I could mail them off today. I spot them and slow my steps. "Nope. Not yet." I take a breath, grab my keys, and get the door. I'm stepping out when I bump into Ben and Shannon, who seem to be on their way out too.

"Hey, neighbor," he says. "Heading somewhere?"

"Yup. I'm in search of a gym and food. You?"

"I was going to hit the gym while Shannon sits at the doctor's for her glucose test, then we're getting lunch. Want to join us?"

Normally, I wouldn't want to intrude, but considering this is a new state and these are the only two people I somewhat know here, I agree. I've got to start somewhere, and they seem nice enough. Here's to making new friends.

# Chapter Fourteen

I SIT IN MY new agent's office, waiting for him to come back in. Today is my first day on the job, and as much as I'd love to go home and crawl back into bed, I have to make a good impression. I showed up to his office a whole twenty minutes early, clean face, hair down, and ready for whatever they throw at me. Meeting here isn't normal, but considering we have paperwork to take care of before I make it to set, this seemed like the best option. Oliver—my agent—said he'll be taking me to my first job right after we finish here. I guess they like to hit the ground running. I've been in New York for a week and have felt awful the whole time. Thankfully, I have an appointment in two days with my new doctor.

"Sorry about that," Oliver says as he walks back in. "I didn't mean to keep you waiting. Pricilla needed my signature on something. Did you have time to look over the paperwork while I was gone?"

I put it on his desk, open to the part that has me questioning. "Yes, I did. I have a concern about not being able to leave the state during my brief employment with y'all. That's got me reluctant to sign." I'm only supposed to have to stay on until I begin to really show and or they find my replacement. "My whole family is in Oklahoma—including the father of my unborn child—and I'd like to be able to visit them when I'm not on assignment. I get that it's only a few months, but still, my time off belongs to me."

Oliver nods. "I can understand your frustration, but with you being on short contract, you will be on call during the time you're with us. I can't change that. When you agreed to our seven-year contract, we stopped seeking out other potential models. The company could have missed out while waiting on you." He looks at his phone as it rings but silences it. "I know it might not seem fair, but you'll still get a partial bonus, along with your moving expenses. Working you so much in the next few months is the company's way of recouping their loss. Now, if you have something come up back home that can't wait, I can be a bit lenient. I can give you a few days' window, but I need you to communicate with me."

I scowl. I have no problem communicating, but this whole situation stinks.

The huff in his voice tells me that Oliver doesn't like having to explain himself, but he continues anyway. "I know you don't like it. I can see it written all over your face, but you did leave us in a pinch. We could take you to court for not fulfilling your agreement. Instead, we're working with you, knowing these kinds of things happen. After we find your replacement or you start showing enough that our clients don't want to work with you, I'll call you back to the office so we can terminate your contract."

I'd rather miss my family for a few months than be taken to court. Maybe I can talk a few of them into coming to me for a visit instead.

I nod. "Okay. I'll make sure to communicate with you." I take his offered pen and sign before sliding it back across the desk.

He takes a check from my file and slides it in my direction. "This is your bonus payment, plus moving expenses. Pay is based on each job and that can be a bit sporadic." He stands and walks toward the door. "Ready to get started?"

I follow closely behind. "Ready."

"Good, let's go. I don't want to be out in the cold any longer than I have to be."

I don't want to be outside either. I just hope they have heaters set up.

New York is so different than what I'm used to. It's fast paced, whereas Okies can be done with their day by five in the afternoon and be moving on to take care of things at home or going out for the evening. Here, it seems like things are just getting started.

We get into Oliver's waiting car and head across town to meet up with the photographer. I don't have time to think, let alone process. I'm rushed into the hair and makeup tent without so much as an introduction, then pulled out of the chair and walked toward the end of the room where wardrobe is. I'm handed some clothes and told to get a move on. I have to suck it in, as this dress isn't the least bit forgiving—either that, or the baby is already making itself known. By the time I'm dressed, I'm being whisked off to the location where the pictures are being taken.

Today, I'm in the skimpiest little rhinestone and gold evening gown and a pair of black stilettos. My hair and makeup are done to the nines. With it being January, I'm freezing. Thank God they gave the models terry-cloth bathrobes. It's not much, but it's better than nothing.

Oliver walks over to talk to the two other models in today's shoot, Marla and Danielle. Making friends at work has always been a rare thing for me. Sure, I have Meg, but she and I knew each other before modeling became a thing. Once done, Oliver runs off to talk to the photographer and the ladies turn my way, sizing me up.

"Morning," I say, extending my hand for a shake. "I'm Kayla."

"Marla." She raises her hand to check her perfect nails.

"Don't mind her. I'm Danielle," the sweet blonde says. "She gets like this when new girls come in. You'll get used to it."

"Nice to meet you. I'm not too worried." I pull the robe as tight around me as I can and blow into my freezing hands.

"Marla!" the photographer hollers.

She walks over as instructed, ditching her robe along the way. Next is Danielle, then me. This guy's not bad. He's straight to the point—snaps and moves on.

"Let's get our group shots. My nips are freezing and I want to go home," Clark, our photographer, instructs.

I'm told to be in the middle. Marla is to hug up to my side so that the camera is to her right side. Danielle is positioned opposite of her.

"I don't understand why *I* can't be in the middle," Marla complains. "I'm the veteran and in the best shape." She snickers my way as she flips her hair, hitting me in the face with it.

Danielle steps in. "She looks fine. Come on, Mar. Let's just get this over with. It's freezing out here."

What could've been done in thirty minutes takes us three hours, and if not for the heaters nearby, we would've frozen. Marla's fussing at every whim gave Clark a headache and that meant he took it out on us. I was worked to the bone and left with stinging skin from being in the cold too long.

"You did good today," Oliver says, as I walk out of the wardrobe tent.

"Thanks." I pocket the Uber card he hands me as I pass. "Do you have another job lined up for me or are you a call-when-you-get-one agent?"

"Right now, we're kind of both. I have one for you in four days. Seeing as you just got here, I don't have you fully scheduled yet. Take the next few days to get things settled. I'll call you if something pops up between now and then."

"Sounds good. Maybe I'll see what New York has to offer."

I take out my phone after saying goodbye and order an Uber. While I wait, I walk to the edge of the park and find a bench. I take out my phone and check my messages.

**Mike:** *I miss you. How's New York?*

I miss him, too, but I'm not sure how to respond right now. We have a child that will need both of us, but being here was meant to help me put my feelings for him behind me. I can't do that if I keep growing more attached.

I put my phone back in my pocket and wait for my ride.

*Being wrapped in his arms is like being home. I feel safe, loved, and cherished.*

*I tug him closer to me and kiss just under his jaw. "That's good to hear, Mr. Buchannan. It sounds to me like you married the right woman then."*

*"I did." Kiss. "Mrs. Buchannan. I couldn't be happier with that decision than I am right now." He brushes his lips against the corner of my mouth.*

*I close my eyes and pull in a breath as joy overtakes me. He moves to my neck, leans closer, and peppers me with open-mouthed kisses just below my ear. "I can hardly get my beautiful wife off my mind. You know how hard it is to work when all I want to do is be home with you in my arms?"*

*I lean my head back a smidge, giving him open access. My eyes flutter shut as he moves his onslaught of kisses to the side of my neck. This is heaven.*

*I let a soft moan slip from my mouth and am met by a growl of satisfaction on my skin as he continues his ascent. The feeling of him surrounding me allows all the troubles outside of this moment to melt away.*

*"I love you . . . I will always love you," Michael says. "Don't you ever forget that, Kayla. You're it for me." His lips find mine in a passionate, toe-curling kiss.*

A loud buzzing sound in the distance makes itself known, threatening to pull me from our heated moment.

*"Ignore it," he says, pulling me back in.*

The buzzing is too loud. It's hurting my ears. I close my eyes tight and put my hands on my ears, unable to ignore it. Feeling the moment escape me, I open my eyes to see that I'm not in Mike's lap. I'm in my new apartment in New York with my alarm blaring loud enough to wake the neighbors.

Though disappointed, I reach over and shut it off before getting up and out of bed. No sense in dwelling on things of the past. If I think too hard on what that dream means, I'll never be able to function.

I walk into my kitchen and turn on the coffee maker, then head for the shower. After scheduling my doctor's appointment, I asked Shannon if she knew how to find the clinic. She smiled big when she saw the clinic's name. I'm seeing a doctor in the same clinic as her. With our appointment times being close together, she agreed to walk with me.

After my shower, I walk to my closet and pull on a pair of skinny jeans. The dang thing won't zip. Again. Looks like I need to hit the gym and the store. It's been nearly thirteen weeks since my wedding night. Surely, I'm not far enough along to need maternity clothes already.

There's a knock at the door. I grab the closest dress and throw it on as I make my way to open it.

"Good morning," Shannon says.

"Morning." I step aside and motion for her to come in. "Have a seat. I'm finishing up now. Would you like a cup of coffee?"

"Is it decaf?"

"No. It's half caff though. I don't know how you can drink decaf. It's so bitter." Since finding out that I'm pregnant, I've cut way down on my coffee intake, but I still can't seem to function without my morning cup.

"I better not. It's not too bad once you get used to it. I'm limiting my caffeine intake, so I'm saving my cup for a pumpkin latte. Thanks though."

"No problem." I grab a cup and add a splash of coconut milk before taking my first drink. The nice, warm coffee is something I look forward to every morning.

I take my cup with me and run back into the bathroom to throw my hair up and put on a little touch of makeup. Next, I grab my shoes, handbag, and coat. "I'm ready if you are."

"Ready," Shannon replies.

I take my cup to the sink, rinse it out, and leave it for later, then make my way to meet a very uncomfortable-looking Shannon at the door. I move to grab my keys from the side table and spot the signed divorce papers that I have yet to send off. I pause a moment, a hitch in my breath. All it will take is me to bring them to the post office and send them to my lawyer, but for whatever reason, I can't.

"You okay?"

I skim the papers with a knuckle as I reach past them and grab my keys. "I'm great." I lock up and we start toward the stairs. "You never told me when you're due. It's got to be close, right?" I ask, trying to get to a better headspace.

She grabs the railing and starts down. "My due date is in three days, actually."

"What?" I ask, shocked. "Where's the father?"

Right before my eyes, I watch this happy-as-a-button woman turn into a pile of mush. Tears pool in her eyes, and she stops midstep at the base of the stairs.

"Oh my God," I say, moving to her side. I put a hand on her shoulder and bend to her height. "I'm so sorry. That was insensitive of me."

"You couldn't have known. It's not like I met you and said, 'Hi, my name is Shannon. I lost my husband to a horrific accident six months ago.'"

One of the neighbors walks by us, not even bothered by her tears.

We start walking again as Shannon dries her eyes, needing to get to our appointment on time.

"For what it's worth, I really am sorry. If you ever want to talk about it, I'm a good listener."

"Thanks. I might take you up on that one day." Her phone begins to ring, so she excuses herself to answer.

We hit the sidewalk just outside our apartment and start walking through the streets. I pull my coat close and remind myself to pick up a thicker one this weekend. This weather is nuts.

While Shannon is on the phone, I pull mine out and dial Leah.

"Hey, sis. How's New York?"

"Cold, but good. I miss you, though. Are you ready for your honeymoon? You leave tomorrow, right?"

"Yeah, in the morning. I'm beyond ready to sink my feet in the sand and get my man all alone for an extended stay."

I chuckle. "I bet. I can't chat long, I'm about to be at the doctor's. I just wanted to check in. All going well? What about the stalker stuff? Have they found him yet?"

"All's good. Mike's been a bit of a pain lately, but otherwise, all is well. The stalker stuff is something Cam and I have tried to put behind us and let Jazz handle. We said if he's not caught by the time we get back, we'll switch gears, but for now, we want to focus on us and building our life together."

I nearly run into someone and sidestep another man coming my way using a walker. I'll never get used to how busy it is here.

Closing in on the clinic, I know I need to cut this short. "I'm glad to hear that, but hey, I better get off here. I'm about there. In case we don't get to talk before you head out, I just want to say I love you and I hope you two have a blast. Remember I look good in copper and gold."

"Don't worry, I know your colors." She laughs. Every time one of us travels, we bring something back for the other. "Love you, too, Kay. Let me know what the doctor says. Hopefully they can figure out what's going on with you."

I haven't told my family about the baby yet and it's eating me up inside. I just want to have doctor confirmation and know where Mike stands first.

"Talk to you soon."

I hang up the phone and make my way inside behind Shannon, following her to the desk to check in. I hope today's appointment goes well. As much as I know that I need to pull back from Michael, I can't help but wish that he was here with me.

# Chapter Fifteen

Sitting in the exam room of my new doctor's office in a paper gown, alone, is driving me crazy. A single tear falls from my eye as I wish I had someone here with me. This is my first baby; I shouldn't have to do this by myself. At the very least, I should be able to tell my family. I'll have to talk to Mike about it later tonight.

Nurse Lane asks me a series of questions, gets my weight, blood pressure, and urine sample; and then sends in my bloodwork. This doctor is thorough. Like I tell the nurse, I'm feeling better now, though I'm still run down at times. I'm glad to know that she's leaving no stone unturned.

Minutes later, Dr. Emmons gives a warning knock before entering the room. She's a cute, older—maybe seventy-something—woman with gray hair up in a bun and the softest brown eyes. She gives off a motherly vibe when she looks at me with a smile. "Good morning, Ms. Covington. It's lovely to meet you." She washes her hands at the sink in the corner, then moves to the computer that's attached to the wall. After pulling up my chart, she takes a moment to look it over. "I understand that you've been dealing with stomach upset for a while and that you took a few over-the-counter pregnancy tests, and they came back positive. Would you mind telling me what you've been experiencing? I'd like to make sure that it's nothing concerning."

Me too. I nod. "It's much better now, but I've been under a lot of stress for the last few months or so. Between getting ready to move halfway across the US without family, my sister's wedding, and my husband drama, there's been a lot. I've basically been living off TUMS and Zofran for the last month. I was barely able to eat for a while. The sight and smell of most foods made me nauseous. It had me so run down, all I wanted to do was sleep." I try to think if there's anything else, but . . . "And now that I'm starting to eat again, I'm feeling really bloated."

"I see." She smiles. "Have you had any other symptoms such as dizziness, swelling in your feet, leg cramps, or more back trouble than normal?"

All these questions are concerning. What if something is wrong? "I have. The dizziness comes and goes, but my muscles have been a bit more achy than normal. No swelling though." I fold my hands in my lap and look back at Dr. Emmons.

"The results of your lab work should be back anytime now. I'd like to give you an exam while we're waiting. Go ahead and lie back on the table and scoot all the way up, please."

She does her thing, listening, pushing, poking, for minutes, then tells me to go ahead and sit up. She goes back over to the computer and starts typing. She steps out for a moment, letting me know that she needs to have her nurse get something.

My hand finds my stomach. "Everything's going to be okay—it has to be." I chew on the inside of my lip in worry. I hate being left out of the loop; I know she's doing her job, but she's also making me want to crawl out of my skin. Tell me already, I want to yell.

Upon walking back in, she goes back to the computer. "Oh, good. The results are back." She looks through them for what seems like forever before she finally looks back at me with a smile on her face. "Well, Ms. Covington, you indeed are pregnant." She pockets her pen, then looks my way again. "Congratulations."

I take a steady breath. Even though I already knew, hearing it from a doctor makes it that much more real. I look up when I feel a hand rubbing my shoulder. Dr. Emmons is standing in my bubble, looking at me with concern.

"I see hearing it aloud came as a shock. Would you like a cool drink? That might help you settle."

"No. Thank you though. I'm fine." All kinds of thoughts swirl around in my head as the reality of my situation sinks in. "Doc, I didn't know for a while there and I'm sure I did stuff that I shouldn't have. I haven't had alcohol since my wedding night, but still have one caffeine drink a day. Can you tell if the baby is okay?"

"I have my nurse getting the ultrasound machine. We'll take a look and listen. Then we should be able to tell, but I'm also going to refer you out for further testing to make sure. We'll get you some prenatals and give you some pamphlets before you leave that can help provide you more information on pregnancy." She moves back to her computer and types something in before looking my way.

"Hang in there and we'll get you taken care of. I'll be back in a bit. The ultrasound tech should be here soon."

Minutes later, a woman in blue scrubs wheels in an ultrasound machine and asks me to lie back, handing me a blanket for my lap. I feel a chill when the goop is applied to my stomach. The technician presses a wand to me, and suddenly, a whooshing noise fills the air.

"Good baby," she says.

There, on the screen, is a tiny baby. *My baby!*

Tears fall down my cheeks as I can't hold them back any longer. This little one might not have been planned, but he or she is there, in black and white. Our little bean. I so wish Mike were here to see this, our baby, one created in love.

The tech pushes her machine out the door when she's done. I clean up, but remain lying down, my hand on my stomach.

"Momma loves you, Bean. I know your daddy does too—he's just scared. Give him time. I'm sure he'll come around." I can only hope. Even if he doesn't, we'll be okay. There isn't a thing I won't do for them. Even if that means raising Bean on my own.

"Knock, knock," Dr. Emmons says. She walks in with a smile on her face and a hand full of pamphlets.

I sit up and wipe the tears from my cheeks so I can focus on what she has to say.

"Everything looks to be well with your little one. You appear to be just about thirteen weeks. That's right along with the date that you told me. That'll put your due date at July eleventh." She puts down the paper she was looking at and back to me. "I have the sex if you'd like to know. We put it in an envelope so that you can keep it a surprise if you'd like to wait."

I shake my head. "Can you keep the gender quiet so that I can share it with my husband first?" *My husband.* I know he signed the papers, but for whatever reason, I still haven't filed them. I can't bring myself to do it.

Dr. Emmons nods and hands me a CD, pictures, a stack of pamphlets, and a referral slip. "This is a recording of everything we saw today on your ultrasound. I can continue your care, or you can switch to an ob-gyn now that your pregnancy has been confirmed. I'd like to see you again in a month if you decide to stay with me. Otherwise, you can cancel that on your way out. Your appointment card is with the referral. I've already sent a prescription for prenatal vitamins to the pharmacy. Do you have any questions for me?"

I shake my head. I'm sure I'll have a million running through my head on the walk home, but right now, I can't think of one.

She smiles and pats my knee. "Congrats again. See you in a month." She walks to the door, closing it on her way out.

After getting changed, I make my way back to find Shannon waiting for me in the lobby. "Are you ready to head home?" she asks.

"I have to find the pharmacy first. Then I'll be ready."

Ready for parenthood? I don't really know, but I do know that the moment that I saw my little Bean's image flutter to life on that gray screen, I was in love. There isn't a thing I won't do to protect it. So ready or not, I will be by the time Bean makes their appearance.

Waking from my nap has me feeling groggier than I did when I fell asleep. I had to turn my phone off so I could get a couple hours uninterrupted sleep. That's become a bit of a challenge lately. After coming home, sleeping was the only thing that I wanted to do. Crawling into bed felt amazing, but now . . . I almost wish I hadn't. The clock shows 7:37 a.m. No wonder I feel like crud. I slept the whole night away.

"I better get up and get something to eat." I stand and start my journey to the kitchen as I power up my phone. The constant ding as it loads up has me a little concerned. I normally have a few notifications, but I'm being blown up. I set it down on the counter and move to the restroom to relieve myself while it finishes loading.

As I'm washing my hands, there's a knock at the door. I walk to get it, grabbing my phone along the way. I open it to find Shannon and Ben standing there with a couple of carryout boxes and a movie.

"Come in. Did I forget that we were getting together for breakfast?" I ask.

"Nope," Shannon says. "This is a spur-of-the-moment thing. I wanted to have one last hurrah before Lizzie comes. I hope you don't mind. We're all early risers. We didn't think that you'd care."

"Not at all." I point to the kitchen and pull up my missed calls on my phone. Fifteen from Uncle Joe, ten from Mike, and three from Janet. "Help yourself. I think something's going on back home. I have to check in. I'll be just a minute."

I walk over to my bed and sit on the edge as they take plates out of the cabinet. I hit Dial on Uncle Joe's contact. Voicemail. That's odd . . . I try again. Voicemail again. I try Janet and get the same thing. Finally, I try Mike.

"Kayla. Thank God! I'm glad you called," he rushes out.

"Mike, what the heck is going on? Is everyone okay?" A lump forms in the back of my throat at the worry in his voice but I can't bring myself to freak out just yet. I need to hear what he has to say first.

"No. Cam is leaving the hospital. He called and said that Leah had been taken by her stalker. There are people out searching for her and any clues that could lead us to her whereabouts."

A wave of nausea strikes me with no warning. I double over, and the taste of bile fills my mouth. I stumble from the bed, barely making it to the bathroom before my stomach heaves once more. Ben is here within seconds, holding back my hair while putting a cool washcloth to my neck. Through my retching haze, I can hear Shannon talking to someone just outside the door. Her voice is filled with worry. Oh God, I can't do this. I need to get back to Oklahoma, but I'm under contract. This can't be happening. How can Leah be gone? I never got the chance to tell her that she's going to be an aunt. Tears hit me full force. This cannot be happening right now.

After what seems like forever, I finally sit back, no longer feeling the need to empty my stomach. Ben hands me some mouthwash, and I hand it back once the taste is gone. He scoops me up and carries me to my bed. Shannon sits next to me while Ben moves around the house, taking care of things.

"Where's my phone? I need to call Mike back."

"He said he would call you. Mike went out to join the search. He said that practically all of Baycliff Valley is searching right now. They'll find her."

"I don't understand how this happened," I cry.

"From my understanding, your brother-in-law was drugged. They were at the airport on their way to their honeymoon when they were caught off guard," Shannon replies.

I sit up in bed and look at her. Ben joins us on the bed, handing us each a water.

"He's okay, right?" I ask.

"Yeah, I think so. Your husband said that Cam took the IV out of his arm and checked himself out of the hospital. He's apparently going nuts trying to find his wife."

"Good," I reply. "Not that Cam is going nuts, but that he's looking for her. I know he won't stop until she's found."

"You have a husband?" Ben asks.

I nod. "Long story short . . . he was a longtime friend and crush. Michael asked me to marry him in Vegas. I did, but when we woke up, he regretted it. I'm here, he's there. Not much more than that." Then it dawns on me—there is . . . *a lot* more. "Oh, and I'm pregnant."

Ben looks shocked for a split second. "Wow. That's a lot. I hope you don't mind me asking, but if he's not even here for you and he has regrets, will he even want the kid?"

I barely know Ben. He has no right to say these things. "He might not want it, but I do. Mike doesn't have to want me to want his kid." I have to brace myself—the time may come that he tells me he doesn't want this kid. No matter what happens, I love our baby. That'll have to be good enough.

"He's crazy. If I had a girl like you, there's no way in hell I'd have regrets."

My brow furrows in confusion. "Thanks, I think." That's a bold statement for a new friend to make.

Shannon puts out her hand for help up. Ben is quick to jump up. "I'm hungry. You need to eat, too, Kayla. You might not feel like it, but I'm sure that baby needs it."

Even though I want to roll my eyes and refuse, I know I need to take care of me and Bean. I move to the kitchen and make myself a plate of eggs, bacon, and fruit—not exactly what I want, but it'll do for now. I eat my meal without uttering so much as a peep. By the time they finish, I feel like a bad friend.

"This was supposed to be your last hurrah. I'm sorry I brought you down with me. What can we do to celebrate?" I ask Shannon.

"Nothing. Spending time with you two is enough. I don't want you celebrating me when you only feel like checking in on your sister. I'm sure Ben wouldn't mind going back to my place to watch the movie. If anything happens and you need us, you know where we are."

They load their dishes in the dishwasher and head across the hall. I'm left with a quiet home and a sour stomach. I need to talk to Mike and tell him about the appointment, but I don't want to take the focus off Leah.

I walk over to my bed table, grab my phone, and sit down, ready to make the call. I hate feeling so weird talking to him.

I hit Call on his number and wait for an answer.

"Kayla? Are you okay?"

"I'm okay. Is Leah?"

"I don't know. They haven't found her yet. Tom called saying that he thought he had located her, but he isn't answering anymore. Cam is gathering a team and heading to his location now."

*Oh, thank God!* "Keep me posted, please. I need to know that she's okay."

"Will do . . . Hey, Kay. I know it might not be what you want to talk about right now, but can we talk about therapy real quick? It's not like either of us can do anything for Leah and I don't want you stressing."

I *so* don't feel like chitchatting but he's right—there's not much else I can do, so why not? "Sure. Anytime."

"I've been a few times already, and I go again tomorrow. It helps a lot. But when you've been in survival mode for so long and you finally start trying to heal, it's like everything goes haywire. It's kind of rough."

"I bet it is. You can do it, though." I love hearing that he's getting the help that he needs and isn't backing out.

"Do you think you'd want to go with me sometime?"

"Maybe . . . one day. But I think you should work on your childhood before you include me."

"Yeah, you're right." There's a pause. "Hey, let me call you back. I have to take this call."

We hang up and I walk to the window in the corner of the room. I toy with the cord of my blinds as I look outside. Knowing that the same moon I'm looking at is the same one over them helps. Somewhere under the moon's light, my sister is scared for her life while I sit here in my apartment, safe and secure. How is this my life?

I should have never left Oklahoma.

# Chapter Sixteen

I ROLL OVER AND turn off the six a.m. alarm. Today, I have to work, but overnight, I remembered what Oliver said about communicating with him. I know it's a long shot, but I'm going to see what I can do to possibly get back home, even if that means giving back my bonus. Leah is going to need me.

I grab a green juice from the fridge and make my way back to my bed, pick up my phone, and hit Call on Mike.

"Morning, beautiful."

I'm taken aback at first. He hasn't called me that in a while. It used to be a nickname that he called me a lot.

"Morning, Michael. I was calling to see if you got any news about Leah."

"Last I heard, they were closing in on the location, and then it's been radio silence. Butch has been keeping me updated. Let me call him and find out and I'll call you right back."

I hate not knowing if they found her or not, but then again, knowing that they're closing in helps a lot. I stand from the bed and pace the floor, waiting for Mike to call me back. *What takes so long to make a call?* I'm sure it's only been a minute or two, but it feels like twenty.

There's a knock at the door. I speed walk to it and let Ben and Shannon in.

She leans against the wall across the way with a smoothie in hand while he yawns, coffee at the ready. "Morning, Kayla," she says as she pushes past a sleepy-looking Ben.

He smiles softly. "Morning."

They make their way to my couch while I head toward my closet to grab some clothes. The two of them have decided to tag along with me to set today. I think they're worried I'll have a breakdown if they don't babysit me. I love the fact that they care enough to join me. Afterward, we're going to go sightseeing. In two days, Shannon will go in to be induced, so she wants to get out as much as possible before she's homebound for months.

My phone rings from my room. I fling open the bathroom door and rush to get it. "Hello? Mike?"

"It's me," he says, sounding dejected. "Can you video call me? I need to see that you're okay."

"Yeah, but . . . you're scaring me. What's going on?"

"Accept the transfer to video and I'll tell you."

I look at the phone in my hand as it begins to beep. Mike is trying to swap over. I hit Accept and sit back on my bed. "What's all this about? Mike, just tell me."

He looks down and nibbles at the inside of his cheek. "Kayla," he says, running a hand through his hair, "Leah was hurt badly. She's been in surgery for hours."

Tears sting my eyes and threaten to fall. "Okay." I look at him, still fidgeting. He's nervous. "What aren't you telling me?"

He looks up at me and hesitates a minute before speaking. "From what Butch said, they lost her once already. I'm about to head over there, but . . . if you need me, I'll be on the next flight out."

There's no holding the tears back now. They come fiercely. My heart in my throat, I can hardly breathe, let alone talk. I shake my head no, in hopes that that's good enough.

"Look at me, beautiful. I need to see that if I don't come, you'll be okay. I need to see your eyes."

I snap. I don't mean to, but it's out before I can stop it. "I'm *not* okay, Michael. How could I be? My sister is fighting for her life and I'm not there. I don't need you here; I need you *there* with her." I take a breath and try to calm myself. "I'm going to try to get out of this no-fly contract and come home. I can't make any promises, though. I'll let you know the next time we talk. Go! Go to the hospital and keep me posted. *That* is where I need you right now."

"Babe," he argues.

"No. Don't do that. I *need* you there. I need you to be there in my place. I'll do all I can to be there soon. *Please* Michael. For once, don't fight me on this." He starts to say something, but I continue. "I have to go. Keep me posted. I have a gig in an hour. I'll call you after if I haven't heard from you by then."

I hang up the phone, toss it on the bed, and walk out to the living room. Once they see me, Ben walks my way after helping Shannon stand. I melt into his open arms the moment I reach his side. Shannon plays with my hair, cooing at me like a baby. How can this be happening right now? Leah has to be okay. She has to. There's no way around it. Life without her in it isn't life worth living.

"Shhh," Shannon says. "We've got you."

"We're not going anywhere," Ben utters.

These two perfect strangers have quickly become an important support system for me. I just hope that one day, I can return the favor to them. I snuggle deeper into Ben and let it out—the pain of being so far from my family and of knowing my sister is fighting for her life. How much can life throw at one person before they crumble?

I allow myself to break, but soon enough, my alarm is letting me know that it's time for work. Drying my eyes, I grab a cool cloth and put it to my cheeks to lessen some of the puffiness as I rush to get ready. I grab the doctor's note that I set near the still-there divorce papers and shove it into my bag. By the time I'm ready, the three of us head out the door. We grab an Uber, and in no time, we're pulling up to my next shoot. I direct them to where they can go to stay out of the way and rush to get ready.

Three hours and a lot of fussing later, I'm done. I was not on my A game at all, but who would be in my situation?

I step outside of the wardrobe room and find my friends across the way.

"O-M-G," Shannon says. "That was amazing!"

"Thank you." I catch sight of Oliver and excuse myself so I can catch him. "Oliver!" I holler before he can make his escape.

He stops midstep, turning to face me. He smiles kindly as I catch up to him. "Afternoon, Kayla. Is there something you need from me?"

"Yeah, there is. My sister has been in surgery for a while and is fighting for her life. I'd like to get home and be by her side. I know that I signed the contract, but this is a true emergency. This is me communicating with you. Oh, and . . ." I open my bag and grab my pregnancy confirmation and hand it to him. "Here's the confirmation you requested."

Oliver looks taken aback at that rather large information drop. "First, I'm sorry to hear about your sister. I can't get you out of the contract, but I can give you a small window. How about you take time off until Monday? I'm sorry I can't give you more time, but if I don't work you, it'll get noticed."

I throw my arms around him in thanks, then pull back quickly. "Thank you. I'll take it. I owe you one."

"You don't owe me anything. Go, be with your sister." I turn and take out my phone as I walk toward Ben and Shannon. There's a flight leaving at three. Seeing that it's already noon, I better hurry. I book it and order an Uber.

"What'd he say?" Ben asks.

"I'm going home. I have to be back by Monday, but I get to go be with her. My plane leaves at three. I'm sorry I can't hang out today, but I need to catch a flight." We start walking toward the exit to wait for our ride. "I'll miss Lizzie being born. Send me pictures?"

"Of course. You can meet her when you come back. Leah needs you right now. I have Ben. We'll be fine."

I pull her in for a quick hug. I'm glad she understands. I mean, I'd still go be with Leah, but I don't want to lose what could possibly be my best friends in New York either.

Our Uber pulls up out front, and Ben gets the door for us, then follows us in. "Let's get you to your plane on time, shall we?"

By the time we get back to the apartment, get ready to go, and get to the airport, it's just after two o'clock. We make it just in time for me to say a quick goodbye and I'm off.

Before I get in line to board my plane, I take out my phone and call Mike.

"Hello?"

"Mike?" He sounds different.

"No, sorry, it's Drew. He's dealing with something in the office. Give me a minute and I'll take him his phone."

"Okay, thanks." Drew is one of the new cooks at Uncle Joe's. From what I've heard, he's a good one.

I sit in the chair with my bag at my feet, waiting for Mike to get on the phone. I hope he hurries up. I need to get in line soon.

"Kayla?"

"Yeah, it's me. I'm fixing to get on a flight home. Do you think you or D can pick me up? I should get there by seven."

"Of course. I'll be waiting. How long will you be here?" The hope in his voice makes my stomach flip.

"I have to come back on Monday. I'll be in New York for at least a few more months still. That part I can't change. Oh hey, they're calling my flight. I have to go. But Mike . . . we need to have a talk while I'm there. Do you mind if I stay at your place? I can always ask Meg if it's too much." I stand and grab my bag, heading off to get in line.

"You're always welcome, beautiful. I'll see you tonight."

Once I know that Leah's okay, I need to talk to Mike about the baby. I don't expect this to go well, but I guess we'll see. I check my bag to ensure I have the papers. Depending on his reaction, I might be filing them while I'm back. I will always love Michael, but I know now that no matter what I feel, he needs to work on him. This kiddo deserves to have a good home. His or her daddy will always be welcome, but I need to show them that home is a happy place, not a place of sorrow.

I find my seat in economy. Of course, I got the last ticket, putting me right between two big ole guys. I wouldn't mind, but it seems that they know one another and kept this seat empty so that they'd have stretching room. *Sorry to put a damper on that, guys, but I need this spot.* They make room for me to take my seat and I accept. I strap in, put in my earbuds, lean back, and will the plane to get to Oklahoma in record time. 7:07 p.m. can't come soon enough.

I feel the guys on either side of me stand. Cracking an eye open, I see others standing and I can't be more grateful that flying knocks me out nearly every time. Minutes later, I stand and grab my carry-on and make my way to the exit.

"Welcome home," Mike says as I make it to baggage claim. He pulls me into a hug, then looks for my bag.

"Thanks. Any news on Leah?"

"They have her in the ICU on a ventilator. At this point, Cam is the only one who can see her. I told them that you were flying in for a few days. Cam said he'd make sure you got to sit with her a bit while you're here." He grabs my bag and turns back to me, wrapping an arm around my shoulder. "Let's get you home so you can rest. I have the next couple days off, so I can take you to the hospital whenever you want."

"Thanks, Michael. You don't think there's any way I can see her tonight, do you?" I know it's a little late, but if there's a chance, I'd love to take it.

He shakes his head. "No, I already asked. Cam said that visiting hours are over by six. We can be there at eleven tomorrow morning—that's the earliest they allow visitors—and you can stay as long as you want."

Mike gets us loaded up into his Chevelle and heads down the road to his place. He glances at me, then back to the road. "What is it that you wanted to talk to me about?"

I look down at my hands in my lap. "I had planned on seeing Leah first, but since I can't see her 'til morning, how about we talk when we get back to your place? I need the bathroom and a drink first."

"Sound good. Are you hungry? I can stop and grab something if you want."

"I'd love to have a jalapeño grilled chicken burger."

"Done."

Mike takes us through the drive-through and then to his place.

I'm tired, but I'm always tired nowadays. It's time to show Michael his baby. I just hope he doesn't blow his top.

He takes my bags to my room while I rush to the bathroom. Once I'm back at the table, we dig in, but rather than talking, I start sending text replies.

"I'll let the others know I made it, then we can talk."

He nods and gets to work on his burger.

I open the family text chain that we set up for Leah's wedding and send a message.


**Me:** *I made it to Oklahoma. I'm crashing in Mike's guest room if you need me. I'll check in tomorrow. Night, all.*

**Uncle Joe:** *Glad you're home. Love you.*

**Cam:** *I'll let Leah know you made it.*

**Me:** *Love you too. Thanks, Cam. Tell her I love her, please.*

**Cam:** *Will do.*


I take a steadying breath and move on to Meg and Damon.

**Me:** *I'm back for a few days. At Mike and Damon's now. Will I see you two while I'm here?*

**Damon:** *Welcome back. I'm painting the new place tonight. How about I pick up pizza and we do dinner tomorrow night?*

**Megan:** *I'm out of town on a shoot. Dinner tomorrow sounds good to me. I'll be back by three.*

**Me:** *See you guys then.*

I look up from my phone and see Mike watching me intently.

"One more and then I'm all yours. Promise."

I pull up Ben and Shannon and let them know I made it.

**Me:** *My plane landed. I'm back at Mike's now. Talk soon. Good luck, Shannon. Send me pics when little Lizzie makes her debut.*

**Shannon:** *Will do =) Good luck to you too. Hope all goes well.*

**Me:** *Thanks.*

**Ben:** *I'll send as many pictures as I can take. Glad you're safe.*

**Me:** *Thanks, talk soon.*

I put my phone down and look at Mike. "How's work?" I take a bite of my sandwich. I've never been one for small talk, but I don't know what else to say right now. I don't want to get into the heavy stuff while we eat.

"Work's fine. Did you file the papers yet? My lawyer hasn't sent me anything."

I flinch. I didn't realize he was that eager for the divorce. "No, I haven't, but I have them in my bag. We can drop them off while I'm here if you want. I didn't realize you meant for me to file them the moment I got them. I've been kind of busy getting settled."

"It's fine," he says. "No rush. I was just curious. I thought you would have filed right away."

I set down my sandwich. "Michael, it's not like I'm trying to rush into a new relationship or anything. I'll get them to my lawyer while I'm here. I just didn't have time." Shaking my head, I attempt to get us back on track. "I don't want to argue with you." I take his hand in mine and look into his green eyes. "I really do have something to show you."

Mike nods. "Okay then. Go ahead."

"I saw the doctor and she confirmed that I am pregnant. I know I told you after the home tests but now it's doctor confirmed. No more uncertainty."

I sit back and wait. Other than the initial flinch, there is no response. None.

I give him more time. I don't know if I broke him or what, but if his chest wasn't moving, I'd think I'd killed him.

Standing, I go to the kitchen, grab a juice, and come back.

There's still nothing, not a single movement.

I know when Dr. Emmons told me, it was as if I was finding out all over again. Maybe that's what's happening here.

"I know it's a lot to take in. The way I see it, we have a few options," I start.

When his eyes move to look at me, I take that as a good sign. He's listening, so I continue.

"One, I don't file the papers, we can go to therapy, and we give us a real chance. I know that's highly unlikely, but I figured I'd throw it out there. Two, we can draw up custody and visitation papers and go through with the divorce. We can both be attentive, loving parents, just not together. Or three, you can sign over your rights and I'll raise Bean on my own. You can be a cool uncle when you're around. Not ideal, but I don't really know where your head is here. If you have another thought, just let me know. This is all new to me."

I sit back and take a sip of my juice in hopes that he'll say something, but I swear it's like I've been talking to a brick wall. I get up and go to the sink, cleaning out my cup. By the time I return, he's still how I left him.

"Michael, I love Bean already, so as long as you don't ask me to abort, I'm up for listening. Either way, I'm starting to show, so we need to come up with a game plan."

When he still doesn't say a thing, I stand, grab my bag, and drop the papers on the table. "I'll give you time to process. See you in the morning."

It's still early, but I head in the direction of a bed. I thought for sure he'd respond, say something, maybe even yell at me. This not saying a thing? This is new.

# Chapter Seventeen

I turn over in bed when the light of the morning hits my eyes and throw the blankets over my head, not wanting to get up. Maybe if I tuck back in, I can sleep for another hour. "It's too early for this," I grumble. Flying always takes it out of me. Thankfully, when I came to bed, it was early. I could hear Michael's muted voice as he spoke to someone on the phone and the floor creak as he paced the hall. He doesn't have the need to come down this hall since his room is on the other side of the living area. Even though I couldn't get my mind off Michael, a hot shower helped. Once I was relaxed from the hot water, I crawled in this soft and fluffy bed and was out in no time.

Now, there's a knock at the bedroom door and I peek out from under the covers as it cracks open. Michael sticks his head in and smiles softly. I sit up and scoot to the head of the bed, motioning to the foot.

He walks in and takes a seat, then turns so his knee is on the bed but both feet are off as he looks at me. "I'm sorry about last night. I should've responded to you. I did try, several times, but I'm trying to think before I speak, and nothing sounded right."

The reaction bothered me last night but it's understandable. "Okay, I can appreciate that."

He takes my hand in his and grins. "I still don't really know how to respond. It's like I'm having a battle within. Part of me wants to jump for joy and spin you in circles, because this is huge!"

"Please don't." I chuckle. "I can imagine how sick that'd make me."

He grins, but it becomes serious quick. "There's this other part . . ." He looks at the bed and frowns. "Look, this therapy stuff is still new. I'm working through a lot, and I'll make sure to work with Richard on my feelings on this, too, but I can't tell you what I want to do yet. I won't abandon you, though. Anything you need, just say it and it's yours. Can you . . . give me some time?"

I nod. "Of course. But Michael, my clothes are already getting tight. What do I say when I can't hide it anymore? Surely, you've had time to think while I've been gone."

"We tell them that it's mine. I'm not going to deny it. I just hope by then, I'll have answers."

"Okay." Knowing that he won't deny Bean makes me happier than he could imagine. This is an improvement for sure.

"Now, get dressed. We leave in an hour, and you need to eat before we go."

He steps out and I run to the restroom before my bladder bursts. I quickly shower, then dress in my stretchy yoga pants and a baggy hoodie. Mike knows about Bean, but the others can't know just yet, so I gotta hide my tiny bump somehow. When I'm done, I step out of my room and make my way to the kitchen. I'm famished.

"Have a seat," Mike says, pointing at the barstool across the island. "Breakfast will be done soon, then we can head out." The smell of bacon and eggs fills the air.

I stand and go to the fridge, pour myself a tall glass of juice, then grab the jar of salsa and some strawberries before returning to my stool. Mike slides a plate in front of me.

"Thank you," I say around a bite. "This is so good."

A few bites in, I look up to see him staring at me. "What is it?"

"You seem ravenous. You're eating in New York, aren't you?"

"I am. I'm just starving. You know, now that I'm not emptying my stomach contents daily, I feel like I'm making up for lost time."

Mike nods and drops it. We eat up and then head to the hospital.

Mike opens the waiting room door for me. I walk in ahead of him and am pulled into the arms of Uncle Joe right away. We stay this way for a few minutes before he pulls back and checks me over head to toe.

"I'm so glad you got to come. A month is too long to go without seeing you."

"Has it really been a month already?"

"No but it feels like it," Janet states. She raises her brows and pulls me in for a hug. "We've got some catching up to do."

I'm a little confused at that reaction but I'm sure she'll let me know what I did soon enough.

"The doctor is in with Cam and Leah now. He said he'd come out in a bit and give us an update. How about you walk down with me and get everyone some coffee?"

I look around to see Cam's best friends, Mark and Becca; Cam's parents; and Tom. Maddie is sitting next to Tom, rubbing his back. I nod and head toward the door.

Once we're down in the cafeteria, Janet looks around, and when it looks clear, she pulls me to a stop. "When were you going to tell me?"

"Tell you what?" I question.

She looks down at my covered stomach and then back at me. "You can't tell me that you're not hiding something behind that three-times-too-big-for-you hoodie. Come on, you might be able to fool Joe, but you can't fool me. Is it Mike's?"

"Who else's would it be? He's the only man I've ever slept with." I put my hands in my hoodie pockets and look down. "Mike doesn't know how he wants to handle it yet, but he's not abandoning me financially, at least."

"Oh, Kay. I'm sorry, sugar." She pulls me in for a hug, then sits down, taking me with her. "Please tell me you're coming home. We can help. I don't know how Joe will handle this, but please let us be close."

"I plan on coming home as soon as I can get out of my contract. I'm in a three-month clause, so it shouldn't be long."

"Good. You don't need to be alone in all this. When do you plan on telling everyone else?"

"I'd tell the others right now, but Mike asked for some time first. So I guess whenever that is. I don't really want to take the focus off Leah right now, though."

"I'll leave that to you, but with you already showing, it won't be hard for them to find out."

She and I stand and make it to the drink line, where we get everyone a cup of coffee and me a water.

"I know. Thank God it's winter and I can be bundled up for now. That buys me some time."

"I guess."

After we pay and make it to the elevator, she pulls me aside one more time. "In all seriousness, I'm happy for you. I just wish this were under better circumstances. Call me anytime, day or night, even if it's just to scream. The least I can do is provide a shoulder."

"Thanks, Janet."

By the time we get to the waiting room, Cam is there. He sees me and pulls me in for a big hug. "Your sister would want to see you," he says. "You can come back with me if you want. You'll need to be ready, though. She's in rough shape and in a coma. I believe she can hear you, but she can't respond."

I nod and follow him down the hall to Leah's room.

When the door is opened, I feel my mouth drop. I stop in my tracks and take it all in. Leah has so many machines and tubes hooked up to her that there's barely a spot that's not touched. I wipe a fallen tear and step closer as Cam shuts the door behind us.

He puts his hand on my upper back and guides me in. "She's a fighter," he whispers. "She'll come back to us. You need to believe."

I nod—I do. But seeing her so pale, just lying there unresponsive when she's always been so full of life, hits hard.

Cam walks to her side and leans in, kissing her head and running his finger along her cheek. "I love you, sweetheart. You have a visitor all the way from New York."

He looks at me and I walk that way. I take her hand in mine and nearly beg for a response. There is none, so I follow his lead and lean in to kiss her cheek. "Hey, sis. It's me. You need to get up, Leah. I could really use my big sis right now. I so badly need you to fight this. We know you can. You're the strongest woman I know. You got this." I dry my eyes and move her hair from her cheek.

I turn back and place my bag on the chair behind me and grab a comb and hair tie. "Do you mind?" I ask Cam. When he shakes his head, I grab the coconut dry shampoo she loves and spray the comb before running it through her hair. I teach Cam how to braid her hair the way she does mine, and then put a little ChapStick on my finger before putting it on her lips.

"There you go. You always say you feel more human when you're clean. I bet you feel a million times better. I bought some things for Cam to take good care of you while you're here in bed." I grab her caddy and put in her favorite body spray, lotion, dry shampoo, and nail polish. I leave the comb and ChapStick too. I know these things won't do anything to make her better, but it's all I can think of doing right now. "You come back to us, you hear me? I'm coming home soon. I spoke to my agent. I'm obligated to fulfill a couple more months, then I can come home. I'll be here to pick on you before you know it." I sit back in the chair and hold her hand.

"That scent—coconut something. It reminds me of the weekend I asked her to be my girl." Cam smiles and scoots closer to Leah. "Do you remember that, sweetheart? That little purple bikini." He laughs. "You know, she wanted to wring your neck for sneaking that in her bag, but in time, it made its appearance more than any other she owned. So much so that it was in her bag, ready to hit the beach on our honeymoon."

I chuckle. "I got the riot act over that one, but I'm thrilled that she ended up loving it."

Cam tells Leah about their honeymoon that never was, about their private hut over the ocean, and I can't help but tear up. They've missed out on so much because of a man I brought into her life.

"You okay?" Cam asks.

"I can't help but wonder why I make the choices I do. John was only there because of me. It's me that should be in this bed. Not her."

Cam shakes his head. "I can hear her now. She would be chewing you a new one." He laughs. "I hate that she's in this bed just as much as you do, but there is no way that this is your fault. She wouldn't want you thinking like that."

I nod. He's right, though—she would tear me up if she heard me talking like that.

Cam and I sit in the quiet, listening to her heart monitor and ventilator as the time passes. I get out a book that I borrowed from her a while back and start reading out loud. When we were small, Leah would read to me. Though it was never a romance book then—more like sports or something Barbie if she took pity on me.

By the end of the chapter, I lean back in the chair and let the memories of our childhood wander. I chuckle at the thought. "Leah was so proud of this yellow ribbon that she borrowed from Kim. She couldn't have been more than twelve at the time. She wouldn't let me touch it. Being the younger sister, I wanted everything she had. I snuck into her room one day and took it. She was mad at me for months after that." I look over at Cam, who has a small smile forming on his face. "I wonder if Uncle Joe ever found it. I tucked it in the pages of some old romance novel on the shelves. At such a young age, I don't know how I thought to hide it there." I giggle and look at the clock.

A few hours have passed, and Damon and Meg should be coming soon. As much as I hate to leave, I know I'm not the only one who wants to see Leah.

I stand and stretch my back. "I'm going to head out. Thanks for letting me visit."

"Of course, Kay. Anytime." Cam stands and pulls me in for a hug.

"I'll come back tomorrow. I leave Monday morning, but I'll be here every day until then. If there is any change, please let me know."

"Will do. Thanks for coming. I know Leah would be thrilled that you did."

I walk down the hall to our waiting family and stop just outside the room to take a minute. The tears fall at a rapid pace. How could something like this have happened to such a good person? I need her to be okay. I'll never be able to get the image of her lifeless body lying in that bed out of my head, but if she comes back to me, I promise I'll do all I can to make this the best life possible for her and me.

I open the door when I think I've finally gotten control. Seeing everyone's concern, I can't help but lose it again. Leah has always been the strong one. How will I make it through this without her? She's got to be okay; she just has to be.

Sometime later, I'm able to pull myself together and promise that I'll return tomorrow. Uncle Joe insists that Michael take me home. I don't argue.

Mike opens the door to his truck and helps me in. He rounds the hood once I'm seated and hops in behind the steering wheel. Instead of starting the truck, though, he turns to me and takes my hand in his. He doesn't say anything, just sits there and lets me make the next move. Without hesitation, I scoot in and lean on his shoulder, letting the tears fall.

A few minutes go by, and Mike nudges my chin so I'm looking at him. He kisses the tip of my nose and wipes my tears. "Care to tell me about it?"

I tell him about it all—the tubes coming out of her mouth that's hooked up to the air thing that pumps and makes this swooshing sound with every breath, the IVs, the purple and black coloring all over her skin. "How could someone do that to her? She was beaten so badly that I could barely see skin not covered in a bruise or scratch."

"The guy was evil," he says. "I met John and never got those kinds of vibes from him. He hid it well. But from what Tom said, Tillie—John's girlfriend—seemed to be the true evil behind it all."

I tense. All this makes me want to scream.

"We need to focus on her healing now, though," Mike adds. "Cam has got everyone focused on that. He wants no negativity falling on her when she wakes up. She's going to need all of us."

I nod, then I tell him how sweet it was watching Cam take care of her. I might have taught him how to braid her hair, but he already knew how to bathe her. When a nurse came in, rather than doing it herself, he took the items from her and simply thanked her before getting to work. He even told Leah what he was doing before he made a move. That man is so in love with her. I hope she comes back to us . . . to him.

"To have a love like that is more than I could have asked that she find," I say with a sigh.

"I agree. Though I've never had an example of it, nobody can deny that those two are madly in love."

My phone beeps with a text. I pull it out to make sure it's not Uncle Joe or Cam.

**Ben:** *Lizzie is here! She's the most precious bundle of red hair I've ever seen.*

I pull up the three attached pictures and can't help the smile that stretches my face. This is what I needed! I know my emotions are due to the hormones, but this baby is so beautiful. Through watery eyes, I type out a reply.

**Me:** *Aw! Give her kisses for me. Tell Momma good job. I'll see you guys Monday.*

I put my phone back in my pocket and scoot over in my seat so I can buckle up. Life right now is a bit of a rough ride, but seeing that beautiful little bundle of joy reminds me that I have something to look forward to. I said I wanted to take this time to grow up—now I have extra incentive.

# Chapter Eighteen

When we got home from the hospital, I needed to take a nap. I asked Mike to take the envelope with the gender to the local bakery and get cupcakes for tonight. After a little debate, he agreed. We're sharing the baby's gender with Megan and Damon and asking them to be his or her godparents in case anything ever happens to either of us—or so Bean will have a man besides an uncle or grandpa in their life in case their daddy won't step up. Already, Bean has more men in their life than Leah and I did. That makes my heart happy.

The smell of pizza hits me as I step out of my room.

"Afternoon, sleepyhead. I was about to wake you. Damon and Meg just parked and are on their way up now,"

Mike says. He walks over, handing me a green juice. "Drink up."

"I'd much rather have a coffee right now." I chuckle, but start drinking anyway. I don't think I'll ever get used to not having my coffee all the time.

"You're the one who said you can't have that much caffeine; I'm just making sure you have what you need." He smiles.

The front door opens and in walks Megan and Damon. She pushes him out of her way and runs over to engulf me in a swaying hug. "My God, you're a sight for sore eyes." She looks me over and smiles. "Did you just wake up?"

I look down and, yeah, I'm not put together like I normally am. Not many people see me like this, but considering literally nothing fits me right now, I'm happy with my look. I have on Michael's shirt that I kidnapped all those months ago and a pair of sleep shorts, my hair up in a top knot, and not a stitch of makeup.

"I did. Do I really look that bad?"

"No," Mike says. He clears his throat and steps away.

Megan chuckles. "I guess not. Come on, tell me all about New York. Did you ever make it to the doctor? Are you really pregnant?" She takes my hand and pulls me along with her to the living room. I look over my shoulder at Damon and wave.

He smiles and nods in return.

My phone rings. Since it's on the other side of the room, Mike answers for me.

"Hello? . . . Yeah, hold on a minute." He walks over, arm stretched out, phone in hand. "Ben wants to talk."

"Thanks." I nod and take the phone. So that he knows I have nothing to hide, I put it on speaker. We are still married, after all. "Hey, Ben, what's up?"

"Shannon is awake and wanted to see you for a minute. You busy?"

I look to the others and then reply. "Yeah, a bit, but if we keep it brief, I can video." I click it over and he accepts. I see his face come on the screen and he smiles brightly. "Hey . . . where's Shannon?"

"Just inside the room. I wanted to make sure you could talk before I got her all excited."

Megan leans over, lying on my shoulder so that she can see better. Ben smiles her way and then pushes open the door to her room. He turns the camera so that it shows Shannon lying in bed, holding Lizzie.

"Aw, Shannon. You did such a good job. How are you feeling?"

She looks up at the phone and smiles brightly. "Thanks. I'm tired but good. She has some of her daddy's best features. I can't keep my eyes off her." Shannon wipes a tear from her cheek, then takes Lizzie's tiny hand in her fingers. "I can hardly wait 'til you get home and get the chance to spoil her. How's your sister doing?"

My smile drops and Mike sits down next to me, putting a hand on my knee. "She'll pull through, I'm sure of it. It's hard seeing her like that, but on the bright side, she's still with us." I shake my head. This is supposed to be a happy time for her and here I am dragging it down again. "I'm going to get. Give Lizzie kisses for me. I'll see you guys Monday."

"Will do. Good luck," Shannon says.
Ben turns the phone toward his face and smiles. "Let me know when your plane is due, and I'll come pick you up. See you Monday."

"I can call—" Before I can finish, the screen goes black.

"She is so precious," Meg starts, "but that Ben guy's got the hots for you." She looks at Mike, then smirks at me. "I guess if you're a free agent, you can see what it's like to date a New Yorker."

"Megan," Damon scolds.

"First, he's not a New Yorker. He's from Oklahoma, somewhere near the Red River. Second, I'm not really a *free agent*. I'm still legally married, so no dating for me."

Her eyebrows go up. "I thought for sure you guys would've filed by now. What's the holdup?"

I grab a piece of pizza from the box in front of me and look at Mike, who's already stuffing his face. "Mike gave the signed papers to me at the airport, but I've been busy. Plus, my lawyer is here. But considering that we thought I was pregnant, I needed to wait for the confirmation. During a divorce, you're asked if there were any children during your marriage. Now that I know for sure, I figured I'd talk to Mike before we decide what to do next." I take a big bite of my pizza, knowing that I'm about to be bombarded with questions. This will buy me a moment to process.

They both seem shocked by this new information but seem to be understanding. They look between Mike and me, almost as if they're in sync now that they're together, and then Megan settles in on me.

"So many questions are running free in my head right now."

"What I want to know," Damon starts, "is what you plan to do now that you know that your *wife* is for sure pregnant.

You've had a while to think on it. You should know what you want to do."

Even though I would normally agree, Michael has been in therapy, working on his holdup. When I feel Michael tense next to me, I jump in.

"He and I had a talk," I start.

Mike stops me by placing a hand on mine. "I'll be financially supporting her while she's pregnant, as much as she'll let me. When the baby comes, he or she then too. As far as relationship-wise, I'm not sure. Part of me is thrilled and I want to jump and shout it from the rooftop, and another part of me wants to run and push her as far away as possible."

Megan stands up, causing me to slide into Mike, who steadies me. "Push her away? Again? I've sat by and watched you treat her like crap, Michael. You've run her off and obliterated her heart. You say you don't want to be with her because you want to protect her from what you grew up with—"

I stand. "Megan—"

"No, Kayla. I love the both of you. If he can't handle a dose of honesty from someone he's close to, then what can he handle?"

Mike reaches up and takes my hand, tugging slightly so I sit. "I'm good," he says. "Let her say her piece."

I start to argue, but Meg starts back up, drawing my attention away from him.

"Look at her, Mike. My best friend, my sister, standing up for the man she loves, even though right now, he doesn't deserve it. You have the love of a good woman, one that has gone through hell and back to prove it to you. She's carrying your kid and you're still willing to let her walk away?" She tosses her hands in the air and then slaps them down. "You don't deserve her." She plops back down on the couch, grabs her beer, and chugs it.

Damon scoots in and takes her hand in his, bringing it to his mouth. He doesn't say a thing. Either he is playing it smart or he agrees with her. Either way, I leave it be.

The four of us eat in silence. I'm not sure how to handle what just happened. It takes a lot for Megan to blow up like that, but when she does, it makes people take notice.

"Well," I say. "If everyone is willing to set aside their emotions, I had Michael pick up some cupcakes. If you guys would like to know the gender of your godchild, we can find out."

"What?" Megan screeches. "God baby?"

Damon pulls her into his side, holding her close and kissing the side of her head.

"It's all behind us. I've said my peace now."

"Good, because I spoke to Mike about it, and he agrees with me. You two were there from the start, no matter how bad. This baby will need people he or she can count on when their parents can't be the people they want to go to. Sure, they'll have aunts and uncles, but a set of good, strong godparents is so valuable. If you say yes, I'll expect you to be there for them, just like I will be, and in the event that something happens to me, it'll be the two of you raising Bean."

Damon nods and smiles brightly.

Megan is in tears. "I want nothing more than to be god momma to your baby."

"Then it's official. Bean has godparents." I smile and wipe the tears coming from my eyes. The only thing that could make this better is if his or her daddy would wake up and be a part of this in every way.

"Now," Damon starts, "can we please find out what we're having?"

I chuckle. "You sound like a proud papa."

"I am a very proud god papa, and until the day their dad takes his place, Bean will be spoiled rotten by the three of us." He looks over at Mike, who's still on the other side of me. Damon makes his feelings known by the heat in his eyes, and I can only imagine what will be said when us ladies are out of earshot.

Mike hands me the cupcakes and I nearly second-guess sharing this moment with them. This is a moment we should be happy about, and I am, but I'm also torn. I'm happy that they are taking up for me and making it known that Bean deserves better—that I deserve better—but at the same time, I hate that Michael is basically being verbally beaten on. That's not okay either.

So I make it known.

"Before I hand these out, thank you both. For everything. But what happens between Michael, Bean, and I needs to be respected. He's dealing with a lot right now, and us beating on him isn't helping. Mike needs to see that he can count on those who claim to love him. I'm not saying to tell him he's right when he's not, but I am asking you to give him some grace. We'll figure this out. No matter what we decide, I'm going to be okay. So will Bean."

I don't give anyone a chance to reply as I open the box of cupcakes and pass them out. "One cupcake will have blue or pink icing in the center. We'll take turns until we find it. Care to make bets?"

"Girl," Meg says.

"Boy," I retort. "I've always dreamed of having a boy first."

"Boy," Damon adds with a nod of his head.

Finally, Mike adds, "Girl."

We start off with Damon, who bites into the first and then the second. Neither has a color inside. Megan is next. She bites into hers, grumbling when there isn't a filling.

"The suspense is killing me here," Damon says. "Bite your cupcakes already."

Mike looks at the cupcakes in hand, assessing them both. He weighs the options and smiles. "This one—" he holds up the one on the left, "—is lighter. I bet it's not it." He bites into it, and sure enough, it's not filled.

"Just bite the other one already," I fuss. "If it's really heavier, we know you have it, and I want to know."

Mike chuckles and motions for me to bite mine. I do and come up empty. He teases us by rolling the remaining cupcake around in his hand. Without thinking, I pull it down to my face and take a big bite out of it, pulling back as I do.

*Pink!*

Mike smiles at me as I wash the cake down with my drink. He turns the cupcake so the others can see the inside. "It's a girl!"

I start bouncing and laughing, but no matter how happy I am right now, I can't help but feel alone. Megan and Damon are hugging and laughing. Mike is still sitting there with a smile on his face.

Meg looks my way, sees the tears on my cheeks, and realizes that I'm no longer celebrating. She pulls out of Damon's embrace and has me turn to look at her. "What's wrong? Aren't you happy? Now we can talk baby names."

"I am, I just . . . I thought things would be different." I shake my head and paste on a smile. "Don't mind me—it's just the hormones." Baby names? How could I possibly choose a name without Mike?

Not buying it, she glances at Mike, then back at me. "How so?"

"Hmm?" I look up to her imploring eyes.

"How did you think things would be different?"

"It's fine, Megie. Just leave it be." I take my phone out of my pocket and check my texts. Anything to get out of this. Mike's been beat on enough.

She takes my phone from my hands and puts it on the

coffee table. "Leah is fine. Everything else can wait. What's going on in that head of yours?"

I shake my head.

Mike stands in a huff and walks off, Damon following suit.

I look over my shoulder to see Mike standing in the kitchen, running his hand through his hair. Damon walks in behind him, and they start having what appears to be a heated conversation.

Megan stands and pulls me up with her. She leads me to my room and closes the door behind us. "Now. Tell me what's wrong?"

"What's not? That would be a shorter list right now. My sister is in a coma, and I live on the other side of the US. I'm pregnant with my first child and I have to keep it a secret from most everyone I love so that my so-called husband can process and figure out what he wants. I watched you and Damon laugh and hug when you found out it's a girl and . . ."

"Aw, I'm sorry. Come here." She pulls me in for a hug.

"I thought when I settled down and got married, had a baby, that at least my husband would celebrate with me." I sit on the edge of my bed and put my face in my hands and let loose. "What is wrong with me? Am I really that unlovable? Do I not deserve to have a family of my own?" I take a breath and look up into Megan's worried eyes, also filled with tears. "You know, all I've ever wanted was a family. Bean was not something I planned for, but I'll love her until my dying day. How can he not?" I sob.

I should be out telling my family, buying maternity clothes, and thinking of baby names, but instead, I get to lie and hide my joy behind baggy clothes and excuses while Mike takes his time to decide what's right for him.

"How is this fair?" I nearly growl. "I thought I was okay with it all, but . . . it hit different when I had nobody to celebrate the news with."

Megan drops to my side and pulls me in for a hug, then sits back, nudging my chin to look at her. "You have a few months in New York. You'll finish up that time and come home. In the meantime, I'll start looking for a bigger place. If your so-called husband won't step up, I will!" She rambles on about how she and Sadie have been wanting to move anyhow and that there is no way she'll let her goddaughter live in a home with no love—meaning here.

I love her for it, I really do, but she and Damon are just starting out. If I let her do this, she'll be so focused on me and Bean that she'll push him away again. I won't let that happen.

"I love you, but I can't let you do that. We'll be fine, I promise. By the time she comes, I won't be here. I have enough money stashed away from my inheritance that I can buy something that'll be big enough for the two of us."

She looks at me as if she's gauging the truth of what I said. She finally nods.

"You know that house on the other side of Becca and Mark?" I ask.

"The cute little purple Victorian?"

It really is cute—old but cute. I fell in love with it the first time I went out that way.

"Yeah, the Victorian. Becca told Leah that the older couple that own it are planning to move to Colorado to be closer to their grandbabies."

"So you're thinking of buying it? Doesn't it need a lot of work?"

"I am and it does, but it's not like I can't live in a travel trailer on the property until it is done being remodeled. "And I love the proximity to my sister. The property isn't small—Leah said that it's twenty-plus acres. Between that and the remodel of the house, it might be too much for me to take on. It would be a dream come true if I could do it, though.

My marriage may have failed but finding a place I can call home so close to family gives me hope that I can still have a bright future. Even as a single parent.

# Chapter Nineteen

SITTING HERE IN SHANNON's living room, holding little miss Lizzie, I can't help but smell her. *Is it weird to smell a newborn?* I wonder. Well, if it is, I don't want to be right.

I've been back from Oklahoma for a little over three weeks. In that time, it's pretty much been radio silent from Mike except his weekly text—*Do you and baby have everything you need? How about financial needs? Do you have any of those? I hope you're doing well.* It's pretty much the same every week. I think he copies and pastes it. I'm grateful he's willing to take responsibility in that way, but it takes more than money to take care of a baby. Thankfully, she's still in my belly and not feeling the pain of abandonment. I hope not, anyway.

"What's the plan for today?" Shannon asks. She's in the kitchen with Ben making us breakfast. I got put on baby duty and am more than happy to do so.

"I have to see Dr. Emmons at ten. Otherwise, I figured I'd go shopping. Nothing I have fits me anymore." I stand and walk to the changing table in search of a fresh diaper. I'm getting pretty good at this; Shannon likes to remind me that I need the practice. Though I think it's more like her chance to not have to do it all herself.

"Want some company?"

"Sure," I reply.

"Do you mind if I join?" Ben asks. "I'm taking the day to work from home and really need to get out of the house for a while."

"The more, the merrier," I reply. "Though you might get bored. I need to buy maternity clothes." I lay Lizzie down once I locate what I was looking for and get started changing her nasty butt.

"I have sisters and nieces," Ben replies.

I chuckle. "I also kind of want to look at the baby stuff. I don't want to buy much since I'm not staying, but an outfit or two won't hurt."

Shannon chuckles. "I'm sure once you buy one, you won't stop so easily. Girls are fun to buy for."

"I can carry the bags," Ben says. "If it'll get me out of the house, I'll take it. Plus, it'll give me an excuse to treat you ladies to a nice lunch."

I glance his way and smile. "You don't have to do that, Benny."

"I do. It'll be like you two doing me a favor. How many guys do you see out to lunch with two beautiful women on their arms? Come on, cutie, do me a favor and have lunch with me."

I put the dirty diaper in the can nearby and join them in the kitchen, Lizzie on my shoulder. "We'll have a baby with us and I'm bursting out of my clothes. Unless you're trying to convince people that you're potent, I don't think we'll be doing you any favors."

"You could walk into the fanciest restaurant in Manhattan wearing a potato sack and still be the most beautiful woman there . . ." He trails off, then looks down at Shannon. "Next to this one here, of course."

Shannon chuckles. "Nice save." She comes over and takes a sleeping Lizzie from my arms and heads toward the crib. "You're laying it on awfully thick lately, Benny boy.

I'm game, but if you two would rather have some privacy, I don't have to go. If you want to ask her out, just say the words. I don't need to be a chaperone."

Ben smiles shyly my way and then gets back to the eggs.

"I'm still married. I can't really date anyone," I say. "Besides, I'm pregnant. It's not like anyone would want to go out with me even if I could."

"I would," Ben says under his breath. He starts plating the eggs, adding toast and bacon to each plate before turning and setting them on the island.

I can't keep my eyes off him. How did I not know that Ben is interested in me like that?

"Come and get it before it gets cold," he hollers over his shoulder, then grabs his plate and makes his way to the couch.

"You just registering that he's been crushing on you?" Shannon nudges. "I could tell from day one. Our Benny here will be an amazing husband and father one day. Poor guy. Always comes up empty in love." She grabs her plate and heads off in his direction. I grab my plate and head that way too.

"Ben," I start. "If I weren't married. . ."

"It's fine," he says. "You owe me nothing. I shouldn't

have even said anything. Let's not make this weird, yeah?"

"Yeah," I reply.

But the rest of the time spent at Shannon's, I can't help but wonder what life would be like if I were able to give myself to Ben—a man who wants me—rather than a man who can let me go.

I step across the threshold to my place and kick off my shoes. Yesterday's shopping trip was a hit. I got a week's worth of clothes that fit me—then I couldn't help it and bought ten outfits and a slew of bows for Bean. Shannon was right and couldn't stop laughing when she saw how much I was getting. Then, Shannon dropped the news on us last night—she's thinking about moving back home. Her mom and mother-in-law are in a debate about wanting her to move back home with each of them. She brought it up at dinner.

*"These two are driving me crazy!" she states.*

*"Who?" Ben asks.*

*I take a bite of my steak and nod in agreement.*

*"My mom and Chad's mom. They both want me to move in with them. It's not that I wouldn't mind the help, but Texas and Kansas are two completely different states. If I choose one, the other gets hurt. Besides, I don't know if I can stand the thought of living with either of them again when I'm finally on my own."*

*Ben begins stuffing his face with bread, not wanting to add his two cents. I can't help but laugh. Most of the guys I know back home would do the same unless it was concerning their girl—or sister, rather.*

*"Not to add to it," I start, "but why don't you move to Oklahoma?" She starts to object, but I cut in. "Hear me out for a minute, then I won't say another word about it."*

*She nods, so I continue.*

*"You said choosing one would hurt the other and you don't want that. Plus, you don't want to live with them, but you can use the help. I'll be moving back in a month or two, and if the price is right, will be buying a home—fingers crossed. I put in an offer already, I just haven't told anyone. So not to jinx it, but you can move in with me, or even get a place nearby. The rent prices are right, and my uncle is*

*always hiring, so that's a guaranteed job and sitter. Plus, it's halfway between the moms. If you think about it, it's a win-win."*

*She looks at nothing as if she's thinking about it. "Not for me," Ben adds. "It's a big loss. All my girls are leaving me. Whatever will I do? I just started liking New York."*

*I feel bad for the guy. He really is a good friend, but with his crush on me, I could see it becoming an issue if he came with us. Though if Mike does end up wanting a divorce…*

*"Come with us," Shannon says. "I couldn't imagine life without Benny nearby. Plus, how will Lizzie get along without her uncle?"*

I'm snapped out of my thoughts when my phone starts ringing.

"Hello?" I grab a water from the fridge before moving toward the living room.

"Hey," Mike says. "How's the baby? How are you?"

I put my hand on my fast-growing bump and smile. "We're fine. I'm surprised that you called. I've kind of gotten used to your weekly text. How are you?"

He clears his throat as I put my phone on speaker and lie back on the couch. "Can we video chat? I haven't seen you in weeks." He sounds glum.

"Sure." I get up and run to my bookshelf in the corner and grab my tripod nearby and set my phone up. When I see the request to switch to video, I accept and settle into my rolling chair near the window. Since it's Michael, I make sure that he has a whole profile look so he can see just how big I'm getting. When I do this with the others, I only show chest up.

He looks down at my stomach and smirks, but it fades fast. "What's up?"

"It's just . . ." He huffs, and his shoulders deflate. Michael looks down at the ground, then back to the screen. "It's been a rough three weeks. I didn't want to get you wrapped up in the mix and I thought not calling would help, but it's not. You're the only person I want to talk to aside from Richard."

Seeing as he called, he must want to talk now. Not wanting him to stop, I don't say a thing. I put my feet up on the nearby stool and wait.

"After you left, I went to therapy, and it was intense. I felt ill for a week—almost like I had the flu. When I went back, I realized just how bad my trauma was. It's almost as if I have been living under a cloud. A lot of my life doesn't make sense. I can recall a lot but most of what I remember has been since I met you and Leah."

"Are you okay?" I shake my head. "Dumb question, sorry. Of course, you're not okay. I can ask Oliver if I can fly out for a couple more days if you need me."

He chuckles. "Always my protector. I'll be fine. This is just part of the process."

I lean back in my chair, put my hand on my stomach, and wait.

He takes a drink, then settles on the couch. "Anyway, long story short, I've been struggling pretty bad. I've been having nightmares, panic attacks, and bouts of anger. I don't want you to worry, and I don't want to take it out on you again. That's why I've taken a step back." Mike leans his head back on the cushion, letting his chest rise. When his eyes open, I can see that he has gone to a darker place—one I don't like.

"Kayla, I've been remembering things that I have suppressed for years. I don't really know what to do with it all. The beatings from her boy toys and the hurtful words were one thing, but the abandonment was another. How can you let your kid think that they aren't deserving of love, no matter how tainted that love is? She let them take me and didn't even fight it. I still remember her words in court—'Your honor, I'd rather not try and get him back. Please. Let him stay in the group home.' I've never forgotten that." He sits up and looks at the phone. "I can't fight the demons in my head and be there for you. I'm no good for you and Bean."

I wipe my eyes. I want to argue with him, but I can't. He needs help, no matter the cost.

"I'm sorry. I didn't mean to unload on you like that."

"I'm glad you did." I smile softly. "Surely, you can see that it was her, not you. Michael, *you* are loveable . . . *You* deserve to be loved . . . *You* are capable of loving others. I know being in that group home did a number on you, but there is nothing we can do to change that. You can heal. If not for you, then for your daughter. Learn to heal and move forward. I am *so* proud of you for taking this step."

He smiles softly. "I'm working on it." There's a knock at his door. "I better get going, Kay. Can I call you tomorrow?"

"Sure . . . and Michael, thank you for sharing with me."

I hang up the call and rub my belly once more. "It looks like your daddy is struggling. Hopefully, he'll feel whole again soon. I don't want him to miss out on you. He loves you so much, Bean. Please don't ever question that." I stand and start putting up my tripod when a knock at my door sounds.

A delivery man is standing there, holding a bag of food. "Kayla Covington?"

"Yes. What's this? I didn't order anything."

"It's paid for and has your name on it."

"Okay . . ." I take the bag and shut the door. Moving to the kitchen counter, I look at the receipt on the bag. It's from a local Southern restaurant called Mama Pearl's. In the memo it says, "Enjoy your meal, beautiful." How on earth did he do that? I open the brown bag and nearly cry at the smell.

Fried chicken, mashed potatoes, fried corn, and corn bread! Oh my God, I'm in heaven. I didn't even know this place existed. I move the platter aside and go to throw the bag away but feel something else shift. I look back inside and find one more container at the bottom, along with all kinds of sauces and salsa. I grab it out and open it. "Seriously?" Banana pudding. Oh my God, I hope it's as good as Uncle Joe's.

I take a picture of the spread and move to the table. I take a bite of everything and have to text Mike.


**Me:** *You are amazing! I can't say it enough. This food is so good. I swear the owner must be from back home* *or something. It's almost like I'm sitting at Uncle Joe's dining room table with all of you. Thank you!*

**Me:** *I really miss home. I can't help but cry ugly tears right now. It feels like a nice warm hug.*

**Me:** *Sorry, sorry. I'll leave you alone now. I'm just lonely and really missing home. I hope you have a great night. You deserve it, Michael. Thank you again, for taking care of me . . . and Bean.*

I put my phone down and open my laptop as I scarf my dinner down—not exactly ladylike, but who's watching? Opening the call app, I see that I have seven minutes left until my call with Tom and Maddie, so I load in and wait for them to join. It's become a thing with them since I left. They have dinner with me, or we play cards or something and chat, mostly about Leah, but there isn't really a cap on it. I stand and run to the living room to grab my deck of cards, remembering last time they said we'd play tonight. I stop off and grab a drink on the way back. By the time I get back, I see that they've joined the room and are watching me move around the room intently. But what doesn't register right away is that they aren't looking at me—they're staring at my not-hidden belly.

Crap.

"I can explain. But until I do, you need to keep this between us."

# Chapter Twenty

I STEP ONTO THE treadmill at my gym around the corner from my place and set my pace. Gunnar should be calling me before long, but considering I have a shoot in a couple hours, I need to get moving now. No time to waste. At first, I thought I'd have to stop working out so much, but Dr. Emmons ensured me that it is perfectly safe while pregnant. I do have limitations, but nothing like I thought. Before I can even think about starting my book, a video call comes in from Gunnar. With my phone still in the holder on the tabletop of the treadmill, I hit Accept and slow my speed a tad.

"There she is," Gunnar says as his smiling face comes into focus. "Looking good. How's New York?"

"Thanks. It's cold and always busy. I miss you all."

Gunnar sets his pace and looks back at his phone. "I'm sure you miss me. How could you not?" He rubs his knuckles on his shirt and smiles.

"You're so conceited." I roll my eyes. "I do miss you though. This gym is so boring compared to the one back home."

The two of us run in silence for a bit, only sharing jabs occasionally. Two miles later, I need to cut the call short.

"Hey, Gun, I need to get. I have a photo shoot soon and really want to talk to Uncle Joe before."

He smiles softly. "No change in Leah, huh?"

"Not last I heard. That's why I'm calling. Being so far away is driving me crazy."

"I bet. Okay, I'll let you go. Tell Joe to give Leah our love, will you?"

"Will do. Thanks again. Talk soon."

After hanging up, I hit the showers, then head out front to call Uncle Joe and wait on my Uber.

"Hey, Kay," he answers. "How are you?"

"I'm okay. How are you? And how's Leah? Any change?"

He grumbles. "Nothing yet. They've started letting a few of us in at a time, so that's new. The doc said that she should wake anytime now. It's just up to her."

That's good news. I just wish that I'd hear that she's already awake—that would be so much better. "I can imagine that her body is worn out after how hard she fought. She'll come back to us, I know it in my gut."

I hear Janet call out to him and some muffling as if he's covering his phone. "Hey, Kay, I have to go. I'll call you back."

"I'm on my way to work now. Call me tonight."

"Will do. Love you."

"Love you too." Before I can finish saying it, the line goes dead. I hope everything is okay. He's not one to normally hang up on me.

I pocket my phone and step up to the curb when my Uber pulls up. Hopefully everything's okay back home, but right now, I can't dwell on that. Today, I'm working with Marla and Danielle again. Danielle and I have worked together a few times since my first shoot here and we're cool with one another. Marla, on the other hand . . . she can't stand the sight of me.

A short ride later, we pull up outside the studio where I'm meeting them for today's shoot. Oliver is supposed to meet me here at some point today and give me the information for my next shoot. It has been almost six weeks since I moved here. I'm ready to go home already. Bean is starting to show, and all I want to do is tell my family and pick baby names. That'll have to wait, though.

"Hi, Kayla," Danielle says as I walk past her.

I nod, saying a quick hello, and head toward hair and makeup. Of course I had to get a chair next to Marla. I swear I don't know why she's so catty—it's not like I'm after her job.

"Oh, great," Marla sneers. "Do you really have to keep showing up like this? You know these shoots would go a lot smoother if we didn't have to tape your fat self into every outfit change we have. Go home already. You're not wanted here."

I don't move for a minute while my lip stain is being applied. "Nice to see you, too, Marla. Don't worry about me, I'll be out of your hair soon enough." There's a loud clap behind us, causing me to jump. The guy doing my makeup gives me side-eye. "Sorry," I whisper.

"Ladies," Oliver says. He walks toward us and plants his butt on the makeup table in front of us. "Today, you two need to be on your best behavior. This shoot has the large potential of leading to other shoots that can line your pockets for months." He smiles and then looks at Marla. "Do as the photographer says. No arguing, and do not mention

Kayla's stomach. Get in, do as you're told, and get out. Is that understood?"

After he is sure that we'll be on our best behavior, he leaves. If only he could have that talk every time I have to work with Marla.

Surprisingly, she's pleasant to work with this time—not one remark is made.

Three hours later, we're sent back to change. I walk out of wardrobe with my makeup still on. Normally, I'd wash my face, but today, I'm meeting Shannon and Ben for dinner at a fancy restaurant. Tonight, we have something to celebrate, so when Ben said we needed fancy, neither of us argued. I brought my little backless black dress that hit midthigh. Even though I'm pushing eighteen weeks pregnant already, I've got to say, I still look good. My little bump is so cute—not quite big enough to rest a cup on yet but still noticeable. Reaching into my day bag, I grab my phone to see if my Uber is here yet. I ordered it before going in to change. Seeing that it's pulling up, I head out. I told Ben and Shannon that I'd walk, but Ben insisted I not. He doesn't want me walking that far—eight blocks—alone in the dark.

I spot my Uber and hop in, on my way to Franko's—Shannon swears they have the best lobster that she's ever eaten—a small highly rated restaurant that her husband took her to once before his passing. Pulling up out front, I catch a glimpse of them both waiting for me near the building. Ben walks my way, opens my door, and extends a hand to help me out.

"Wow," he breathes. "You look amazing."

I giggle. It doesn't matter if I'm dressed in the fanciest dress I own or in my joggers and baggy T-shirt, he always has a way of making me feel seen. Michael had set the bar so high that I thought no other man would ever reach it, but Ben can skim it if he's on his tiptoes. Though, given the years I've had with Mike versus Ben, I'm sure that bar might be obtainable in time.

"Thank you," I say as I take his hand.

"You look amazing in that dress," Shannon adds upon approach.

I look at her and am in awe of her beauty. Not even two months ago did she give birth, and I'd never be able to tell if I didn't know better. "Look at you. You give the phrase hot momma meaning."

She chuckles. That's when I notice that there is one very important person missing.

"Where's Lizzie?"

"Not long after you left for work, my sister showed up

at my door. I didn't even know she was coming." She smiles brightly. "I tried to ditch y'all tonight since I haven't seen her since Chad's . . . well, I haven't seen her in some time, but she wasn't having it. She kicked me out of my own home."

I chuckle, knowing Leah would've done the same thing.

"As she should," Ben says, giving us each an arm. "You need a night out and I'm going to make sure you get it."

A gentleman opens the door for us and nods to Ben as we walk in. Ben goes to the hostess stand and gives his name. She walks off to make sure our table is ready before coming back to lead our way. Once there, she lights the candle and pours us each a glass goblet of water.

"Your server will be with you in a moment."

"Fancy," Shannon says. "I still can't believe they serve water in a wine glass. When I was here last time, I took a picture of it and sent it to my sister. Chad laughed at me something fierce. I figured it was bragging rights. Where I come from, this isn't a thing."

Ben laughs. "It's not a wine glass, Shan. It's a goblet, or as my sister says, a stemmed water glass. I'd probably have laughed too." He picks up his menu and starts his perusal. "I think steak is in order for tonight. What do you ladies think?" He looks over the top of his menu at the two of us.

"I think I can find a good steak in Oklahoma," Shannon replies. "I'm leaning toward lobster. I don't know when I'll get the chance to have another good one."

Shannon took me up on my offer of Oklahoma. I put her in touch with Uncle Joe and he guaranteed her a job with a flexible schedule for little Lizzie. I also put her in touch with Ella—my realtor—who found her a few rental homes within fifteen minutes of the restaurant and close to my new home. Speaking of, my offer was accepted. They did come back with one minor change, but I was more than happy to keep the old playhouse out back. Sure, it'll need a bit of work, but I can only imagine Bean getting a lot of use out of it when she's older.

"What about you, Kayla?" Ben asks.

"I think I'm with you on this. Steak it is."

Ben smiles and places our orders as the server makes it to our table.

When I was at work earlier, Uncle Joe left a voicemail saying that Leah is starting to wake up. I immediately texted Ben and Shannon to let them know.

"Have you heard anything more about your sister?" he asks.

"No, but I do have a call with Tom and Maddie later. If I don't hear from anyone by then, I'll ask. I hate feeling like I'm bothering everyone, so I've limited myself lately. I send out a text twice a day to Uncle Joe and Cam, and then I have my nightly video chats."

"I'm sorry," Shannon says. "I know that's got to be hard, but it's so good to hear that she's trying to come out of it now."

I rub my finger along the top of my water glass as I search for the right words. "I've had my fair share of breakdowns. All I want is to be by her side, but this contract is in the way of that." I shake off the glum feeling and smile. I know Leah wouldn't want this to break me. "None of that. Tonight, we celebrate."

"Hear, hear," Ben says in cheers.

Dinner is amazing! No wonder Shannon had to have Franko's—this place is so good.

The server brings the check to the table. I reach out a hand to get a look at my damage, but Ben grabs it, handing it back with his card.

"My treat."

"I can't let you do that. I splurged tonight. Let me pay you back."

"Not happening." He smiles. "If you want to pay for something, we can walk the park and you can buy me dessert."

Shannon smiles. "I'm going to catch a ride home. I want to spend some time with my sister before she leaves, but you should go. The park is amazing this time of year in the evening. You might not get the chance again."

I look over at Ben.

He raises his hands as if to say, *Don't look at me.* "I'm not trying to do anything funny. Just friends. I thought Shannon was going to come too. If you don't want to go, we'll catch a cab home. No hard feelings."

We make our way out front and put Shannon in a cab home. Since we're two blocks from the park, we walk. There's a chill in the air that wasn't there before. It's late January, after all. Ben takes off his blazer and wraps it around my shoulders. I smile at him in thanks.

"It really is beautiful here," I say.

"It is. I've been here going on seven years now and there's still so much I have yet to see."

We step around a mom kneeling to wipe her child's face. I can't help but smile. That'll be me one day. This mom thing is more appealing to me now than it ever was before.

"Do you think you'll take Shannon up on her offer to room with her and Lizzie?"

He nods to a churro cart in the distance, and we start that way. "I've been thinking about it. The first six years of being here, I was lonely but focused on making a name for myself. I worked sixty-plus hours every week, came home, slept, and repeat. On occasion, I'd fit in a date, but nothing ever stuck. When Shannon and her man moved in, I picked up on their accent right away and felt a tingle of something."

We make it to the cart and order us each a churro. I take out some cash and hand it to the vendor and thank him. Then we turn and start walking again.

"I was so busy with work, I never really got to know Chad, and when he passed, I couldn't help but feel for Shannon. I'd come home from work and hear her crying through the door of her apartment. She was so depressed and lonely that my heart hurt for her. I started by picking up an extra meal at dinnertime, just to make sure she ate. One day, she told me that the night of the accident, she told Chad that he was going to be a dad. Everything in me changed. The man dreamed of being a dad and he got it moments before his life was taken in such a way."

Pushing through the sleeve of the blazer, I reach my hand out for his. It can't be easy sharing this with me. "What happened?"

"That's something for Shannon to tell. But for her to have witnessed the love of her life slip away and still be the bright and beautiful woman we know today, that just speaks to the woman she is. I'm in awe of her every day. Nothing will ever happen between her and me, but if I'm being honest, I can't imagine my life without her in it. She's my closest and best friend, a sister from another mister, as she says."

I chuckle. I've heard her say that a time or two.

We stop at a nearby trash can and throw away our wrappers, then find a nearby bench.

Ben grabs my hands and brings them to his mouth to blow warmth on them. My hands are always cold. "I never thought I'd leave New York, but now that she's leaving, I can hardly imagine staying."

I lean my head on his shoulder and let my mind wander. I can't even begin to imagine what Shannon has gone through, but having Ben there seems to have done wonders. "I can't speak for Shannon, but I know for me, you've been amazing. I came here a mess; I thought my life was over—well, life as I knew it, anyway—but you found your way in and showed me that it doesn't matter what I've been through. I still have people who care. It's because of you that I was able to pull through when I found out

that my sister was taken. You, Benjamin, are a good man."
I lean in and kiss his cheek, seeing it turn a light shade of
pink when I pull back. Maybe I shouldn't have kissed him
like that, but it truly was friendly. "Let's get a cab. It's
getting cold, and I still have to check in with Tom."

Ben stands and extends his arm for me to take. I gladly
accept and head back to the exit on our way home.

This man deserves the best. Part of me wishes I could be
her, but my heart still belongs to Michael.

# Chapter Twenty-One

I grab my clothes from the closet and make my way to the shower. I love how fast the water in my apartment heats up. I'm used to it taking a few minutes before I can jump in, but not here, it's almost instant. Moments after hopping in, my phone rings from the counter across the way.

I hop out, dry my hand on a nearby hand towel, and hit Accept. "Hello?"

"Kayla?" Mike questions.

"Yeah, it's me. Sorry, you caught me in the shower. I have soap in my hair. Is this about Leah? Did she finally wake up?" I wouldn't normally answer while I'm indisposed, but knowing that Leah is close to waking up, I have my phone with me all the time.

"No, not about Leah, but I did hear that she's been mumbling and twitching. They said she could wake at any moment."

"Yeah, that's what Uncle Joe said yesterday. I'm thrilled to hear it. Give me a minute." I hop back in and rinse the soap clear and turn off the water. I step out of the shower and towel off, wrapping one around me as I make my way to my bed. "So, what are you calling about? I haven't had an appointment since we spoke last." I put my phone on the tripod and dry my hair.

"Is there any way we can swap to video? I hate not being able to see you right now."

"Sure, let me grab a shirt real quick." I run to my dresser and grab Mike's shirt and throw it over me before switching us to video. While waiting on him, I grab my brush.

"Hey," he says as his face appears.

"What's up?"

Mike sits on his couch and leans his head back. Eyes closed, he takes a deep breath and runs his hand through his hair.

I grab a pillow and set my brush aside, hair forgotten.

This is not a good sign. "Michael?"

He looks back at the screen and the look of defeat on his face breaks my heart. "Kayla, I took the papers to my lawyer this morning. I'm a mess and I don't want to drag you along any more than I already have."

I nod, unable to say anything. My heart is breaking, and I can't even hate him for it.

"I had therapy yesterday and I lost my cool. I didn't hit anyone or anything, but something we spoke about triggered me and I wanted to. In that moment, I was that angry teen that was let out of the home with nowhere to go and nothing to my name but the bag on my back. If I have that much pent-up anger in me and can lose my cool that easily, I can only imagine how I could treat you or Bean if triggered. I can't let that happen. I told my lawyer to give you full custody." He stands and starts pacing. I have to look away as it starts making me dizzy.

The tears flow free, and I can't be bothered to stop them. Seeing him like this hurts.

"I will be giving you spousal support until Bean turns five or you remarry. At that point, it will transfer to be an additional support for Bean but in way of a college fund. I will also be sending you child support. But if that's not enough, we can renegotiate. I want to do right by the two of you."

"I don't need you to support me, Michael, just help me take care of Bean. But that's not what I'm worried about. You're making this decision hot off a traumatic experience. Are you sure this is what you want?" I feel nauseous and want to scream but that won't help my case any.

"There will be months that you can't work, and even then, I'm sure you won't want to go right back. Me supporting you allows you to have that time with her. Please, don't fight me on this." He sits back down and grabs his beer, taking a drink. "No. I'm sure that this isn't what I want, but this is what I need to do to make sure that you and Bean are safe. I still want to see her and be a part of her life, but I can't be left alone with her, Kay."

"You would never hurt our daughter," I cry. "Look at what you're doing. You're sacrificing your own happiness for us. That's an act of love, Michael." Why can he not see that?

He nods and wipes his cheek. In all the years I've known him, I have never seen him cry. My tears hit even harder, seeing that.

*He's really doing this.*
*He's letting us go.*
"I will *always* love you, Kayla. I'll always love Bean too.

Thank you for giving me this gift. I never dreamed that I'd be a dad one day. Seeing you sitting there carrying our child makes me want to be a better man. You are *so* beautiful." He inhales and seems to shake himself. "But I know that I can't bring you any more pain. You deserve better, so it's time to move on. I want you to be happy, and being with me won't bring happiness. After we hang up, I'm going to go to Joe and talk to him. He's meeting me for a beer nearby and I'm going to tell him everything. You can tell him about Bean, but he will hear from me about you being my wife. No more hiding, beautiful."

"What about you?"

"Me? What about me?" He shakes his head. "I'm checking myself into this program that Richard suggested. It's six weeks long—give or take, depending on me. It helps people heal with traumatic experiences. I can't have any calls until I level up, but I'd like to put you on my list to talk to, if that's okay."

"Of course. No matter what happens, I'll always be here for you. I've said this before, and I'll say it again—I am proud of you, Michael. No matter how much I wish things were different. I am proud of you for fighting to take your life back."

I don't know how I'm able to stay so strong. All I want

to do is crumble. This hurts so much worse than it did before. I know that there's no coming back from this. Once he hangs up, Michael and I are over.

"Thank you." He looks off toward the wall where I know his clock is hanging and then back my way. "I have to go now. I love you, Kayla. You and Bean both. I'm sorry I hurt you. Please know you deserve the world, and if I were a better man, I'd be more than happy to give it to you."

Before I can respond, the call is cut.

I stand and pace the floor, tears rolling down my face. "Why?" I scream. "Why can't you love me enough to give us a chance?" I swipe a trinket off my dresser and throw it across the room. Why am I not enough? I sink to my knees, put my face in my hands, and cry.

There's a loud bang at my door.

I ignore it, but then it gets louder.

"Go away!" I yell.

"Kayla!" Ben says from the other side.

I'm up on my feet, throwing the door open. He takes one look at me and sees the tears falling. Before I can say a single word, he lifts me bridal style, kicks my door closed behind him, and finds his way to my couch. He sits and holds me tight to his chest.

"I've got you," he says, his lips in my hair.

I don't know if it's my broken heart or knowing that when Ben says he's got me that he does, but sitting there safe in his arms, I cry myself to sleep.

I roll back over in bed and pull the covers up to my chin. Today, I deleted my wedding photos. Michael wants me to move on from our marriage, and while I will always love him, I have to let go . . . starting with the pictures.

There's a small knock followed by my front door opening.

"Kayla?" Ben's voice carries in from the other room.

"I'll be out in a minute," I return.

I throw the covers back and make my way to my closet to grab some clothes. After I'm decent, I head out to the living area. Shannon and Ben are sitting on my couch with breakfast on the coffee table in front of them. They make room between them, and Shannon pats the seat for me to sit. I do as instructed.

"Neither of us have anywhere to be. We are all yours," she says.

I don't need to be told twice. No longer than her words are out, I open my mouth and tell them all about the call. By the time I finish, tears are flowing from my eyes, but I don't feel as hurt as I did last night. Now, I see that he is doing this for us—not to hurt me, but to keep us safe.

Everyone is silent for what seems like an eternity.

"I can't imagine giving up my family for anything," Ben starts. "I've got to give the man props for what he did."

"I've never liked him," Shannon says. "I didn't think he is good enough for you. I mean, who gets their wife pregnant, then sends her away? But now that I hear this, I think I'm Team Mike now. Sorry, Ben."

I stand while the two go back and forth and make my way back to my room to grab my phone. I know after Mike's call last night, I am going to have a lot of explaining to do today. I make it out to the living room and show them my phone.

"Can we take a rain check? I need to check on Leah and do damage control now that my family knows that I'm a married—soon-to-be divorced—woman."

They stand and nod. On the way to the door, Ben

points to the food on the table. "Make sure you and Bean eat. I know you're dealing with a lot, but the baby needs nourishment."

"Thank you, Ben. For everything."

He takes my keys out of his pocket, the ones he must have taken last night to ensure my place was locked up securely after he left, and puts them on the side table as he joins Shannon and steps out.

I make my way to my couch and grab a pancake and bacon. I make a bacon taco and take a bite before I call Uncle Joe. There is no sense in reading his text when I know he will want a call anyway.

"Hello?" His voice grumbles as if I woke him.

"Hey, Uncle Joe. It's me. Are you busy?"

I hear some movement, then Janet asks him what's going on. It takes a minute for him to come back on the line.

"No. Sorry, we were asleep. I'm sure you can imagine, it was a long night."

I feel bad, but there isn't any way that I can change it. If I were in Oklahoma, I would have fought Mike to have been there when he told Uncle Joe. I'm just grateful that he didn't tell him about Bean.

"Kay, why didn't you tell me?" His voice sounds so

dejected that it tears me up inside.

"Uncle Joe, I'm sorry. I wanted to tell you everything so many times, but I knew that Michael needed time to get to that point. It wasn't a normal marriage; it was a mistake." I cringe at those words and toss my food back on the table, my appetite gone. "I guess he told you that he regrets it and has made sure to file the paperwork to end it."

"Michael said a lot of things last night but the one thing that stuck out to me is that he doesn't think he's good enough for you. That man is so in love with you that he is giving you up for your own good. I tried to assure him that we'll support him in any way he needs, but this is something he needs to do. I have to stand behind him on this, Kay. I've never seen him so determined before." He pauses a moment. "Are you okay? I know this can't be easy on you."

"I will be in time. Right now, it's hard. I love the big dope more than anything in this world, but after I had time to let his words sink in, even though it hurts like hell, I can accept his decision." I rub my hand on my protruding belly and smile softly. "There's another reason I called. I'm not sure how you'll take this news. Can you switch us to video?"

"Sure."

Moments later, the phone beeps. I hit Accept and see his and Janet's sleepy faces smiling back at me. I miss them so much. "I wish I was there with you guys."

He nods. "What's the news? I don't know what could possibly top hearing that you're married, other than maybe Leah waking up."

I smile and point my phone down at my belly and rub on it, then bring it back to my face. "You're going to be a grandpa."

His eyes go big as he looks from me to Janet, then back to me. "I'm going to be . . . a grandpa?" He chuckles, then grabs Janet in his arms and drops the phone in the mix. A moment later, they come back on the screen and he looks sheepish. "Sorry. How are you doing? Do you know what you're having? How far along are you? Is it Michael's? Of course it is, I don't know what I'm talking about. Ignore me."

I chuckle and feel my heart warm. This is the kind of reaction I so badly wanted. I know if he were here right now, he'd be making a fuss over me.

"I love you. You know that?"

"I do. Now answer me, please. Don't make me fly out there."

Janet smiles and swats him on the shoulder. "Give the girl time to speak."

He zips his mouth and nods my way.

"First, I'm doing good. I wasn't at the start. This little one really took it out of me—I was so sick. I'm closing in on twenty weeks, and yes, she is Michael's."

"She?" he asks.

I nod my head. "Yes, Bean is a she."

He looks at Janet and leans his forehead against hers, the phone wobbling a bit. "We're having a granddaughter. Can you believe it?"

As much as this warms my heart, it also makes me sad. I want to share this moment with Mike. He deserves this as much as I do.

"Uncle Joe, I'm going to go now. Love you guys. Please don't tell the others just yet. I want to be the one to tell Leah when she wakes up."

He nods, and I hang up. I toss my phone on the table, lie back on the couch, and rub my belly.

"Don't you ever forget—your daddy loves you very much. If Mommy has anything to say about it, he will be a part of your life, even if he can't be a part of mine."

Somehow, I am going to have to learn to move on and build a life without him. I just don't know how. How can you love someone so much and walk away?

I don't know if I can.

# Chapter Twenty-Two

I open the shower door, and once the steam hits my skin, I step in, allowing the warmth of the water to soak me. The last three weeks have been hellish—well, not all of it. Leah is awake, and come to find out, she was eight weeks pregnant—now, closer to ten and with twins. I can still hardly believe it. Leah and I are both pregnant. That's crazy. Much to everyone's surprise, the twins are healthy and thriving. I'm beyond grateful that she's back with us. Therapy, both physical and mental, have been kicking her butt, but she is home and doing well. Everyone now knows about Mike and me, just not the pregnancy yet. I plan on telling them soon. I wanted Leah to have time to adjust after waking up.

Now she has.

Mike and I spoke the day we finalized our divorce—which his lawyer expedited—and the next day, he went to rehab. Since then, everyone back home has been a great support system for me. Maybe too great. My phone has died twice this week due to an overabundance of calls and texts. One of my favorite things is that Tom and Maddie still call me on video every night. We've even started adding Megan and Damon to the mix. Through the divorce and Leah's mess, they didn't want to overwhelm me with calls. They did make sure to let me know that they were there for me, but they didn't want to take up my call time when I needed it for my sister.

My phone chirps from the other room. Seeing as Leah is now awake and I know all is well, I ignore it. Last night, I was told that the four of them—Megan, Damon, Maddie, and Tom—bought plane tickets and plan to come out next week. I can hardly wait; I miss them all so much. Leah said that she'd love to come, but the doctor said no flying just yet. With a few weeks left on my contract, time seems to be dragging by. I have been enjoying my time here, but my heart is back home.

There's a knock on the front door. I hop out of the shower and reach for my towel, then grab my robe and walk carefully to the front door while wrapping it tightly around me.

"Bad timing?" Ben asks. He smiles big and produces a smoothie in his hand.

I grab it and take a sip before stepping back. "Come in. I'll be out in a minute."

I rush off and grab my clothes from my bed and head to the bathroom to finish up. When I'm done, I step out and find Ben in my kitchen making us breakfast.

"What are you making?" I put my hip against the island and watch him at work while I sip my smoothie.

"Banana French toast. You liked it so much last time, I figured I shouldn't mess with a good thing." He takes some bread from the bag he brought in and gets to work. "Are you ready for today?"

"Not really, but I don't have much of a choice." Today, I have my twenty-three-week checkup, then I have to hit the gym before work. I have to work with Marla, the one coworker who likes to make my life hell. Afterwards, Ben is picking me up and we'll be having one last hurrah with Shannon. She's leaving us tomorrow so she can stop off in Tennessee for a week with her sisters and then head to

Oklahoma to make a new life for her and little Lizzie. I'm really going to miss them.

My phone rings. I walk to my bedside table and hit Answer. "Hello?"

"Ms. Covington?"

"This is she. How can I help you?"

"This is Charlie with Home Rehab and Construction. I'm the foreman for your house renovations."

"Hello, Charlie. How can I help you?" Tom said he'd oversee the project for me since I'm so far away. I just go through everything with him on our calls. Charlie calling me is kind of surprising. I put my phone on sp eaker and open my laptop.

"I'm calling because we came across an issue with your plumbing. It looks like it's going to cost a little more than I quoted."

I pull up Messenger on my laptop and message Tom.


**Me:** *Charlie's on the phone claiming I have a plumbing issue at the house. Is there any way you can check in with him? I don't know a thing about this and don't want to be taken advantage of.*

"Do you have paperwork detailing the quote and the changes you're requesting she make?" Ben asks. "We're in New York. Without seeing something, it's hard to app rove that kind of job." He winks my way, then shrugs as if he couldn't help himself. Turning back to the stove, he doesn't miss a beat in finishing our breakfast.

"I don't, but I can get it to you by end of day."

"That would be great, thank you," I reply. "I also messaged Thomas Cameron. I'd like it if you can show him what needs to be done."

"Not a problem, ma'am."

I look at my computer and see that Tom has messaged me back.


**Tom:** *He was supposed to reach out to me if there were any issues. Yeah, I'll stop by in a bit. I'm getting ready for work now. I'll talk to you tonight.*
**Me:** *Thanks, Tom.*


I close my laptop and take a good, long look at Ben. This man has taken care of me from the moment I arrived in New York. Though my heart still aches for Mike, the urge to try things with Ben gets stronger with each time he surprises me like this. Who knows what tomorrow will bring.

I take off my slip-ons and lift my feet up to tuck them in a blanket on the couch. After the day I've had, they are swollen and sore, not to mention my back—I could really use a massage. Thankfully, Shannon chose to stay in tonight. Since her place is full of boxes, we're at my place. Shannon wheeled the bassinet and a sleeping Lizzie across the hall, parking her near me.

I get a message from Tom and click it open.

**Tom:** *All checked out. The price was a bit high but that's taken care of now. It'll take a while longer to get ready, though. You're looking at six weeks to move in, rather than four. I hope that's okay. You can always stay at my place until it's ready.*

**Me:** *Thanks. I'm good. I can extend my stay here and not have to rush packing. When I get back to Oklahoma, I can crash at Mike's. I already have a room there.*

"Well, it looks like the plumbing thing checked out," I say. "I don't have to rush the move so much now, unless Barb needs me out."

"I'm sure it'll be fine," Shannon says. "Didn't she say that the new tenant didn't need it until June anyway?" She walks off to the kitchen and grabs us both a drink.

"Yeah."

"I don't think you have anything to worry about."

Ben walks in and smiles big, holding up a pizza box and a bag.

"Geno's!" Shannon squeals.

I chuckle. Geno's is so good, but she's a bit obsessed with it.

Ben hands me a bag and nods. I open it and find Tropical Skittles, a side of jalapeños, and pineapple.

I look up at him, smiling big. "You're amazing! I hope you know that." The last week, I've not been able to get enough Skittles in my system, and it seems like no matter what I eat, I want jalapeños and pineapples on it. He's always going out of his way to ensure I have whatever I'm craving.

"No kidding," Shannon says. "You're going to make an amazing husband one day." She squeezes his cheek as she walks by, then plops down in my armchair and shoves nearly half a slice of pizza in her mouth all at once.

"Good?" I ask with a chuckle.

"You know it is."

"Do either of you need a plate while I'm in here?" Ben asks from my kitchen.

"I do."

"No, thanks," Shannon replies. She picks up a birthing book from the table and smiles. "Has this one scared you yet?"

"I haven't started that one. Why?" Ben hands me a plate. I nod in thanks and grab a slice.

"No reason. Just be prepared. It terrified me at first." Great. Just what I need. To be more scared of childbirth than I already am.

"It's not as bad as what it says. Well, let me amend that. In the moment it is, but as soon as your little one is put in your arms, it's all worth it." She smiles. "Any names yet?" I flinch. "I know I should have one, but I feel guilty. Mike should get a say in naming her too. I don't know. Maybe I'm just being stupid. I should just pick her name already."

"I don't think so. I had a hard time picking Lizzie's name. Without Chad, it stung. I get it. Maybe you can ask for his input when he gets out of rehab. By then, he should be thinking straight."

"Maybe."

I start to sit up and wince. My back is sore. Today really took it out of me.

"Back hurt?"

"Yeah," I reply. "I did a lot today. The bigger I get, the more my body aches." I can only imagine trying to get around in a month or two. No wonder by the time women are in their final month, they're so ready to have the baby.

"You should ask Ben for a back rub."

I look at Ben and see his cheeks turn pink at her comment. "I couldn't do that. I'll just schedule a maternity massage."

"Why not?" she asks. Then, as if it dawns on her, she looks remorseful. "Sorry. I can see how that could be a problem."

I shake my head, pop a few Skittles into my mouth, then grab another slice of pizza. "It's not that it would be a problem," I say. "I'm divorced now, but I think knowing there's something growing between us . . . this could cross some wires."

Ben looks my way and grins.

"So you admit that there's something between the two of you?" Shannon asks.

Now I see what she's doing. I shake my head at her playing matchmaker. "I'd be an idiot not to see the man Ben is. It has nothing to do with that. I just got out of a marriage and am pregnant with my ex's baby. Plus, you know how I feel about Mike. That wouldn't be fair to Ben." I take a bite and look back at Shannon. "Didn't you say that you're Team Mike?"

"If he'd take you back, then yeah, I would be, but the man ended things and told you to move on. Ben is a good man. The two of you could have something special. If I could see my two besties be happy together, then why not?"

"Shannon," Ben scolds. "Let up, will ya?"

"Fine," she retorts. "You can't fault me for trying to help my friends out. Y'all would be too cute together."

I put my plate on the table, not hungry anymore. "I love that you want us to be happy, but you have to understand that I'm not ready to move on yet. Whether my marriage lasted a day or years, it still hurts knowing I'm not wanted. It does something to someone when they feel less than. I know you want Ben and me to get together. I can't fault you for that." I smile at Ben, then look toward Shannon again. "He's a good man, and an attractive one at that. If life was different, I would've jumped at the thought of being with him. But seeing how things are the way they are, I need to take time to heal. I'm not planning on jumping from a divorce to a new relationship. Ben deserves better than that."

She nods and stuffs her mouth again. Minutes go by in silence, and then she finally speaks up. "I'm sorry. Sometimes I push too hard when it comes to the people I care about. You're right, though—he doesn't deserve that."

Ben grabs a bag near him and produces a to-go container of éclairs. Topic dropped.

I start to sit up but think twice about it. I reach out, making grabby hands. "Please tell me you got me one."

"I did." He chuckles and hands it over.

I take a big bite and moan as the sugary goodness melts in my mouth. "This is heaven," I say around my bite.

"I'll go buy out the case if you enjoy them that much," Ben says.

I take the pillow from next to me and toss it his way. "Don't you go being weird on me now."

He laughs, catching it, then lifts my feet and puts the pillow underneath them. Seeing how attentive he is, I can't help but wonder what these next weeks will look like here in New York.

I rush to grab my phone, which is wailing on the counter. "Hello?" I say, trying to catch my breath.

"Hello, is this Kayla Covington?"

"It is." I put my bag on the counter and start taking the groceries out. Hearing the business nature of the caller's voice, I'm glad I caught the call.

"I have a call from Michael Buchannan. Hold on just a minute and I'll put him through."

I put the cold food in the fridge and move across the room to sit on the couch.

"Kayla?"

"Hey," I reply. The sound of his voice sends a jolt to my stomach. I miss him still, even though I know I shouldn't. "How are you doing?" I pull the blanket off the back and wrap it around my now-cold feet.

"I'm okay. How's Bean? How are you?" His voice sounds so flat, and I hate that I can't see him.

"I'm fine. Bean is good. She's getting big, and I can feel the flutters growing stronger. Dr. Emmons says it won't be long until others can feel her move too."

"That's great. But how have you really been? You don't exactly sound fine."

I lay my head back and close my eyes. "I'm okay. I don't want to drop more on your shoulders. You're there to work on you."

He chuckles. "I appreciate you, but I'd really like to know how you are. No more of this 'I'm fine' stuff. I'm worried about you. I didn't exactly get the chance to check on you after the divorce until now. How are you handling things?"

I stand up and go in search of a drink. "I've been struggling. I know I need to move on. You made yourself perfectly clear on that. It's just hard when I can't shut off my feelings for the father of my baby. I'm working on it, though."

"You have five minutes," a female voice says, cutting in.

I sit down at the table and start again. "How's therapy?"

"Nice try. I know I can't make you move on, Kay, but I don't want you putting your life on hold for me either. It's not easy for me to say that, knowing that I'm giving up both of my girls, but if you can find a stand-up man that will treat the both of you right . . . that I can live with. In time."

I set my drink down and wipe the tears that fall. "And what if you heal and decide you made a mistake in letting me go? What will happen then?"

"Don't do that to yourself. I don't want you waiting for me to get better. You will always have my heart, but I have to accept it when you move on. You deserve so much better than the likes of me."

"Two minutes," the lady says.

"Kayla, listen, I want you to give dating a chance. Try to find a guy who treats you right and go for it." He muffles the phone, then comes back. "My time is up. Take care of yourself, beautiful."

"I will."

"Bye, Kayla."

"Bye, Michael," I echo, and the line goes silent.

Until I said the words out loud, I don't think I realized that I have been holding out hope for him to come back to me. I know he wants me to move on, but I don't know if I can. I'm hurt. While I love Michael still and always will, I don't think I need to be in any relationship at all. I set out to heal and move on. I haven't done that yet and now that I'm a mom, I need to focus on us. Not on a man . . . one that could possibly break me worse than I already am.

He is right though. I do need to move on. Just not with another relationship.

# Chapter Twenty-Three

After loading the dishwasher, I make my way to the living room to relax a bit. Since Shannon left, it's been awfully quiet—just Ben and me. Tomorrow, everyone—Damon, Megan, Tom, and Maddie—will be here. Earlier today, Ben came over and helped me get the place ready for their visit. He brought over a few of his chairs for us to use while they're here, and the place is now spotless. I'm worn out but so happy that I'll get to see some of my favorite people in mere hours. Now that I'm sitting here alone, my hand finds my belly and I can't help but think about the kind of woman Bean will be one day. When I think of her, I imagine a girl who looks just like me but with her daddy's bottle-green eyes.

I'm pulled from thought when my laptop pings with a call.

I stand, and when I see Leah calling, I quicken my step. Today, I plan to tell her and the others about Bean. She's having a game night at her house and wanted me to be a part of it. I'm thrilled and can hardly wait to show them just how big I'm getting.

"Hey, sis," I say as I hit Accept. "HI, everyone." I wave as she pans out so that I can see the others sitting at the table—Uncle Joe, Janet, Tom, Maddie, Becca, Mark, and Cam's other siblings. "You've got a full house tonight."

"That I do. Marie's coming here in a minute. She said she'd be happy to play your hand for you tonight." We have worked it out so that when we play games like this over the phone, someone sits in for me, making the move that I text them in secret after they show me what cards or whatnot I have over the video screen. It can be a challenge, but I love feeling as if I'm being included.

"That's sweet of her." I take in a nervous breath and get Leah's attention. "Hey, sis."

"What's up?"

"I have something I want to tell you. I'll leave it up to you if you want the others to hear or not. It's not something that needs to be kept quiet anymore."

"Okay, shoot. What is it?" She sits down in her recliner at the head of the table and Cam sits on the arm, cuddling in. Everyone else in the room is quiet, so I know they're listening in.

I look down at my table, hating how much I want Michael here with me for this. I try and shake the feeling off, then look back up at my sister. "I wish I were there with you for this, and I am so sorry I haven't told you sooner."

She nods.

"You know Michael and I got married in October."

She nods again. I wipe at a stray tear and find my strength. I don't know why I'm so nervous to tell her.

"Well, um . . ."

"Come on, Kay. What did he do that you're not telling me?" Leah interrupts.

"It's not that he did something. Well, in a way, but that's not what I mean. I just don't want you to be mad at him is all."

"Too late. I love the big jerk. He's like a brother to me, but he hurt you. I'll see past it in time, but *you* are my sister.

He's lucky he checked himself in to rehab. Now out with it, Kay. What did he do?"

Cam tries to calm her, and even though I didn't mean to work her up, I did, and I hate that. It wasn't this hard to tell Uncle Joe, but Leah has been rooting for us to be together for a long time. I hate disappointing her.

"It's not bad, Leah. I'm just nervous to tell you. I know how protective you are of me. I don't want you going overboard is all."

She nods, but I can see her hands tighten in her lap.

There is no other way for me to do it, so I take a steadying breath and spill it. "I'm pregnant."

Her eyes go big and a hand finds her mouth. Cam hugs her to his side and smiles at me before kissing Leah on the head. In the background, I can hear the others talking amongst themselves in reaction.

Leah takes a moment to gather herself before asking. "You're pregnant?"

I nod. "I'll be twenty-four weeks in a couple days." I stand so that she can see just how big I have gotten.

"My God, Kay. You are getting so big." She smiles through her tears. "Do you know what you're having yet?"

I nod. "Uncle Joe brought y'all a cake, didn't he?"

"I did," he says from the other side of the screen.

"Mike and I did a private gender reveal with Bean's godparents while you were still in the hospital. I so badly wished that you were there, so this, in a way, is a replay. When you cut into the cake, you'll find out."

She looks over the screen and then to Cam. "Where's the cake?"

I chuckle. This is such a Leah thing to do. "Don't you want to eat your dinner first?"

"Will the pizza tell me the gender of your baby?"

Cam shakes his head and stands.

"Nope."

"Then I want cake. The pizza can wait."

I throw my head back and laugh. "God, I miss you, sis."

She looks up at the camera. "Then come home. I miss you too. You shouldn't be in New York, pregnant and alone. Come home and get fat with me. Let's do this together."

Uncle Joe saves me by carrying the cake into the shot, while Cam carries a butter knife. They set the cake on the tray table by her side. Leah sits up and cuts a slice out of it. Her head snaps back at me when she sees the pink center.

"It's a girl! Oh my God, it's another Covington girl." She looks from me to Cam, then to Uncle Joe, and back to me. I can imagine the hug that I'd get right now if I were home.

Happy tears flow down both of our cheeks, but my heart still hurts.

I love my family, and knowing that they love Bean this much already means the world to me, but the part of my heart where her dad should be sits empty. No matter how many times I tell myself I need to move on, moments like these make me want to hold on that much harder.

"Who all did you say is coming?" Ben asks as we stand at baggage claim.

"My best friend, Megan, and Mike's best friend, Damon. They're dating. And then my brother-in-law's brother, Tom, and his bestie, Maddie."

"Are you sure you want me to hang around? These are your people, Kay. I should go home," he says dejectedly.

I move to his side and link his arm with mine, tugging him to a nearby bench. "Don't be silly—of course I want my Benny boy here." I giggle.

He chuckles. "You're cute when you get like that."

"Like what?" I question.

"All girlie. Your giggle is my weakness."

"Kayla!"

I hear my name from behind me and turn to see Megan running my way. I stand and turn in time for her to nearly barrel into me, only pulling back enough to not crush my belly.

"O-M-G, I've missed you!" she says. Megan steps back and has me turn full circle. "Let me get a good look at you."

I do as she says, posing at the end. Out of the corner of my eye, I see Ben watching us like a hawk, a smirk on his face.

"There you are," Damon says as he catches up. "You took off so fast, I didn't know which way to go." He looks between me and Megan, then pulls me in for a hug. "How are you doing?" He looks down at my stomach. "And my goddaughter?"

"She's great! Getting bigger by the day."

Tom and Maddie interrupt as they join the party. I'm pulled in for more hugs and belly rubs. Once done, I catch Ben's eye and reach my hand out for him to join us. He does, and I stand next to him to make introductions. I point to each person, allowing him to shake their hands. "Everyone, this is Ben, my neighbor and good friend."

"Nice to meet you." Tom sticks his hand out to shake Ben's.

"Who are we meeting?" a man says behind me.

I turn around and see Uncle Joe and Janet.

"Uncle Joe!" I walk right into his open arms, then pull Janet into the mix. "I've missed you two so much. I didn't know y'all were coming."

"Me too, baby doll. We thought we'd surprise you." Uncle Joe kisses my head, rubs my belly, and then makes his way to the others.

Janet pulls me in for another hug.

"Who is this friend we're meeting? I think maybe we should have a chat," I hear Uncle Joe say behind me. "You're not trying to make moves on my girl, are you?"

"Joseph," Janet says at the same time I say, "Uncle Joe." We pull out of the hug and step their way.

He laughs. "You ladies worry too much. Any man that can take on my girls should have no problem talking to me."

"Ben," I start, but Damon wraps an arm around my shoulder and leads me to the carousel to wait on their bags. I look over my shoulder to see what's going on. Ben winks and puts me at ease.

Damon leans forward and grabs a bag before looking back at me. "This Ben guy, does he make you happy?"

"Ben and I are no more than friends," I say. "He's good to me, but I'm not ready to be with anyone else. Michael did a number on my heart."

"I hate what he's put you through, Kay, but I also know what hell he's going through right now. While I wish the two of you could work through it, I have to respect that he cut you loose. I just hope that he can handle it when you move on." He grabs Megan's bag from the carousel and then turns. "Are you sure you have no interest in this Ben guy?"

I look over my shoulder to find Ben's eyes are still trained on me. "I'd be lying if I said no. He is a good catch, but I don't think he's for me."

"Does he know this?"

"I have been honest with him every step of the way. He has too. I know how he feels, but he also knows that I'm not ready and may never be."

Damon nods as we join the others.

Now that we're on our way out, Ben finds his way to my side again.

"Your uncle asked me to hang out with you guys tomorrow. If that's okay with you, I'd like to come. I told him I wanted to check with you first. I don't want to intrude."

"You wouldn't be intruding," I retort. "I'd love for you to join."

We step out to the waiting passenger van and load in.

I turn, leaning on Ben a little to look at Damon, Megan, Tom, and Maddie in the back row. "Do y'all have a room or do you want to bunk with me? It's small, but I'm sure we can make room."

"A few of you can stay at my place, if need be," Ben adds.

I lean back and look at him, smiling. I don't know what makes him do it, but he leans in and kisses my forehead. I'm taken aback for a moment.

"We have a room," Janet says. "Not that I wouldn't love to bunk with you, but I'm a little too old to sleep on the couch anymore."

"We can bunk with you," Megan says. "I miss you, and I don't plan on leaving your side until I have to." She looks over at Maddie and smiles. "Care to have a girls' night? If Ben is serious about the guys staying with him, I say we take advantage."

"Hey," Damon teases. "You already trying to pawn me off?"

"No, but it wouldn't hurt you to get to know Ben either. He's special to our girl. You should try to include him."

I turn back around so I'm facing Ben. "Are you sure you're okay with that? I know you were hesitant in the beginning."

"I'm sure," he assures me. "If I have any trouble, you're right next door."

I give him an awkward seatbelt hug. "Thank you." I smile. Turning back to the others, I say, "Girls' night it is." I turn to Janet on my other side and smile big. "How are you?"

"I'm good. I've missed you though," she replies. "Our calls just aren't the same as being in person."

"Maybe we can sneak away for a bit while you're here. Just the two of us."

"That sounds like a plan," she replies.

Bean kicks my stomach, startling me. I drop my hand to my belly, gently pushing back where her foot is resting. For the last day or two, she has been kicking harder than she normally does. It used to feel more flutters—like butterflies, really—but lately, she's more active. I chuckle, more to myself than anything.

Janet leans my way. "Are you okay? Mid conversation, you just started staring at your belly."

"We're fine. I promise."

"Why'd you zone out like that?" Megan asks.

"I didn't mean to zone out." I laugh. "It's just Bean. She's become more active lately, especially if I get hungry or relaxed. She's getting stronger, my little fighter, in there jabbing at me."

"Can I?" Janet asks as she attempts to put her hand on my stomach.

"Of course. I don't know if you can feel her yet. I'm not quite twenty-four weeks yet." I take her hand and place it where Bean was just jabbing.

"Oh, sugar!" she cries when Bean moves again. "I hope you know she's going to be spoiled rotten." She turns to Uncle Joe, talking animatedly about the baby and feeling her move.

I chuckle.

This is what I've been missing. Having them here, I don't miss home nearly as much as I did yesterday. Home is not a place—it's the people who have your heart. This van is full of love and it's just what I needed.

# Chapter Twenty-Four

STEPPING OUT OF MY bathroom, I'm met by the smell of Uncle Joe's country omelet, causing my mouth to water. It's only been a night and I already don't want them to go. Girls' night was fun—emotional but nice. I miss them all so much.

"Extra mushrooms?" I ask.

"Of course," he replies.

I pull my robe tighter around me and grab a slice of bacon before making my way to my closet. The maternity pants that I just bought don't fit anymore, so thank God I had my robe in the bathroom. "I need to go shopping. You ladies up for a trip while you're here?"

"We'll all go," Uncle Joe says. "I didn't come all this way to miss out on time with my baby. What are we shopping for?"

Uncle Joe? Shopping? If he's game, I am too. He rarely ever wants to go.

"Maternity clothes." I hold up the pants and wave them around. "These don't fit anymore."

There's a knock at the door. I grab the closest dress and make my way to the bathroom while Uncle Joe gets it, and the guys walk in. I quickly ready myself, then move to my dresser and grab my brush.

Ben walks over with my green juice. He's made a habit of making me one almost every day for the last few weeks. I smile and kiss his cheek in thanks.

"How'd you sleep last night?"

"Good, and you? The guys didn't give you crap, did they?"

He starts to answer but my phone begins ringing, so I hold up a finger and step to my bedside table. It's the same number Mike called from the last time we spoke.

"Hello?" I answer.

"Is this Kayla Covington?"

"It is."

"I have a call for you. Please hold."

I put a hand over my phone and let Ben know it's Mike. He nods and turns back to the kitchen, where the others are gathered. I sit down on my bed and get comfortable.

"Kayla?" Mike asks.

"Yeah, I'm here. How are you? It's been a while since I've heard from you. Everything okay?"

"I'm good. Sorry I didn't call. I've been working on some pretty heavy stuff and didn't want to take it out on you. So, how's Bean? How are you?"

"Bean is good. Janet got to feel her kick last night." I grab my brush and begin running it through my hair.

"She did?" he asks, shocked.

"Yeah, she did."

"That's great. And you? How are you?"

"I'm good."

"Wait. You said Janet. Are you in Oklahoma already?"

I chuckle and lie back on my bed. "No. They paid me a visit—Tom, Maddie, Uncle Joe, Janet, Megan, and Damon."

"That's good. I'm glad they came to visit. Give them hell for me. I miss you all, but this place has been good for me, you know?"

I can hear it in his voice. He doesn't sound so burdened anymore.

"I can tell. I'm glad that you're getting the help you need."

"How have things been since we spoke last?"

I look at the others and smile as Ben catches my eye. "Good, I guess. Shannon moved to Wagon Springs, not too far from Leah, to be closer to her family. Even though it sucks right now, I'll be happy when I move back. My offer on the house was accepted and my place should be ready in about five weeks or so."

"The offer you put on the house next to Becca? You got that one?" he asks.

"Yeah." I look over my shoulder as the others get a little loud. Ben winks at me and then gets back to whatever he was telling them.

I can't believe how well he fits in.

"Kayla, you there?"

"Yeah, yeah, sorry. What was it you asked?"

"Have you found anyone that you'll be willing to give a chance at winning your heart?"

"Michael . . ." I try.

"I need to know, Kay. For my peace of mind, I need to hear it." He's quiet a moment, then tries again. "You've found someone, haven't you? Your tone says a lot."

I wipe a tear from my cheek and muster up the strength to tell him. "I have found someone who wants to be with me. He is good to me, and he knows about you and Bean. We aren't dating, and honestly I'm not ready to be with anyone else but . . . yeah. He's interested, and sometimes I wonder."

"If he asks you out, what will you say?"

I hate that he's pushing me like this. It's so frustrating.

"No. I will say no," I cry. "I should say yes. He's good to me, and I know he wants me. But . . . my heart isn't in it. When I look at him, no matter how much I wish I could, I cannot think of him as anything other than my friend," I huff. A life with Ben would be a good one—I would be cherished and want for nothing—but a life with him would also be a life without true love.

"Five minutes," a lady says, cutting through our conversation.

The line is quiet—so quiet—that I have to check my phone to make sure the call wasn't dropped. "Mike?"

"I'm here. I hate to ask since our calls are so short, but would you mind if I talk to D real quick?"

"Sure," I sigh.

I walk into the kitchen and hold my phone out to

Damon. He scrunches his brow but takes it and steps into my living area. Ben takes one look at me and is at my side in seconds, pulling me in for a hug. I bury my head in his chest and let him soothe me.

"If he can't see what a gem he has in you, that's his problem." He rubs the back of my head and hugs me tighter.

"It's not that. I know this isn't on me, but why would he make me tell him that? It makes me feel . . . mean."

"Tell him what, and why would it make you feel mean if he asked?"

"Michael asked me to move on a while back, and at first, I didn't want to, mostly because I knew he was finally getting the help he needed and I didn't want him to regret his decision, then try to get me back after I moved on. I wanted to avoid that drama."

Meg hands us each a plate and we move to sit on my couch.

"When he filed the divorce papers, I decided it was time to put me first. To put relationships aside and to heal from everything that has happened. I didn't want to jump from whatever we shared to another relationship." I take a bite and hum at the goodness that is Uncle Joe's cooking. I tell Ben what happened during my call with Mike, then put my hand on Ben's. "It's not that I don't find you attractive—I do, and you know you're a good-looking man. It's just that my heart isn't in it, and I can't go there with you unless I know I could give you my heart."

Ben nods and turns his hand over, linking our fingers together. He remains quiet and lets me get it all out.

"Mike couldn't even give me ten minutes," I cry. I put my fork on my plate and take a drink.

Ben shakes his head. "I hate that for you and I'm sure it hurts. But as a man, I can only imagine the pain he must be feeling right now. You said that he admitted his love for you but let you go because he didn't want you or Bean to get hurt."

I nod.

"That's a sacrifice that any man—or woman, for that matter—would feel deep in their bones." He sets down his plate and covers our hands with his other. "I can't claim that I'd do the same in his position, but I am grateful that he's willing to give you up when he knows he can't give you what you deserve. He sounds like a good man. I hope one day he finds his happiness and that he can be there for his daughter. You both deserve to find your happy."

"What if he never lets himself get close to her? I can take him pushing me away, but if he shuns Bean, that's another story. I don't know if I can deal with that."

Ben nods as Damon and Megan walk in from behind me

and sit on the edge of my coffee table. I pull my hand from Ben's and turn their way.

D hands back my phone and smiles weakly. "That's where we come in. You chose us as godparents. We'll make sure she's loved—so loved that she'll be begging us to leave her alone."

Megan chuckles but nods. "What Ben said," she starts, "shows me what a good man he is. I'm glad that you have him by your side while you're here. Mike walked away. Though right in his mind, it might not be by everyone. Give him time to adjust. If you find anyone who grabs your interest between now and then . . ." She trails off, smiling at Ben, "Michael will just have to learn to live with that."

Ben grins but takes a bite to try and hide it.

I hate that Mike is hurting over this, but this is what he wanted.

So why do I feel bad then?

I take a bite of my food and try to put Mike at the back of my mind.

Shopping is fun, but the nap . . . that is so needed. Damon and Megan bought so much baby stuff that they'll have to buy another suitcase or ship it home. Uncle Joe bought a rocking chair for me when he noticed that I couldn't stop looking at it. This rocking chair looks like something that belongs in a Victorian home but was updated with white paint and the softest pink material I've ever seen. I'm still trying not to buy much but I did get some really cute shoes and a couple blankets. I couldn't help myself.

After the shopping trip, Uncle Joe took us to lunch at a nearby pizzeria that Janet wanted to try. Ben and I agreed that Shannon would have loved it if she were still here. Uncle Joe took Janet sightseeing while I napped. Now that it's closing in on dinnertime, we're all meeting soon.

I throw on my shimmery black dress but can't get it to zip. Sticking my head out the door, I holler out for Meg. "Can you help me zip up?"

She runs over and begins zipping, but once it gets to midback, it won't budge.

"Seriously, Bean." I thought that once I bought maternity clothes, that was it—they would stretch until I gave birth, Boy was I wrong.

"Baby girl is getting big," Meg says. "Do you have another dress?"

"I bought one earlier but it's not nearly as nice." I run into my closet and strip out of my black dress and grab the long blue sundress. It's cute but not anything fancy enough for tonight's dinner.

Megan eyes me as I slip it on and hollers over her shoulder at Maddie. "Run next door and ask Ben if we can borrow a navy or black blazer." She looks back at me. "Where's your jewelry?"

I point her in the right direction and smile as I grab my slippers. I've missed my people so much. Thirty minutes later, Meg and Mads have done wonders in helping me pull together something presentable enough for a fancy night out.

By the time we're ready to leave, Damon, Tom, and Ben are standing at my door, ready to escort us to the restaurant.

"Ladies." Damon smiles.

"Looking good," Tom adds.

Ben smiles brightly. "Our car should be here in ten."

"Do you mind if we cancel it? I need to get my steps in. Besides, I don't know if I'll ever get another chance at a New York evening," Meg says.

"I'm with Meg," I reply. "I haven't gotten to the gym today and have to get in my steps also."

"You still have to hit the gym?" Damon asks. "You're

pregnant. Shouldn't that be a free pass?"

Megan and I both laugh.

"Being pregnant isn't a free pass," Maddie says. "If Kayla wants to bounce back after having Bean, it's important to keep up with her routine. She just needs to modify it a bit. Plus, it helps ease labor pains."

Tom's gaze meets hers. "Just how do you know all that?"

She shrugs. "I have older sisters."

I link arms with Ben as we start walking. Four blocks later, we spot Janet and Uncle Joe standing outside Franko's, waiting on us. He takes her hand to his mouth and kisses it. When he lowers it, I see her stare into his eyes as if he hung the moon, just for her. That is the kind of love I want.

We make it to them, and I'm pulled into a hug immediately. Uncle Joe steps back and pulls Janet to his side. He smiles brightly, then lifts Janet's hand to his mouth once more. He's being awfully lovey-dovey tonight.

Then I see it.

My eyes grow wide, and I snatch her hand from his. "When did this happen?" I ask.

On her left ring finger sits a platinum band with a simple princess-cut diamond in the center.

I look up at them with a smile growing on my face. "Y'all

got engaged?"

She nods happily while he smiles at me brightly. "We did," he replies.

I pull them both in for a group hug and laugh. "It's about time. I'm just so happy for you."

The others make their way over and give hugs.

"I want to hear all about it."

We are shown to our table moments later. Once we put in our order, Janet shares the story of how Uncle Joe took her on a ride around Central Park in a horse-drawn carriage. She wanted a pretzel after and when they came near the pond, he took a knee—she got her pretzel and a ring.

"I never would have expected anything like that from Joe. I thought he'd take me for a ride on the back of his bike and stop near the lake or something." She giggles. "This was perfect. Right out of a romance novel, if you ask me."

I fight to hold back tears, but neither Janet nor I are successful in doing so.

"Woman, you are ruining my reputation in front of the guys here," Uncle Joe scolds.

"Not at all," I retort. "If anything, you are showing them what women really want—a man who is willing to step out of his comfort zone to give his woman what he knows she will cherish forever. That is a dream man. Maybe you should teach some classes." I chuckle.

The girls join in. The guys seem indifferent but not set apart in anyway.

"When do you guys head out?" I ask.

"We have an early flight, two days from now," Janet says. Megan nods.

"Tom and I leave tomorrow morning," Maddie adds. "We're flying back home for my nephew's birthday party tomorrow evening."

Ben puts his hand on my knee and squeezes lightly before retracting it. I appreciate the support, but I am going to miss them all so much. Thankfully, Oliver has me booked with back-to-back gigs for the next couple weeks. Hopefully those will help me pass the remainder of my time here. I'm looking forward to the day I can walk back into his office and sign the termination paperwork. I'm ready to go home.

# Chapter Twenty-Five

I take the final step onto my landing, pulling out my keys from my handbag. Once inside my apartment, I toss my bag on the entry table and plop down on the couch. This has been a crazy busy week. I'm worn out! It has been nearly four weeks since my family left, and I have barely had a moment to myself since. Oliver warned me that he had me booked with back-to-back gigs, and I will never doubt him again. This morning was my final shoot here in New York, and I've been thinking . . . it might be my last gig ever. I think I want to slow down now that I'll have Bean. Maybe I'll take my spot in the family business.

Who knows, but right now I'm going to take some time to focus on me and my baby.

Speaking of, Bean kicks, and my hand instinctively covers that spot. "Momma loves you, Bean. I really should give you a name. I can't keep calling you Bean forever." It's not for a lack of thinking of baby names—I have a few that I like but I cannot bear the thought of narrowing them down without her dad's input. "Daddy will be out soon, and we'll talk. I promise."

There's a knock at my door. I stand and go open it.

Ben stands there, holding out a tropical smoothie for me with a smile on his face. "Ready?"

I huff and let my shoulders deflate. "I guess."

Ben chuckles. "I know you've been working hard lately but look at it like this. After you sign those papers, you're done. Then we can get you packed for the move."

"You have a good point." I grab my bag and smoothie, slip my shoes back on, and follow him out. A brief time later, we're at Oliver's office, where I sign the termination papers and gain my freedom once more. This day really is looking up.

"It has been a pleasure working with you, Kayla. If, down the road, you find yourself wanting to work again, give me a call," Oliver says.

"Thank you. I'll keep that in mind."

I turn and head out of his office, only stopping in the waiting room to collect Ben.

"What now?" he asks.

"Well, I have a call with Leah after my appointment with Dr. Emmons, but I still have plenty of time before then. Let's hit up that baby store my uncle went to with us. I want to see if they still have that fairy-tale bedding set. I should have bought it then."

He raises a brow at me in question. "You want me to go baby shopping with you?"

I feel bad that he even questions that.

"I'm sorry if I made you feel like you couldn't." I stop walking and turn to look at Ben. "You are one of the closest friends I have. Of course I want you to go shopping with me.  I love how much you want to be there for me and Bean, but there has to be boundaries. I do not want to lead you on."

"Okay. I can accept that. I never meant to overstep. If I did, I'm sorry."

"You haven't. Now, if you don't hate me, I'd love for you to go shopping with me."

"I could never hate you." He takes my hand in his. "I know I'm not her dad, but I have been here every day since you told us about her. I love that little girl. Think of me as Uncle Ben. She's gonna be so spoiled."

I pull him in for a hug. "Thank you for being so understanding. The last thing I want to do is hurt you."

He steps back from our hug and smiles. "Let's go baby shopping, shall we?"

He and I link arms and walk in silence. Two blocks later, we're standing outside the biggest baby store I've ever seen. I smile and open the door. I already have to hire movers, so what are a few extra boxes?

Let's do some damage.

Ben points the phone—which has Leah on video call—at me. Since I decided to let loose a bit and allow myself to shop, I couldn't help the excitement and had to share. Ben told me to put her on video and took my phone. I smile and show her every outfit in my cart. I found the cutest boy outfit—I recently found out that my Leah is having a boy and girl—and had to get something for my sister too. "Look at these shoes! I can't not buy them."

"Agreed, they are adorable, but isn't that a boy outfit? I thought you were having a girl."

I smile. "I am, but I'm also having a niece and nephew."

"Aw, Kay. You don't have to do that."

"I know I don't, but you know me. I'm going to anyway." I smile up at Ben and realize how rude this is. Even if he suggested this call, I should wait and call her later tonight. "Hey, sis. I'm going to get; I'll call you tonight like planned."

"Okay, sounds good. Love you."

"Love you too." I take my phone back from Ben and tuck it into my pocket. We continue through the aisles, only checking out once I have looked at every inch of the store. Even though I have several bags, I am not leaving with the fairy-tale bedding set that I so badly wanted—it was sold out.

Ben walks ahead of me, arms loaded with bags. I ordered an Uber since I bought so much. He goes to the trunk and starts unloading his arms as I step out of the store and into the mix.

Screaming fills my ears.

I turn and spot a man running after snatching someone's purse. He barrels into me before I can react, causing us both to tumble. My arms flail in desperation for something to grab on to.

"Help!" I yell.

Ben appears with his hands outstretched, ready to save me. I reach out with one hand and curl in around my stomach with the other. Bean could be seriously hurt if I don't protect her. I can't let that happen. As I make contact with the ground, pain shoots through me like a bolt of lightning. I barely avoid hitting full force, thanks to Ben. I just hope it's enough.

Please, *please* let Bean be okay.

I look at my shattered phone and tuck it into my bag as I'm loaded into the ambulance. "Is my baby okay?" I ask.

The paramedic is busy checking my vitals, but replies, "I'm not sure, ma'am. We'll get you to the hospital so they can check you out. Is there anyone I can call for you?"

I start crying, and she just pats me on the knee and continues to work. "Everyone I know except Ben is out of state." I furrow my brows. "Where is he?"

"The man that was with you said that he would meet you at the hospital."

"Thank you." I lay my head back and try to rest.

I'm jumbled from side to side as we make our way down New York streets. It doesn't take us long to get to the hospital, but once there, nobody will give me answers. I feel like I'm crawling out of my skin and nobody's answering my questions. But they sure do have a lot of their own.

"How far along are you?" someone asks.

"Twenty-eight weeks."

"Have you had any contractions?" the nurse asks.

"No, just some pain in my lower back, close to where I landed. The only sharp pain I felt was upon impact."

She nods. "Any bleeding or leaking of fluids?"

"Um . . . I don't think so. I haven't been able to move or even check." Ben wouldn't let me stand, and once the ambulance got there, EMTs put me on a gurney and loaded me up. I haven't stood on my own since the fall.

I lie here with all kinds of machines hooked up to me, thankful when I hear Bean's heartbeat. They run test after test, draw blood, and leave me in a room with nothing but my thoughts. *Where is Ben?* I wonder. There's not one person here holding my hand, and I'm scared out of my mind. The tears won't stop at this point. I wish Mike were here, but when I spoke to Damon last week, he said Mike was due for discharge in a few days. I wonder if he made it home yet, though I haven't heard from him. I'd assume he'd try to video call me if he was. Someone pops in every ten minutes or so and checks the machines, but nobody is telling me what's going on. Lying back, I close my eyes and try to rest.

This stress is good for no one.
I feel a faint tug on my arm and look at the clock on the wall. 9:13 p.m. By this point, I've been here almost ten hours. I thought Ben said he was meeting me at the hospital.

Why am I all alone?
If my phone wasn't shattered, I could call someone, but I don't know their numbers.

The nurse smiles at me as she swaps out my IV bag.

"Can you tell me what's going on? I've been here a long time. Is Bean okay?"

"Things look stable from what I can tell. I can ask the doctor to come in next time she's this way."

There's a ruckus outside, so she excuses herself.

I lean my head back on my pillow and put my hand on my belly. "I need you to be okay, baby girl. *Please* don't leave me." I keep my hand there and let the tears fall as I picture what it would be like to hold her in my arms, to put her in Michael's for the first time and watch the joy spread across his face. I have no doubt in my mind that if he would just be open to being a dad, he'd be the best. Tears come stronger at that thought. "I love you with all my heart, and I know your daddy does too. He's just struggling right now. Give him a chance. He'll be the best daddy in the world. I know he will." I reach up and dry my face. "Hang in there, Bean. Mommy and Daddy love you very much." I rub circles on my stomach, willing her to fight.

"Sir," a woman says, causing me to open my eyes and look toward the door.

Standing there is a sight I would've never imagined seeing—a very disheveled Michael is staring back at me.

"Can I help you?" the nurse behind him asks.

He shakes his head. "No, ma'am, sorry. I came for my wife and kid."

*His wife?*

Bean moves, and my attention flies to my stomach.

"Nurse," I say excitedly. "My baby just moved!"

Mike rushes to my side, worried, then hesitates.

I take his hand in mine and put it on my stomach.

"It's okay. Talk to your daughter. It seems she needed to hear your voice."

He sets down his bag and pulls a chair up to my side as a doctor comes in and checks the monitor. She smiles at me, then Mike.

"Is she okay?" I ask.

"Her vitals seem to be steady, but I plan to keep you here for observation for a while longer. You took a hard fall. Things are up in the air right now. Just try to rest. I know it's nearly impossible, but don't stress."

After she leaves the room, Mike looks at me, then my stomach. "When Ben called me—thank God Damon gave him my number—saying that I needed to rush here, I nearly had a heart attack. I called so many hospitals to find you. I'm so sorry. I know that this isn't my fault, but if I were the man I should've been, I would've never let you go. You'd be home safe and in my arms right now."

My breath catches and I don't know how to respond.

He leans down to my belly to kiss it, then starts rubbing. "Your momma is right, you know. I do love you, with all my heart. Hang in there, Bean. Momma and Daddy are here, waiting for the day we get to bring you home. Keep fighting, little one."

Will the tears ever stop?

Mike lifts a hand and wipes my cheek. "You rest, beautiful. I'm here now and I'm not going anywhere."

Not strong enough to argue, I do as he says.

I close my eyes and feel him run a finger over my arm. The zaps cause goose pimples to form. Tears sting the back of my eyes—I have wanted this for so long. I'm thankful to not go at this alone, but I can't help but wonder when he'll run next.

I'm awoken when a nurse pats my arm. I smile as she begins to take the IV out. She looks at Mike on one side and Ben on the other. Late last night, Ben finally made it to the hospital. From what I heard, he wanted to give Mike and I time to talk before checking in on me. I was surprised that he even called Mike at first, but Ben being the man he is, I shouldn't have been.

"Which of you two will be taking her home?" the nurse asks.

"We both are," Ben states.

The nurse looks at me.

I just shrug.

"Okay then. I'm going to go over the doctor's orders and give her prescription to you, then she'll be free to go. One of you can pull the car around and I'll wheel her out."

Ben squeezes my hand. "I'll order a car and meet you two out front."

She nods, then goes back to the paperwork on her clipboard. "Dr. Smith ordered you to be on activity restriction with extra rest. While you heal, you need to take it easy."

"What's activity restriction?" I ask.

"You can't stand or walk for more than about ten minutes at a time to start. Reduce your typical activity—no stairs, no lifting or bending, and *no* sex."

My cheeks burn so hot, I know I'm beet red. "No problem," I utter.

"Every two hours, she wants you lying down to rest. You need a pillow between your knees and at your side, like we've done here. Make sure you're up three times a day to walk, and take advantage of that ten minutes on your feet. We don't want you to overdo it, but you do need to be moving."

I'm trying to take it all in, but this is a lot.

"How long will she need to be on this restriction?" Mike asks.

"She'll need to follow up with her doctor in a week. That'll be up to her. Do you have any more questions for me?"

I shake my head no and sign the release papers.

"Do you need help getting dressed?"

"I can manage, thank you."

"I'll be back in a bit with your chair." She steps out of the room, and Mike follows.

I slowly stand and realize maybe I should have asked for help after all. I'm a lot sorer than I thought I'd be. I manage to get my sports bra and boy shorts on before I have to take a breather. At least I'm decent enough now. I sit in the guest chair, clothes in hand, but am completely zapped of energy.

There's a tap at the door and then it cracks open. "You okay in there?" Mike asks.

"I think I bit off more than I can chew." I chuckle and immediately wince.

"Do you want help?"

"You can come in if you want. I have enough on to be somewhat decent." Considering I've worn less in photo shoots, I think I'm fine.

Mike opens the door and steps inside, then shuts it behind him. He walks my way, hand out for my clothes. I hand him my pants. He takes a knee and begins slipping them over my feet. I smile softly when he sees me looking.

"Okay, let's stand up."

I have to lean on his shoulder as he helps pull up my pants. Can this get any more embarrassing?

"I bet you didn't think you'd be helping me dress at such a young age, did you?" I laugh and wince again. "Ugh. I've really got to stop laughing right now."

"I'm happy to help." He kisses me lightly on the nose. "Anything you need."

He is really confusing me.

Michael is looking at me with so much love, and the way he's caring for me melts my heart, but just the other day, he was begging me to move on. What gives?

If we weren't at the hospital right now, I'd be making him talk.

After he has me dressed, he grabs my shoes. Without saying a thing, he kneels and takes my foot in hand, then puts on my sock and shoe, taking his time with each. Looking up at me, he smiles softly. "Is that too tight?" he asks as he ties it.

I shake my head. "No."

Mike's hand rubs my ankle, causing a current of electricity to run through me, our eyes still locked with one another's. "Kayla . . ." he starts.

"Alright, Ms. Covington. Let's get you out of here," the nurse says as she wheels a chair in the room.

I take my eyes off Mike's and smile her way. He helps me to stand and walk to the waiting chair. I don't know what he was planning to say, but the way he was looking at me makes me question everything that has happened between us.

What was he going to say?

I get the feeling that he's done pushing me away. A little voice in the back of my head tells me to run, but my heart warms at the thought of being in his arms again.

The battle within is brutal.

# Chapter Twenty-Six

MIKE AND I ARE on the way to see Dr. Emmons. Tomorrow, I have to be out of my place. We'll see if I'm able to travel yet, considering that I can walk much better—not for a full ten minutes yet, but close. If I know her as well as I think I do, the doctor won't approve of any travel until I'm back on my feet. I just hope we can find a place to stay in the meantime.

It feels weird going down the sidewalk in New York being carried, bridal style. Though it is odd, I'd have thought more people would look our way than they do. In

Oklahoma, we would've had a few people stop and comment, but here, nothing.

Someone opens the door for us, and we walk inside the office. I check in once Mike puts me on my feet, then take a seat and wait my turn.

Nurse Lane opens the door and smiles at me. "Come on back."

I return her smile and stand, Mike following suit. He said he would not miss another appointment. I started to argue but thought better of it. He deserves the chance to be a part of the pregnancy—a chance to be a father.

"How are we doing today?" the nurse asks. I slip off my shoes and hand Mike my bag. "I'm okay. A little sore, but better."

"That's good. I'm sorry to hear about the fall. Thank God the little one's okay." She turns and starts heading toward the bathroom. "You know the drill. Leave me a sample. We'll be in room four when you're done."

I do as she says and make my way to the room. I'm a little tired by the time I get there, but nothing too bad. Once in the room, she checks my vitals and hands me a lovely paper gown. Mike steps out and lets me change. Once done, I crack the door open to let him back in.

Michael takes one of the chairs and moves it closer to my side. His eyes wander the room before settling on me. He takes my hand in his and fiddles with it. "I'm sorry you've had to do this alone for so long."

"We can't undo the past. I'm just glad you got help before she came."

"Knock, knock." Dr. Emmons sticks her head in the room and smiles as she walks toward the computer. "I heard you took a hard fall. I'd like to run some tests while you're here, just to check on Baby."

I nod. "Thank you. Not that I like the tests, but they'll put my mind at ease."

Mike squeezes my hand, and I look his way and smile.

"Dr. Emmons, this is Michael, Bean's dad."

She walks over and shakes his hand before washing hers. "Nice to meet you." She dries her hands and gets the stirrups ready. "Scoot on down for me. Unless you'd rather he leave the room."

I look over at Mike. "As long as he stays up here, I'm fine."

He nods, and I scoot down.

Dr. Emmons does her exam. "I'm ordering some lab work to be done and I'll have them wheel in the ultrasound machine. While you wait, I'll check in on a few others. I'll be back in time for the results. You two get comfortable."

Twenty minutes later, Bean is making herself seen on the screen. Tears fall as I see her moving around. Not long ago, I was begging her to move like that. I look over at Mike and see him wiping his cheek too.

He brings my hand to his mouth, kissing it. "I still can hardly believe the two of us made her."

The tech finishes up and hands me a cloth to clean up. I wipe the goo off my belly and Mike helps me to sit up.

"Is it weird having me here for all of this?"

"Not weird, just different. I got used to doing this alone. Well, in a way." His brow furrows, so I explain. "Ben or Shannon—before she left—always made a point to come with me. They'd stay in the waiting room while I came back so I wasn't completely alone."

Mike runs a hand through his hair, takes a breath, and then looks at me with a smile. "As much as it pains me to admit it, he's a good guy."

"He is."

This conversation, though he started it, seems to make him nervous. His hands run up and down his pant legs. "You see him as long term?"

"We are only friends, Michael. I know you wanted me to move on, but I couldn't do it."

We get quiet while the lab tech comes in to take my blood. Once they leave, I lie back on the bed and put my arm up over my eyes to block out some of the light.

"All I ever wanted was your love. You were it for me . . . my soulmate, the one that no matter how hard I tried to walk away from, I felt drawn to." A tear slides into my hair, and I hate that I'm crying over this again, but I need him to hear me, and all we have is time. "You tried to push me away so many times, but I couldn't let go. I'd wait for you no matter how long it took."

"Knock, knock."

I wipe my eyes and Mike helps me sit up. Dr. Emmons looks between him and me. I smile, trying to hide the tears.

"Baby girl is looking good. Big, actually." She types something into the computer and clicks around for a bit. "It looks like we have a healthy baby, though she still hasn't turned. We still have time."

"That's great news."

Michael nods in agreement.

"Do you think I'm okay to travel? I was set to move back to Oklahoma tomorrow."

She looks at me and then at my chart. "I'd like to see you walk for me. From what I see, the fall you took left you on soft bed rest. If that's the case, I cannot okay your travel. Not yet."

I stand and have to hold the wall for a minute to get my bearings. She opens the door and has me walk with her up and down the hall. We do two laps, then make it back to the room. Mike extends a hand to help me get back on the bed.

"I'd like to see a little more improvement before I release you. I don't think you need to be on bed rest, but I do think you need to be on light duty. No lifting over twenty pounds, walk several times a day to get your strength back, but don't overdo it. You know when you're getting tired. I'd also like to see that nasty-looking bruise lighten up a bit." She types something on the computer, then looks back at me. "You already have an appointment for next week, your thirty-week scan. Keep it and we'll reassess. But I'll let you know, you're probably looking at closer to two or three weeks before I release you. I know that can be difficult, but we need to make sure Baby Girl will be okay for the trip."

"I agree. Thank you."

Dr. Emmons pats me on the knee and smiles kindly at Michael. "I've taken up enough of your time. I'll see you next week. Try and get some rest." She walks out of the room, leaving Mike and me alone.

He grabs my clothes and hands them to me before he steps out. Once my dress is on, I open the door and sit back down.

"Can you help with the straps?"

Mike gets on his knee and caresses my ankle for a moment, then makes sure the strap is secure. He extends his hand. I let him help me stand before letting go.

I don't know how I feel about staying in New York for another week, possibly three. Will I be left alone again? What if something happens? The thought causes my eyes to sting. How did I ever think being here alone was a good idea?

Mike and I have been back at my place for a few hours now and I've had my daily video call with Leah and Uncle Joe. The movers are set to come in the morning. Instead of calling them off, we decided to go through with it and just get a hotel. Tom, since he already has a key, will meet them at my place in Oklahoma. That led to a conversation about Bean's living situation and Mike suggesting that I stay with him while we get our bearings.

The conversation came to a stop when my phone chimed with a text from Ben, letting me know that he'll see me for dinner. "When Ben gets here tonight, would you mind giving us time to talk? Maybe you can run out and pick up dinner?"

A few nights ago, the three of us were sitting around watching a movie. I—like normal—cuddled up to Mike without even thinking about what I was doing. Ben got up from the couch and left without saying a word. I didn't mean to hurt him and wanted to try to go talk to him but didn't want to push. Since the fall, he's been around less than normal.

"I wouldn't worry too much," Mike said. "He's probably got a lot to do with the move and all."

I tried to blow it off, but it's been bugging me more than it should.

"Sure. How does pizza sound?" He walks toward the living area, two plates in hand. Mike hands one to me, then sits in the chair across the way. "I'm not causing issues, am I?"

"Pizza sounds good." I take a bite then continue. "No, you are not. I think something's up with Ben. I just want to make sure that he's okay. It's not like him to be so distant."

Mike and I eat lunch, then clean up. I pack the rest of my closet—I guess I should say *he* packs it while asking me what I need left out—leaving enough for a week to put in my suitcase. If I have to stay any longer than that, I'll just have to do laundry. Mike makes sure each box is labeled. All furniture that I bought is covered or wrapped.

At six p.m., Ben still hasn't shown up Mike heads out, saying that he'll buy some time and stop in at the supermarket while he's gone.

Finally, there's a knock at the door before a key is turned. I look at the clock. 6:42.

"Sorry I'm late," Ben says. He walks my way, then sits across from me in the same chair that Mike just left, leaving behind the smell of booze.

Oh yeah, something is going on for sure.

"Everything okay?" I ask.

"I should be asking *you* that. How'd things go at the doctor's?" He looks around the room as if he's just noticing something. "Where's Mike?"

Scooting up to a better position so I can see him, I look his way. "I had him run out for dinner so we could talk."

Ben flinches. "The dreaded we-need-to-talk speech, huh?"

I furrow my brow. "What do you mean?"

Ben walks off to the kitchen and grabs a beer from the fridge, then comes back and pops the top. He chugs the whole thing, then looks my way with a smile on his face. "Can we talk tomorrow?"

"Um . . . sure, I guess."

I'm not used to this Ben. I've never seen him like this before. It's a bit worrisome.

"Are you sure you're okay?"

His eyes flash as he snaps. "No, *Kayla*. I'm not!" He cringes and closes his eyes, pinching the bridge of his nose as he tilts his head back.

"Ben . . ."

"You really can't wait, can you?" he growls.

A tear slips down my cheek. "I'm sorry."

He looks my way, but instead of softening, he looks more frustrated at my tears. "I really thought you were the one." Ben shakes his head in frustration. "I should've known better. You're still in love with a man who doesn't even *want* you. I've tried—I've tried *hard*—to be what you want me to be. Yet, you won't even give me a second look. You know how much it hurts to fall for someone who only sees you as a *friend*?"

I flinch. "I'm sorry, Ben, I really am. I . . ."

He stands in a hurry, causing the chair to fall backward. "I'm going home." He walks to the door and opens it, looking back my way. "We'll talk tomorrow after I've had time."

He shuts the door behind him, and I sit there, head in hand as I let the tears fall. If not for the urge to use the bathroom, I'd huddle down and stay forever. I never meant to lead him on. I told him time and time again how I felt.

My phone begins to ring. I grab for it and answer. "Ben?" I say, without looking to see who it is.

"No, it's me," Mike says. "Are you okay?"

"No."

"I'm on my way."

By the time Mike makes it back, I'm a blubbering mess. He sets the food on the counter and hurries my way. He sits next to me and starts looking me over for anything that could be wrong.

"I'm not hurt," I cry. "Physically, anyway."

He nudges my chin to look at him when all I want to do is hide. "What's wrong?"

I look down at my hands in my lap and fill him in on what went down with Ben. "I didn't mean to hurt him, Michael. I really didn't, I promise," I cry. "What is wrong with me?"

"There is nothing wrong with you. You're beautiful, kind, loving, and smart. You also have the biggest heart of anyone I know." He takes the pillow from my hands and smiles at me. "It's that big heart that gets you into trouble. I can't speak for Ben, but with me, you saw beneath my problems to the real me and fell for me. I was the idiot who messed things up. Not the other way around." He tucks the pillow behind his back. "I know you say what you and Ben have is just friendship, but from the sounds of it, he thought it was more." He smiles softly. "What do *you* want, Kayla? If Ben is the man you want in your life, you need to let him know."

Mike stands and walks to the kitchen, grabs our dinner, and brings it back. "I'm going to stay long enough to finish packing, then I'll go get a room for the night. You need time to think about what you want. I'm not going to be around to influence you in any way. I'll only be a phone call away if you need anything."

I nod and pick at the slice of pizza in front of me. What do I want? I thought I knew where I was headed, but

with Mike back and Ben snapping at me, I'm so confused.
Maybe some time to think is just what I need.

I open the door to find Ben standing there with a bouquet
of flowers. He looks down at his feet before finding my
eyes and handing me the gift. I step aside and motion for
him to come in. He steps around me.

Last night gave me a lot to think about, and I'm not sure
how I feel, but I do know that his actions were uncalled
for, and that is not something I'm willing to allow in my
life or Bean's.

"Where's Mike?" he asks.

"I'm sure he's still at his hotel. He'll be here when the
movers get here." I grab my water bottle and look over at
Ben, who stands in the entry as if he's never been here
before. "Ben," I huff. "Can we not make this more
awkward? We're both adults here."

"I'm embarrassed is all. Sorry I'm making this weird."

I raise a brow and wait. We have a lot to talk about, but until he makes things right for how he spoke to me, there's nothing to be said. Part of me feels petty, but I also have to set boundaries.

Ben pulls me in for a hug. "I can't begin to tell you how sorry I am." He takes my hand and walks me to sit in the living room, where he turns to look at me head-on. "I let things get to me instead of talking to you like I should have. The guys and I went out for a celebratory drink after work, and it led to way more than I should have had. That one drink led to so many that I lost count. All I wanted to do was drown my sorrow."

Does he have a drinking problem? I take his hand in mine. "Have you done this before? The drinking? Ben, that . . . I don't even know. It was like you were a different person. The way you spoke to me, that's not okay."

"I know it's not. I hate that I did that to you, but no. I've never drank so much or acted like that before, but I did watch my dad come home drunk like that often. Before he and Mom split, he'd have long nights at the office and come home smelling of booze. He never hit any of us, but he wasn't too nice either." Ben takes my hand in his and links our fingers. "I really am sorry that I let it get to the point of being mean. That's not me. I can promise it will never happen again. Kayla, I'm going to take a step back from whatever this is between us."

Tears well up at the thought of losing him. He really has become a good friend these last few months. I don't want to lose him.

He clears his throat and lets my hand go. "When Mike is in the room with you, I can feel the tension. You two have something special. No matter how much I want you, I cannot compete with that." Ben sticks out his hand and wipes the tear that falls down my cheek. "I've seen the way you look at him, the way you shiver when he's nearby. I can only hope to find that one day." He smiles. "I think Mike is here to win your heart back. Maybe you can hear him out?" He leans in and kisses my forehead.

Did I lead him on? I shouldn't have cuddled with him or kissed his cheek. I did this to him. I caused him this pain and I can't stand it.

"Ben," I cry.

He stops me. "I'm not going to take calls, texts, or visits for a while. I'll have Shannon let you know when I make it to Oklahoma, but I need to move on. Maybe one day, we can be friends again."

I want to argue but I can respect what he's saying. I hate that I hurt him, even if I didn't mean to. "I'd like that," I say. I wipe at my rapidly falling tears.

My front door opens, and Ben helps me to my feet. We walk in that direction.

He stops near Mike and looks at him. "You take care of these two now." Ben turns back to me and kisses my cheek. "Please let yourself be happy. *You* are worth it. Your little one will be looking to you to show her how." Ben gives me one last hug, then lets me go and walks to the door, pulling it shut behind him.

I stare at it a moment longer than needed and sigh.

Michael reaches out, pulls me into him, and lets me cry.

Ben may see that Mike is trying to fight for me, but I know him. When things get hard, he runs. Just because he's here now doesn't mean he always will be.

# Chapter Twenty-Seven

I step out of the bathroom, towel-drying my hair. Mike and I have been staying in a nearby hotel for just over a week now. My last appointment with Dr. Emmons went about as well as expected even though she didn't release me yet. She did schedule Mike and me to take birthing classes while we're here. I'm kind of excited about that. My next appointment is scheduled for next week. I will be thirty-one going on thirty-two weeks by then, and she expects that I'll be able to travel.

Mike and I have taken the last few days to discuss baby names but are stuck between two. He likes Tanya, while I like Lily. I guess time will tell.

I'm just about to make it to my suitcase when he opens the door that joins our rooms and waltzes in, carrying take-out containers.

"Do you mind?" I fuss, pulling the towel tighter around me.

He looks over his shoulder at me, then turns back toward the table. "Don't mind me. I didn't see a thing. You get dressed while I set up breakfast."

I do as he says and get dressed. I throw on a pair of joggers and one of his shirts that I took while he wasn't looking. At this point, his clothes are more comfortable than mine. Besides, I don't think that he'd mind. I brush my hair and teeth, then step out and take a spot across from him at the table. I take a drink of juice and grab a piece of bacon.

Then I see it—Mike is holding one of my baby books in hand.

"Did you really already finish that?" Before the movers came to get my stuff, he grabbed a stack of my baby books and said that he had a lot of reading to do. I love that he's trying to be a part of Bean's life now.

He smiles. "I did. I told you; I have a lot of catching up to do."

"What's this make now, four?"

"Five," he replies. He takes a bite of his biscuit and takes a moment. "I have an appointment with Richard in a half hour. Want to join me?"

I don't understand why he keeps asking me. "I don't want to intrude. I'll just read."

Being thirty weeks pregnant doesn't allow for a quick retreat anymore. Not to mention that Bean already takes after her daddy and is a big girl. She's measuring closer to sixteen and a half inches rather than the normal fifteen. Though looking at both of our heights, I kind of expected her to be tall—but she's not just tall, she's overall big. I'm a little worried. I've always been petite, so having Mike's big ole baby won't be easy.

"You wouldn't be. It might be good for us," he adds.

"For us?" I question. "Michael, we aren't even a couple. Why would you want me there?"

He cringes. "I know, I just thought it could help us communicate better."

"I think we do fine when we aren't together," I huff, then take a deep breath, trying to calm myself. I know I'm not being fair, so I try again. "I'm sorry. I didn't mean to snap like that. Michael, what is it that you want out of this? I should've asked sooner but we've had so much going on.

Now all we have is time." I smile apologetically. "You are giving me mixed signals and I don't know how to take it."

He puts down his fork and looks my way. "Right now, I want to earn back your trust. I want a chance to be a father, and your friend. If you're ever feeling generous enough to give me a chance to be yours again, I'd love that too. But I won't push it—I want to do this right." He stands and grabs the trash. "I'm going to my room. If you need anything or decide you want to join, you know where I'll be."

He brushes past me, skimming my arm on his way. The goosebumps I get from his mere touch piss me off. I know he's trying, but I don't know how to act. This man has hurt me more than any other. What am I supposed to do? It might not be fair, but I can't help being mad at him. He pushed me away for months and now that he's here, what? I'm just supposed to be okay with everything. I want to trust him again, but last time I did . . . I don't know if I can go there again.

I walk to my bed and lie down, hoping to settle in with a good read. At the very least, maybe I can get a moment of peace.

It's three in the morning when I wake from yet another nightmare. Unable to fall back to sleep, I get up to make me some herbal tea. I haven't had much sleep in days, and I know I'm walking a thin line between reacting and overreacting. When I drop a spoon, causing a ruckus, Mike comes into my room. He finishes making my drink for me while urging me to have a seat and then joins me at the table. He sits there watching me sip my hot tea. Mike suggests that he give me a foot massage to help me relax . . . and I snap. I don't know if it's the hormones or the lack of sleep, but I can't help it. My mouth and head are at war. Part of me wants him to hold me and make it all better and yet the thought of him touching me right now . . . "Just stop. I don't want you touching me."

Michael looks at me, hands raised in surrender. "I promise I won't touch you in any way you don't want me to. But, Kay, you need to sleep."

I sigh. I know he's right, and I hate it. Since the fight with Ben, I haven't slept much at all. What he said hit me hard—*You're still in love with a man who doesn't even want you.* I hear his words nearly every time I settle. It was hard enough to hear it once, but repeatedly . . . I'm struggling. I know Mike said that he'd like another chance, but how can I be so sure that's what he *really* wants?

A tear falls down my cheek, and because I don't want to have this conversation, I stand and find my way to my bed. "I'm fine, Michael. Go back to bed. I'm sorry I woke you."

Between Bean kicking and making it hard to breathe, my body aching, and the constant replay of that night, I don't see sleep coming any time soon.

"You're not fine. How can you say that when you're lying there crying? At least let me try to help."

Seeing as my back is to him, I look over my shoulder at him and scowl. If I could sit up quick, he'd be in real trouble. He's lucky it's harder than normal for me to move around right now. "Just leave me be!"

"Come on," he tries. "If you don't want my hands on you, fine. I won't touch. What about a nice, warm bath? Let me do *something*, Kay. I'm trying here."

I try and sit up, wobbling a bit until Mike gives me a hand. "Why can't you just leave me alone?" I stand and start pacing. "You're the one that left me. You begged me to move on," I cry. Tears pour down my cheeks as I pace. "How is it that you could be gone for months, out of the picture, and I do fine, then one day! All it takes is one look, one touch, and I'm lost again." I turn and face him, wiping my tears frustratedly. "What is it? You saw me happy and you didn't like it? You saw that another man was trying to move in on what you once had and you—what? Got jealous? So . . . because you can't have me, nobody else can either? Is that what this is?" I walk over to him and pound his chest. "It's all your fault. You did this to me."

Michael doesn't move—he just lets me break.

In time, I lean my head against his chest as the tears come full force. I pound one more time, finally losing steam. "Why couldn't you just love me? Am I really that unlovable?"

He wraps his arm around me, pulling me to him. "I'm sorry, Kay. So sorry. You have no idea how much I hate what I've done to you." He rubs the back of my head, then lifts me off my feet, holding me to his chest. Michael finds a chair in the corner of the room and sits, holding me tight.

My head is buried in his chest as I cry.

"I don't know why I can't stop loving you. I hate what you did to me. I hate that I can't let you go," I gasp, trying to catch my breath. "Ben said I'm still in love with a man that doesn't even want me. You know how that makes me feel? Knowing that he's right hurts."

I feel him tense beneath me. He takes a long breath and settles back in the chair. "Kayla, I need you to look at me when I say this."

I shake my head. I don't want to hear it. I don't want to hear his empty words again. I can't take it anymore.

"Then I'll wait."

He runs his hand in comforting circles until I cave, pulling back enough to look at him.

He tucks my hair behind my ears and dries my eyes. "I'm not worth your tears. I don't even deserve to be in the same space as you. What I did was cowardly." Mike clears his throat and tries again. "Instead of getting the help you asked me to get while I had the woman of my dreams by my side, I ran." He shakes his head. "I can never undo what I did. I hurt you, and I can never forget that. You didn't push me away. This is not on you. You have an amazing heart and don't need to change a thing. Look . . ." He points between the two of us. "I gave you every reason to leave me, to never let me back in your life. Look at us now. I know you don't trust me, but I'm not going anywhere. You fought for me, and now it's my turn. Kayla Covington, you are strong . . . you are beautiful . . . you are deserving."

I didn't know he knew what I say to amp myself up.

He smiles. "I've always admired how you can look yourself head-on, say those simple words, and come back looking ten feet tall."

"You have?" I question.

"I have. You're one of the strongest women I know. Heck, you Covington sisters are fierce. Our daughter is lucky to have you as a mom and Leah as an auntie. I'm a little worried that I might be wrapped around her little pinkie already. But it'll be worth it. Watching a little mini you grow up into a strong, beautiful woman will be an honor."

"So you're really going to stick around for her?"

Mike nods. "I'm here for the two of you. I should've never left."

I nuzzle back into his chest. It's time to try. Our little family deserves that much. "If your offer to do counseling together still stands, I'd love to go." This will not be easy, and I still have my doubts, but I need to try to accept this for what it is—Mike trying.

He takes a deep breath and wraps me in his arms once more, holding tight. A beat later, he loosens his grip. "Let's get you to bed." Instead of letting go of me, Michael carries me across the room and lays me in bed. He takes a knee and kisses my belly. "Daddy loves you, Princess. Be good to your momma and let her sleep." Then he kisses it one more time before tucking me into bed and pulling the covers up to just below my chin. He leans down and kisses my head, then reaches out to turn off the bedside lamp. "I'll be in my room if you need me."

I reach out to take his hand in mine. "Will you stay until I fall asleep?"

Mike nods, then sits on the bed beside me. I turn and put my head in his lap. He takes one hand, placing it on my belly, and the other finds my hair.

"I'm sorry I hit you. I shouldn't have done that."

"Maybe not, but I'm glad you let it out. It's not good to hold it all in like that." He rubs my stomach as Bean starts moving around. Mike leans his head back against the headboard and does something I've only heard him do a few times in all the years I've known him—he sings. But it's not just any song. He's singing the very song we danced to the night I kissed him for the first time—"Wanted" by Hunter Hayes.

Tears that I didn't know I still had in me fall. This time, they're not of anger but of hope. I have to wonder, *What if he really has changed?*

By the time I wake and grab my phone, I see that is almost noon. I haven't slept like that in a long time. I get up and stretch, looking around the room for Mike, but don't see him. I run to the bathroom and take care of business. When I come out, I grab a water and take my vitamins. Going to the table, I see a note.

*Good afternoon, beautiful,*
*You looked so peaceful, I couldn't stand to wake you.*
*I've gone to the gym and the grocery store. I'll be back soon.*
*If you need me for anything, I have my phone on me.*
*Love, Mike*

I smile and grab a banana and sit down at the table, kicking my feet up in the chair across the way. I scroll through social media and give myself a moment to wake up, then grab a change of clothes before heading off to the shower. By the time I'm done, Michael is walking in from his room with a bag of food. My stomach growls loudly, causing him to chuckle.

"You smell good," he says.

"Not as good as that food," I retort.

I meet him at the table as he pulls out two burgers and a tray of fries and onion rings. He opens the other bag, full of all kinds of peppers, pickles, and condiments.

"I got us an appointment with Richard if you still want to join me."

I nod and shove a fry into my mouth.

"Good. Eat up then. He'll be calling in an hour."

I swallow my food as nerves take flight. He really does move fast. I only just agreed.

In no time, the hour is up and we're both sitting on the bed so I can elevate my feet. Mike grabs his laptop and signs in.

*Am I doing the right thing?* I wonder.

He takes my hand in his and squeezes lightly. "Thank you for doing this." The screen lights up, and he hits Accept.

Richard, a friendly man in his midforties, takes up the screen. "Afternoon, Michael, and I'm guessing you must be Kayla. It's nice to meet you." He looks toward Mike. "How are you doing?"

Mike gets to talking. He mentions that his mom has come to mind a lot lately, but he's been able to work through it. I've never heard him talk about her so calmly before. "It also hurts to know how much pain I've caused Kayla. I don't think I realized just how much until last night." He tells Richard how I lost control and let it all out. I'm ashamed that I lashed out like I did, but I'm glad that it's brought us to this point. "Everything around me is changing so much."

Twenty minutes in, Richard shifts the conversation. "Can you tell me why you've decided to bring in Kayla? Are you wanting to work toward rekindling things, becoming friends and co-parents, or just finding a good space to walk away in?"

I look over at Mike in question.

He smiles at me, then looks at the screen. "I'd love to get to the point where Kayla is willing to give me another chance."

I turn to get a good look at him.

"How does that make you feel, Kayla?" Richard prompts. Mike nods his head at the screen.

"I'm not sure," I say, turning to look at the laptop. "If he'd said that he wants to learn to co-parent or walk away, I would've known what to do. I think. Mike wanting another chance . . ." I trail off. How *do* I feel? "I trust that he does—don't get me wrong. I will always love Michael, but he's hurt me, not just once. I know he's done a lot of work on himself in therapy and I'm proud of him for that, but that doesn't take away all the times he's pushed me away." I wipe at the tears that have begun to fall. "What's to say that if I give him another chance, he doesn't grow tired of me and make me leave again? I have to think of our daughter. She needs a good home. I don't want her to get used to him being around only for him to leave. It tore me up, and I can only imagine what it would do to her."

"Kayla," Mike says. He urges me to look at him, so I do. "I am never leaving your side again. I can promise you that. I'll regret the way I did you every day of my life. I'm here, and no matter how long it takes for you to believe me, I'm not going anywhere."

Tears well in my eyes and the butterflies are present. I know that he means what he says. But it's just so hard to let go of the pain. Bean kicks in that moment and I take that as a sign. I can learn to forgive if it gives her the family I have always craved. I just hope that he won't hurt me ever again. I nod my head. "Okay, Mike. I'm in."

# Chapter Twenty-Eight

Michael and I are walking back to the hotel from our final birthing class. It really was eye-opening—and a bit terrifying at times. I thought that I wanted a natural birth when I first found out that I was pregnant, but after hearing from some others, now I'm not so sure that I won't want to be medicated. Some of their stories are terrifying. The one good thing that came out of it is that both Mike and I are on the same page. Well, maybe not, but at least he knows what to expect now. Mike thought I was crazy when I said I wanted a natural birth. Though he's supportive of it, he also doesn't want to worry about me and my pain while waiting for his child to come into this world.

"Would you like a pretzel?" Mike asks.

"Yes, please."

About a block from the hotel, there is a street vendor that sells the best soft pretzels that I've ever eaten. Mike is more than happy to keep them coming any time I want. He pays the guy and hands one over to me before grabbing one for himself.

"Thank you."

"No problem." He smiles as we start walking again. I feel his hand on my elbow and turn to look at him. "Would you like to go painting with me? I found this little arts and crafts place not far from here. I thought it might be fun."

"Like as in a date?"

"If you're ready for one . . . or . . . we could just go as friends if not. No pressure."

I love that he isn't pushing, and it does sound fun. I haven't done anything like that in some time. "Sure, a date sounds nice. But don't we have an appointment with Richard after lunch?"

"We do, plus I'm sure you could use a nap first. How about we go this evening?"

"That'll work."

He and I start back in the direction of our hotel, only to stop once more and grab a pizza along the way. Finally opening up to Michael and giving us a chance to see where this can go gives me hope that maybe we can find what we once had.

Mike and I sit shoulder to shoulder on his bed in front of his laptop. We've been on call with Richard for the last half hour and things have been going well.

"Kayla," Richard says. "Since the last time we spoke, have you had a chance to think about what I asked? What is holding you back from wanting to let Michael in?

I turn my head and glance at Mike before looking back toward Richard. "I have," I smile, "and I'm working on it. I agreed to go out on a date with him this evening." Mike has been my best friend for years; I shouldn't fear my feelings for him. "I'm not going to lie. I'm scared." I wipe a tear from my cheek. "I can see how hard he's been working on himself. I'd be blind not to. But I can't just dive in headfirst. Trust was broken—I need to know that I can give him my heart again and that he'll care for it. I'll get there but it's going to take time."

Mike turns so that he's facing me. With tears in his eyes, he grins. "All I can do is hope that you can see love in my actions. You gave me the most precious gift when you gave me your heart, and I destroyed it." His hand tightens and he has to close his eyes and takes a moment. "I can never forget the look in your eyes, the morning after our wedding. It killed me to walk out on you the way I did. I was fighting demons, and they won. I wasn't strong enough back then to fight for us."

The reminders of one of the worst days of my life hurt. We can't keep bringing that up—it's like opening a wound that's trying to heal. "If we're moving forward together, we both have to learn to let that go. No more beating yourself up over it. I never want to go back to that, and the more I dwell on it, the more it hurts." I look down at my hands in my lap.

He puts his finger under my chin and nudges it, so I look at him.

"Thank you for giving me this chance to show you that I can be the man that you deserve and the father that Bean needs. It won't be easy, and I know that I'll mess up, but I will never walk out on y'all again. That is a promise." He adjusts the strap on my dress when it falls and continues. "The night Ben called . . . I . . . Kayla, the thought of losing you and Bean?" Actual tears slide down his cheek, catching me off guard. "I can't imagine a life without the two of you. From the moment that I got the call to the minute your eyes met mine, my whole world was in chaos. I couldn't get to you soon enough. You are it for me, beautiful. You are my world."

In that moment, a little piece of my heart is healed.

I can see the torment in his eyes over his actions. While I don't want to cause him pain, knowing that he has remorse makes me feel like maybe, just maybe, we can find our way out of this mess and into a new, healthier future.

I reach over Mike and grab some of his green paint. He smiles down at me and kisses the side of my head. I freeze in place a moment, accepting the warmth of his actions before moving back to my easel. Since the session with

Richard a few hours ago, I have allowed myself to hope. Though I am not yet ready to move forward in a relationship, I am ready to give him a chance to date me as we should have in the beginning. I know Michael, and the man that I married was the unhealthiest version of him that I have ever seen.

"What are you making?" I ask.

"Honestly, I'm not sure. It kind of looks like a blob." He laughs.

I chuckle. It does look pretty bad—it's a big brown spot in the middle of his canvas with two green dots. "What did you have in mind when you started out?"

"It was supposed to be a dog. Is it really that bad?" Mike turns to look at me, eyebrow raised with a teasing smile on his face.

I cover my mouth, trying not to laugh, and shake my head.

He leans in, looking at mine. "Yours makes mine look like child's play." Mike chortles. "I guess mine really is that bad. Nice barn."

"Thanks." I take his brush from him and reach over to his canvas and add four stick legs, floppy ears, and a tail. I can't help the giggle that comes from within. "There. All better."

Mike looks from the painting to me and back as if he's assessing my work and snickers. "This is for sure being hung in the living room when we get back home. I think it's some of our best work."

"Sure, it is." I laugh. I turn back to my canvas and get back to painting. I can feel his eyes on me but all I can do is smile. I love this side of him.

"How about dinner and a movie?"

"Rain check? I really want to put my feet up. It's been a long day."

"We can take it to go."

"Now, that I can do." Mike and I clean up our areas and head out. There's this Mexican restaurant not far from the hotel. We stop there and place an order that is ready in no time and make our way back up to my room.

I sit down at the table and open the container and breath in the heavenly smell of chicken fajitas with extra onions and my mouth waters. "Oh man, this looks good."

"I know right. Wanna bite?" Mike got carne asada tacos and a side of rice.

"You wouldn't mind?" He scoots his tray over and I lift a taco to my mouth and take a bite, moaning at the deliciousness of the meal. "That is *so* good."

"I thought so too." He pops the last of his taco in his mouth and takes a moment to chew. "What do you say to a spa night instead of a movie? I know you've been talking about it the last couple of days now."

I'm taken aback. "You'd want to do a spa night with me?" Tears sting my eyes. Nobody but Megan ever does one with me. I love at-home spa nights.

"If the only woman I have ever loved likes this kind of stuff, who am I not to give it a try? Besides, I better learn to embrace girl-dad life now."

*The only woman he has ever loved . . . girl-dad life?* He sure isn't holding back anymore, that's for sure, and I'm here for it. "She's not even here yet," I remind him.

"No, but you are."

Mike cleans up our dinner mess while I locate the items needed for a face mask. I pull my hair back and get to work on applying the mask. *Is he really going to do this?* I wonder. Sure enough, he picks up the tube and squeezes some on his hand and begins applying it to his face. I nearly laugh out loud at the contorted face he makes the moment the cool gel hits his skin but hold back. After washing my hands, I go to the fridge and grab the cucumber slice patches I picked up and make my way to my bed. Mike joining me soon after. He sits on the opposite side of the bed, sweatband holding back his

hair, mask in place, and cucumber slices over his eyes.
I laugh so hard I nearly wet myself. "When did you get to
be so goofy?"

"I'm just happy. It makes a world of difference when
you're not carrying around years of trauma wherever you
go." Mike links his pinky with mine as we sit in silence a
moment, waiting on the alarm to tell us when to wash.
"What's next?"

"Nails, I guess. You can paint my toes, and I'll do your
fingers," I tease. In all the years I've known him, I've
never seen his nails painted. I doubt he will start now.

"Done," he says. "I'm not into that kind of thing, but
hey, if you or my daughter wants to do it, so be it. I'll
show them off to everyone I know."

That reminds me of this one dad on a social media
post that I saw sitting at a little table playing tea party
with his daughter in a tutu and painted nails. It was the
best thing I had seen in some time. Now, hearing Mike
of all people say that he'd wear painted nails with pride
for his daughter and me . . . Taking things slow with him
saying stuff like that might be an issue. I couldn't care
less about the nails—it's the fact that he'd go to such
lengths to make us happy that hits hard.

A moment later, when the alarm goes off, I stand and make my way to the bathroom to wash my face. I grab my nail polish bag and walk past him toward the table. "You're laying it on kind of thick tonight, don't you think?" I smile.

Mike washes his face and then joins me. "I'm not trying to do anything other than show you that I've changed. I can be the man that you deserve."

"I don't want you to be someone you're not. If I'm going to be with anyone, I want them to be genuine. Be you."

Mike takes my hand and gains my attention. "That's just it, Kay. I *am* being me. Before, I was trying to push you away. Now, I live to see that smile on your face. It makes me happy to see you happy."

"Michael . . ." I pause. "Those words are everything I could have ever wanted to hear. But take things slow with me. Okay? I'm trying."

He sits on the floor and takes my foot in his lap and starts to rub. "We can take this as slow as you want. Just know, I'll never stop trying to show you just how much you mean to me."

Pregnancy hormones are no joke. I cry at everything nowadays. I wipe the tears as they fall and smile. I have faith that as long as he's patient, we'll get there in time. I grab the navy blue nail polish from the table and hold it out.

He nods and takes it. "Just your toes?"

"Just my toes," I echo.

I hit Answer on my now-ringing laptop and give Leah my practiced smile. Mike paints my toes while I carry on a conversation that I'm only half into with my sister. I can't take my eyes off of Mike. After he finishes my toes, he sits across from me at the table with a far-off look on his face.

Ten minutes later, Leah says she has to go. I close my laptop and hold my hand out for the nail polish. He yawns, stretching his arms above his head. "I'm going to call it a night. Rain check?

"Sure."

He stands and makes way to his room, only stopping at the door long enough to look my way. "Good night, Kayla. I had fun tonight. Thank you for giving me this chance."

"I did too, Michael. Thank you for asking me." I smile. "Good night."

I cannot wipe the smile off my face as the door closes behind him. All I can do is hope that this lasts. I'm already in deep. I pull back the covers and crawl in. Then I pull them up to my chin and stare into the darkness as I will myself to sleep.

I wake in a fright, tears flowing down my cheeks. Falling asleep again won't come easy. I had another nightmare. This time, Michael was the star of it. The memory is vague, but I know I lost both Mike and Bean. I had nothing left; my family was gone. Realistically, I know I would have Leah and Uncle Joe, but in my dream state, that didn't matter.

*My* family was gone!

I stand and find my way to Michael's room. He left the door ajar in case I needed him. Seeing him sleeping so peacefully, I try not to wake him as I pull back the blankets and crawl in. He stirs, and I cringe. I didn't want to wake him.

"Kayla?"

"Shhh. Go back to sleep. I had a bad dream and don't want to be alone."

I crawl in, facing the outside of the bed, and reach back for his arm, grazing a bare chest. My first thought is to run, but knowing how comfortable I feel in his arms, I push on. I lift his arm and scoot back while he moves forward. We meet somewhere in the middle, and he holds me to him.

Mike moves his hand to my belly and rubs in loose circles. "I've got you, beautiful," he whispers.

With him being so close, his breath hits the back of my neck, causing a shiver to run down my spine. I know he feels it.

He leans in and kisses my bare shoulder, then lays his head back on the pillow. "Nothing can hurt you now. I'm here.

A tear slips from my face to the pillow beneath me. What if the one thing I'm most afraid of is what I want the most?

# Chapter Twenty-Nine

Michael opens the door for me and holds out his hand to help me in. We've been cooped up in that hotel for far too long. Sure, we go on small walks and  do things nearby, but I haven't been more than a block or two away since we checked in. It's driving me crazy.

We had another session with Richard yesterday and have another coming up soon. At our last session, he gave us homework—get out of the hotel, go for a drive, have a picnic or something. Keep it simple, but just the two of us. Talk and see where it goes. Mike went with it, and before I knew what was happening, he had today planned.

"I feel like I should rethink my wardrobe for this," I say. Mike rented us a powder-blue, white-top, 1957 Chevy Bel Air in mint condition. It is beautiful! Years ago, he and I went to a car show held by one of the local casinos and there was one of these cars there. I took out my phone and made Mike be my photographer.

I was in *love*.

Michael looks at me and smiles. "You're perfect just the way you are."

I pat his chest and get in. He shuts my door and rounds the hood, getting in behind the wheel of the car. Man, he looks good.

"I can hardly believe you pulled this off. I didn't even know you could rent a car like this."

He turns the key and starts the engine. It purrs—such a beautiful sound. I couldn't fight the smile on my face if I tried.

"When Richard suggested us getting out, I remembered seeing an ad somewhere about classic car rentals. As a car guy, I couldn't help but think of the way you lit up over that Bel Air at the car show. I had to try and get one." He takes my hand in his and squeezes, then gestures to the back seat.

I turn and spot a basket.

"We'll find a nice little park or something along the way. If it gets to be too much, let me know and we'll come back." Mike takes his hand back and turns to focus on the road. "Since we don't have an ocean back home, how about we head that way?"

"Sounds good to me. I don't have my suit, but it won't stop me from enjoying the water. So long as you brought sunscreen."

Mike nods. "Of course I did. I know how red you can get."

He's not lying—it can get bad quickly.

Mike pulls out of our spot and heads toward the water while I take it all in. With phone in hand, I take pictures of Mike, the car, our surroundings, and a few of me. The closer we get to the ocean, the fishier and saltier the air becomes.

We finally make it to a place called Jones Beach. I've never seen anything like it before—well, I've been to Galveston a time or two, but this is so different. He drives us toward the boardwalk and starts looking for parking. There are several buildings, places that look like they're for families and entertainment. Though I'd normally be interested, I know we should pass this time around.

After we park, Mike rounds the hood, opens the door for me, and helps me out, then opens the back and grabs the basket and blanket. With one hand carrying the basket, he reaches the other out for mine. Since we've started seeing Richard and have been talking through things, I've realized that my feelings are still there but are intensifying. Sure, I still have some trust issues but I'm working on it and it's getting easier every day. Richard says in our situation that it's pretty normal and not to add stress by pushing too hard. Things will come in time. Just to continue as we are—leaving the past where it is and moving forward.

Mike finds a more secluded part of the beach and spreads out the blanket. He helps me sit—not exactly easy anymore—then joins me. After making sure that I'm slathered in sunscreen, I try to get comfortable.

"How about we play a game?" He opens the basket and starts unpacking it.

"What do you have in mind?"

"We can play would you rather, or one of your old favorites, two truths and a lie."

"Those could be dangerous for us," I reply.

"We can agree to keep our relationship—or lack thereof—off the table if you want."

I pop a grape into my mouth and think. "Don't you think we know each other too well for those kinds of games?"

"Maybe." He shrugs. "Do you have a better idea?"

"We can just talk, ask questions, and get to know things that we might not know. We can always veto if it's too hard."

"Three vetoes?" he questions.

I smile. "Sure. Use them wisely."

"I want you to know everything, so I doubt I'll veto anything."

My brow rises. "Okay then, challenge accepted. But nothing is off the table."

Mike nods and I think about what I can ask. Do I want to start with a big one or something simple? I grab a piece of cheese and put it on a cracker. Mike opens a water for me and then does the same for himself.

"Do you believe in soulmates?"

"I didn't used to," he replies.

"And you do now?" I ask.

He smiles and shakes his head. "That's not how this works. Your turn to answer."

"I do believe in soulmates. Now answer the question."

Mike chuckles. "Even though that's two questions, I'll answer. Yes. I do now."

"What changed your mind?"

He roars. When Mike full-on laughs like this, it is a thing of beauty. My hand itches to grab my camera. With the beach at his back and his neck exposed as he looks to the sky and cackles, all I can do is stare.

He looks at me, all signs of laughter gone. "You did, beautiful. No matter what I did, I could never break the connection I felt with you. It hurt me to hurt you. It's like you and I are one. Your touch brings me comfort and lights a fire in me all the same. It's like I'm home. I don't know how else to explain it." He leans back and smiles. "Damon was kind enough to throw the definition of a soulmate in my face not long ago. It wasn't until then that I actually understood how special our bond is."

I wipe a tear from my cheek. So he does feel what I feel.

"If you could live forever, would you?" Mike asks.

"Oh, that's good," I reply. "That would all depend. If the people I love could live forever with me, sure. If not, no. I wouldn't want to outlive everyone and watch them all pass away. That'd be heartbreaking."

Mike wipes his mouth and sets down his sandwich. "I never thought of it like that. My answer would have been yes, but now I see your point. I have to agree with you."

My back is starting to hurt, and there's no pillow or anything for me to lie on. Mike must notice, because he unfolds his legs and pats the ground between them. I crawl to him and lie back against his chest.

"Better?"

"Much. Thank you." I grab a couple grapes and crackers and start munching. Mike puts his hand on my belly and begins rubbing. I feed him a grape and get back to the game. "What's something that you used to believe about relationships that you no longer do?"

I half expect him to use a veto, but he doesn't. He looks down at me and smiles. "I never thought that I deserved to be in one, that I was deserving of love."

I let that sink in for a minute. So if that's something he *used to* believe, he doesn't feel that way now?

"What about you?"

"I used to believe that one relationship could last a lifetime, but I'm not so sure anymore. I don't have a very good track record, you know." I throw a few crackers out at the seagulls that seem to be getting closer by the minute. If we were in Galveston, they'd be pecking the food right out of our hands.

Mike bends down and takes a cracker from my hand with his mouth, catching me off guard when he lightly nips my finger. The man has yet to remove his hand from my stomach. I look up at him and have to look away. Mike looking down at me with love in his eyes while we're cuddled up like this does things to me that I'm not ready to face.

"It sounds like I have a lot to make up for." Mike nods to the bag of grapes, and I feed him another. "What's your definition of romance?"

I smile. "That's easy. Quality time away from real life. It doesn't have to be candlelit dinners and flowers everywhere—though I do love that. I'm pretty simple. Shocker, I know. But I think that one of the most romantic things I've ever read about was a guy taking his girl for a ride down to the pond where they spent the night under the stars, just the two of them."

Mike leans over to look me head-on. "You, Ms. I-Don't-Want-to-Go-to-the-Lake-Because-Every-Bug-in-Oklahoma-Lives-There, wants a night near a pond under the stars? I would've never guessed that." He chuckles. "I'm filing that away for later." I swat at him, but he just laughs.

"I love this." I wave my hand in the air at our surroundings. "But I also love it when we're back home watching NCIS and cuddling." Bean starts moving around. Knowing that I can see her when she gets like this,

I roll my shirt up. Mike moves his hand briefly then puts it back on my belly.

"What kind of room do you see for our little princess?" Mike asks.

"I've always dreamed of it being like walking into a fairy tale." I close my eyes and smile as I imagine the room. "A castle painted on the wall with little fairies flying around, flowers everywhere, almost as if it's the enchanted gardens." I open my eyes to see Mike staring at me with a big smile on his face.

"Please continue," he says. "I like seeing you like this."

I swat his shoulder. "Don't tease me."

"I'm not teasing, Kay. I love seeing you be all maternal. Plus, it helps hearing that you have Bean's nursery all planned out. Is that why you keep having me stop and see if that castle bedding is in stock?"

"It is. I really hope it's there before we leave. I've never seen anything like it before. I hope you get to see it, Michael. It is so pretty. I can imagine having an entire nursery just like it."

Mike smiles. "I'll keep checking. No luck yet, but if I keep going, we're going to have to hire another truck. I've already got to buy another suitcase just to get the stuff I've bought back."

"Really?"

"Yeah, really. Have you not seen the stack of bags in the corner of my room?"

"No." I laugh. "I guess I haven't paid that much attention. You'll have to show me when we get back."

"Deal." He smiles and leans in to kiss my temple. "You are the most beautiful pregnant woman I have ever seen."

I close my eyes and let the words sink in. Moments like this make me want more.

Mike and I spend another hour talking and feeding the birds. Before long, he finds someone nearby and asks them to take some pictures of us before we load up and head out.

"I bet they have some pretty amazing concerts there," Mike says as we drive past a beach theater.

"If we're still here for the Fourth of July, we'll have to check it out."

He nods and continues down the state parkway.

"I've never seen so many people fishing off a bridge before."

The car gives a jerk, and it begins to lose speed.

"What's wrong?"

"The car died," Mike replies. "Sit back and brace yourself. I've lost all steering and brakes. This thing is a beast." He has both hands on the wheel, sitting up straight, and is concentrating hard.

I put my hand on my stomach and look over the back of the seat. Maybe if I'm careful, I can grab the blanket. With it folded up, maybe it can help shield Bean in case of an impact. I grab it, then look over at Mike's determined face. I know instantly that I could not be in better hands.

I cover my stomach with the blanket. *Just hang in there, Bean. Daddy will keep us safe. That much I know for certain.* No matter what happens, he won't let harm come to me or Bean.

Knowing that I'm safe with Mike behind the wheel, I look out the window and see a sign ahead for a fishing pier and point to it. We are on a two-lane bridge. Breaking down here is not ideal. "Look. Can you get us there?"

"I'll try."

With the momentum and the weight of the car, we are still moving at a decent speed. When the pier comes into focus, Mikes pushes on the brakes. It takes all his strength to get this thing to move, but he manages to get us pulled off the bridge and to the side. He puts it in park and tries to crank it over, but it won't start.

"It's like it's not getting a spark. I better call the rental company."

Mike steps out of the car. I toss the blanket in the back and follow his lead. He walks down the dirt path, making the call while I lean against the car and look out at the water. I guess if we had to break down, at least we are in a nice location.

"They're on the way out with a tow truck," Mike says as he joins me next to the car a few minutes later. "It might be a bit of a wait. Would you like to walk down the pier?"

"I better not. I think I've had enough walking for a bit. It is beautiful though."

Mike grabs the blanket from the back and sets it out behind the car. "This was not in the plans but let's improvise." He sticks out his hand and bends at the waist, bowing in playfulness. "Kayla Covington, would you like to watch the sunset with me?"

I giggle, loving that Mike's willing to be silly with me. "I'd love to."

He grabs my hand and walks us toward the blanket, helping me down before he follows. He settles in behind me, then wraps an arm around to my stomach. "How are you holding up?"

"Other than the rocks beneath the blanket?" I question. "It's been nice. Thank you for today."

I lean back in his embrace and close my eyes. I can picture my life happily in his arms. I tilt my head back, looking up at him. He looks down, smiling. Wrapping my hand around the back of his head, I will his lips to mine. In this moment, all I can do is feel—it feels like my missing pieces are falling into place. Maybe I am ready to go all in.

# Chapter Thirty

Yesterday was my thirty-two-week appointment with Dr. Emmons, where we were given the all clear to travel. When she said, "You're safe to travel," I nearly knocked her over with a hug. All the bruising is gone, I can walk normally, and I'm even back up to walking three miles a day—more winded than normal, but I can do it. I feel good—well, as good as I can for being so far along. Now, Mike and I are standing in line at the La Guardia Airport, ready to finally go home.

We have come a long way since he showed up. I've been thinking about telling him that I'm ready to try again, as an official couple. Though I'm scared, I realize that the fear will never go away fully. I know in my heart that he has changed and that's enough. If he hadn't, he would've left me and gone back to Oklahoma right away.

"You ready?" Mike asks. He locks his fingers with mine and smiles when I cuddle into him more.

"I'm *so* ready."

"I'll kind of miss New York," he replies, surprising me.

"How so?"

Michael smiles shyly. For a man like him to give that look, I'm taken aback. "It's just that things have been so good between us. I have you right next door and all to myself. When we get back, we'll be separated by a whole town and people will be competing for your attention. I'm just . . . jealous, I guess."

I turn and give him a hug. "Michael, we've been working hard to get what we have now. Don't start getting in your head. I'm not going anywhere."

We move forward in line as he wraps his arm around me. "I know. I'm trying. It's just hard going from this to being so far away. What if you go into labor and I'm not there? I know you have family nearby, but it's different. I'm her dad—I should be there."

"I hadn't thought of it like that." It's not like I'm going to have her this week, but I mean, I could. "What if you move into one of my guest rooms until she's here?"

Mike pulls back to look me over. "Don't say that just for my sake. Is this something you're *really* okay with?"

I smile. "I am."

"You're sure?" he questions once more.

"Yes, Michael. I am."

"Heck yeah," he says. "You've got yourself a roommate then."

I grimace, hating the way that sounds.

"What's that look about?"

"Nothing."

He nudges my chin with his knuckle and raises his brow.

"Fine," I huff. "I don't like the sound of that. Having you there sounds good, but roommate? It just sounds so . . ."

"Platonic?" Mike finishes.

I nod my head.

"And you . . . don't want it to be platonic?"

Now it's my turn to get shy as heat rises to my cheeks. I shake my head.

"And what is it that you want?"

I shrug. I don't know how to say the words aloud.

He raises his brow. "I think you do. You know exactly what you want."

I step forward as the line moves.

Mike shifts forward too. "Do you want to be more than roommates?"

I cringe at that word but nod.

He smirks. "But less than married?"

I scowl and hit him on the arm.

"Why, Kayla Covington, are you hinting around that you want to be my girl?"

My cheeks heat heavily, and I look away.

"Can't say we're predictable or do things as they should be done." He looks around the airport at the other travelers. "I guess this is on brand for us."

I chuckle. He's not wrong.

"Kayla Covington, will you be my girlfriend?"

The smile on my face grows. "Yes. I'd love to be your girl." I lean in and give him a kiss.

A throat behind us clears and we break.

Looking over my shoulder, I smile. "Sorry."

"Not sorry," Michael grumbles. "I've waited for *that* kiss for months and it was cut way too short for my liking."

"Aw, poor guy," I tease. "Looks like we'll have to make up for lost time later."

"When we get home, you're mine."

I put my hand to his chest and smile. "We have plenty of time to make out. I want to do things right this time."

Touching my stomach, I look at Mike. "She's counting on us not to mess up."

"Slow is fine. I'm looking forward to a lot of late-night TV watching." He winks.

As we step up to the counter, all I can think is, *Me too*.

Mike and I find our way to baggage claim and spot Damon and Megan instantly. She releases his hand and comes running my way. I step out of Mike's hold and wait for her. Meg slows significantly when she nears me, pulling me in awkwardly for a hug.

"My God, I've missed you. Dame had to dang near hold me back when you got hurt. I'm sorry I wasn't there."

I pull back from the hug and smile. "You called and kept me company when I spent so much time in bed. Megie, you were there."

Her hand finds my belly as she smiles. "I'll never get used to seeing you like this." Meg leans down and kisses my stomach, telling Bean how much she loves her. "Do we have a name yet?"

I look at Mike. "We are at a standstill. He likes Tanya, but I prefer Lily. We agreed to sit on it until we get the nursery together and then we'll discuss it again."

Damon pulls me in for a hug while chuckling. "It might be a good idea to pick one soon unless we're to call her Bean her whole life."

Mike steps in and puts his arm around me. "Not happening." He kisses the side of my head and I see the others looking at us in question. "She'll have a name before she gets here." He and Damon grab the bags.

When Meg links arms with me, I nudge her side and smile. "I've got to tell you something."

"Okay . . ." she drags out. "What is it?"

"Mike is my new roomie."

She raises her brow. "Because that worked so well last time."

I stop and turn back so that the four of us are looking at one another. "I was going to wait to address all this, but I don't want there to be tension between us."

Mike winks at me, and I smile.

"Mike is moving in with me . . . into the guest room. He's also my boyfriend. So there's that too. What happened in the past needs to stay there."

Damon nudges Mike with his shoulder and smiles. "It's about time."

Megan smiles softly. "I need to say one thing, then I'll shut up." She looks at Mike and squares her shoulders. "If you hurt her again, I will *not* hold back next time. You know I love you, Mike, but she deserves the best."

"*Meg,*" I warn.

Mike nods. "I know I have a lot of work to do still, but I will spend every day for the rest of my life showing Kayla just how sorry I am."

That must satisfy her.

We link arms again and head out. Leah wanted to have a lunch when I got back home but I was able to talk her into waiting until tomorrow. I need to settle in and rest a bit. The doctor's orders were to take it easy and not overdo it. As much as I want to see her right now, I also need to listen. Tomorrow can't come soon enough.

Damon and Megan take us to Mike's place so we can get his truck and his mail. Twenty minutes later, we're on the way to my new home.

Home—after all this time, I'm finally here. Not only in my dream home, but in Oklahoma and with the man I thought I'd never have again. How is this possible?

Mike brings in the last of his bags and takes them to his room while I lounge on the couch. When we walked in, Mike took me in his arms and deposited me here and told me not to move. *So bossy*, I thought. But I secretly love it.

The house really is beautiful. I'll need to put my personal touch on it, but it's complete, down to my furniture being put together. I still have boxes to unpack, but that'll come in time.

"Ready to look at the house?" Mike asks upon approach. He takes my hand in his and helps me from the couch.

"Ready."

Mike leads me from one room to the next. My beautiful Victorian has been updated and is up to code now. The rock fireplace—original to the house—still stands in the family room. The first time I saw this place, I fell in love. We make it upstairs and to the room next to mine, which I picked out for Bean. I'm overwhelmed by it all, but when the door to the nursery opens, I nearly break.

"It's *beautiful*." I walk in and turn full circle. One wall is painted to look like a fairy-tale princess kingdom with a castle that looks like our home, butterflies and flowers everywhere, and even a unicorn. I wipe my face as the tears begin to fall. There's a crib, the rocking chair Uncle Joe bought, and a changing table already in place. I move to sit in the rocker and stop dead in my tracks. Inside the crib is the bedding that I had been so sure I missed out on.

I look over my shoulder at Michael through teary eyes. "You did this? " I told him that I wanted our little princess to have a magical kingdom bedroom, down to the fairytale wall mural.

He really listened.

Not only that, but he made it happen.

My heart is so full right now.

"I had some help, but yes." Mike smiles. He walks up behind me and wraps me in his arms, kissing the side of my head.

"Thank you. This all means so much to me. You have no idea."

"We're in this together, Kay." He smiles. "It is my job to give you your heart's desires. I'm just glad you like it."

I turn in his embrace and wrap my arms around his neck. "I don't just like it, Mike. I love it. I don't know how you did it, but this is amazing. Thank you, really."

Mike kisses my nose and steps back. "I missed out on so much of your pregnancy. You better believe, now that I'm here, things will change. You and our little one deserve the best." He smiles.

For the first time in a long time, I actually believe him.

I make it to the living area, tired from our flight and the house tour. Mike insists that we take the rest of the evening to relax and watch TV. Once he has turned on NCIS: Los Angeles and takes my sore feet in his hands, I'm all for this idea.

Ten minutes later, he stops rubbing my foot.

I crawl his way and lie back against him, turning slightly so I can see the TV. I pull his arm off the back of the couch and put it around me, burrowing in as deeply as I can but not feeling like I can get close enough. I trace the tattoo of a shattered heart on his arm. Now that I know how he felt in the past, it makes sense, but I have to wonder if he has any regrets.

"That one's a constant reminder of where I came from, but . . . I'm more whole than I have ever been." He kisses the top of my head and tightens his hold on me.

I let loose a long, deep sigh. This is all I need. We are our own family. We *will* make it. No more hurt feelings, no more drama—just Michael, Bean, and me. It's all I've ever dreamt of.

A tear falls from my eye before I can catch it, hitting his arm. He moves so that he can see me, and when he sees the look on my face, he adjusts so that he's facing me. The position is a bit awkward with my belly, but at least I can look deeply into his beautiful green eyes. The love I see in him melts my heart. No words are exchanged but the air between us is thick.

Michael raises a hand, placing it on my cheek. I lean into his touch.

"I'm not messing this up again. I can't stand the thought of life without you in it. I did that once and I won't do it again, Kayla." He closes his eyes and takes a deep breath, then smiles. "I love you."

To hear those words and know that he hasn't even had a sip of liquor is more than I could dream.

He wipes the fallen tears from my cheek, sending an electric shock through my body as he repeats, "I love you, Kayla."

The tension between us is palpable, heavy like a weighted blanket. My body trembles with desire, longing for his lips to be on mine. Michael doesn't disappoint. When his meet mine, our passion ignites. I turn and he pulls me closer, his fingers tangling in my hair as he deepens the kiss. The taste of mint explodes on my tongue as he takes over, my body floating on a high I don't want to come back from. I pull back just far enough to utter the words, "I love you too," before leaning back in. I lose myself in his touch, his scent, in all things Michael Buchannan.

My phone rings from the dining table. I try to ignore it, unwilling to let anything ruin the moment, but then his phone starts ringing, too, and I know it's a matter of time before this moment is gone. He finally gives in and reaches for his phone on the second ring, leaving me gasping for more. I can't help but let out a desperate moan as we cling to each other, our hearts pounding and breaths heavy.

"Hello?" he growls. There's a pause, then a mischievous smirk. "I know, sorry. My girlfriend and I were a bit busy."

My eyes go big in shock, and I swat his chest.

Mike chuckles. "Yeah, she's here. Do you need to talk to her?"

"Who is it?" I mouth.

"It's fine, Leah. Really."

I reach out and grab his phone, putting it to my ear. "Hey, sis."

Mike leans in and kisses my head. He rubs my belly, but the smile on his face never falters.

"I didn't mean to interrupt. Are you and Mike really back together?"

I groan. "I can't believe I forgot to call you. I'm so sorry, it just happened today. Yes, we're a couple now."

Michael kisses my shoulder, then my neck, distracting me from the call.

"Kayla, did you hear me?"

I push at his chest, getting a laugh in response.

"Sorry, sis. What was that?"

Leah laughs and mumbles something. "Nothing. Go have fun making out with your man. Talk to you tomorrow," and then the line goes dead.

I cover my face in embarrassment. Even though she knows what I've been doing, I can't help the smile that grows on my face. I couldn't be happier than I am in this moment.

# Chapter Thirty-One

We pull up outside Uncle Joe's restaurant that has been shut down for a family get-together—my baby shower. The restaurant staff and so many of our friends and family are all here. Leah let me know that it'd be a packed house. I have never felt so loved before in my life.

I rub my stomach. "This is all for you, Bean."

Friday will make four weeks since we made it back home, and while I've seen my family a few times, this will be the first big gathering. Between Uncle Joe and Janet getting ready for their wedding, Mike's therapy with Richard, and everyone else's busy lives, Leah figured that she'd give them plenty of time for everyone to schedule this in.

Mike parks the truck and turns my way, wiping the tear from my cheek. "Are you ready for this?" He knows how little it takes for me to cry anymore.

"As soon as I find a bathroom again, I'll be more than ready."

He laughs. "Didn't you just go?"

"I'm almost thirty-six weeks pregnant. Give me a break. It's like she's dancing on my bladder."

He chuckles.

We head in. After making a pit stop, we join the party. Mike takes my hand, linking his fingers in mine, and we step through the door.

"They're here!" Leah says.

The room is filled with family and friends and all things baby girl. There's so much to look at, I can't possibly take it all in. Leah really outdid herself.
She pulls me in for an awkward hug, considering we both have decent-sized bellies now, then she moves on to Mike. "I hope you guys don't mind. I figured we might as well do the housewarming party and baby shower together."

"Thank you." I smile. After one more quick hug, I pull back and look her over. "Looking good, sis. Did you change your hair?"

"I did." She smiles. "You can't really tell since it's up, but I cut off about two inches and had highlights done."

"I can tell. It looks good."

"Thanks."

Cam comes over and pulls me in for a quick hug before wrapping his arms around his wife. He whispers something in her ear, and she smiles. "Thank you," she says, before he turns and walks off.

"Come on. Everyone's here. You three are the guests of honor. You have a spot by the windows."

"I'll be there after I make my rounds saying hi." I don't take more than two steps before I'm pulled into a hug with Uncle Joe and Janet.

"Wow. Look at you!" Janet says. "You're glowing. You're even more beautiful today than you were the last time I saw you. How is that possible?" She rubs my stomach and smiles. "It won't be long until we get to hold her and spoil her rotten."

Uncle Joe pushes himself in further. "Not before me," he teases. "It's our first grandbaby. I'm calling dibs."

Janet ignores him as she pulls me in for another hug.

"I'm so glad you're back," Uncle Joe says. "I was ready to lose my mind. I don't think I could've handled it if you gave birth in New York."

"I'm glad to be back too. I missed you all so much."

Gunnar steps to my side and smiles at Uncle Joe. Janet pulls him behind her and walks off to help Leah.

"Welcome home," Gunnar says.

"Thank you. I'm glad to be back."

"Things with Mike okay?" he asks. "I heard y'all got back together."

I look around the room at the others and nod. "Yeah, we're great."

We make our rounds, saying hello to several friends, then head toward the table. Meg and Damon follow us, taking a seat next to Mike, who is right by my side, with Leah and Cam on my other. Seeing so many smiling faces all together in this one room makes it that much more real that I'm home. Some I've seen since I've been back, but many I haven't. Seeing everyone gathered here, in one room . . . it hits me hard.

When things seem to settle, I take Mike's hand and stand. "Thank y'all. I didn't expect all of this." I look over at Mike and smile. "We really appreciate all the support. Bean is a lucky little girl to be surrounded with so much love." I put my hand on my stomach and rub it.

"Are you two *finally* going to make it official?" Xena hollers.

"We already have," Mike cuts in.

"From marriage to baby to dating," Pop says. "That's not how this typically goes."

I giggle. He's right, but I guess Michael and I aren't ones to follow the rules. When I sit down, Mike pulls me in for a quick kiss as Leah and Janet start passing out games.

Leah stops in front of us, smiling. "I always knew you two would be a good match." She motions between the two of us. "I don't care if you have to wheel me down the aisle, I want to be a part of the next wedding."

"You got it," Michael states.

"I never said anything about marrying you again," I say, elbowing his side.

"Didn't have to." Leah chuckles, and walks off.

I guess if I'm really putting the past to rest, I don't see why I couldn't say "I do" again.

After games and opening gifts, it's cake time, and I'm in heaven. The white cake with raspberry filling is beyond delicious.

"This cake is amazing!" I say.

"It really is," Mike agrees. "Thanks, Uncle Joe."

He nods our way, then gets back to his conversation with Pop.

"Those two seem to be getting along better these days," I say.

"I'm glad. They get to share the title of grandpa," Mike replies.

Hearing that makes me smile, but I can't help but wonder what kind of grandpa my dad would've been. I lean back in my chair and watch as Bean pushes up against my stomach. "I'll never get over that."

Leah puts her hand right where Bean is moving and smiles. "I can only imagine how that feels. Mine have just barely started kicking strong enough that their dad can feel. I haven't seen anything like that yet."

"It's kind of trippy," Cam says.

"It was for me, too, the first time I saw it. Now I kind of love seeing a hand or a foot. It makes it so much more real." I yawn. It's been a long day.

"We better start packing up and get you home," Mike interrupts.

"I'm fine," I argue. "I can stay awhile longer."

He turns and says something to D, then looks back my way. "They're going to start loading the truck. Visit for a little while longer, but after they're done, you need to get home and rest. You shouldn't be overdoing it. If you want, I can have them all come out for a dinner or something."

"Fine," I huff. I lift my chin toward the dining room. "Tell them now and I'll go."

He grumbles under his breath but stands anyway. "We're going to get Kayla home now. She's under doctor's orders not to overdo it. We'd like you guys to come out this weekend for a barbeque if you can make it."

"We should be able to swing that," Uncle Joe says.

I get up and start giving hugs while the guys load everything into Mike's truck.

Maddie pulls me aside. "After you settle in, give me a call. We'll have to catch up. I know things have been crazy lately."

"Will do. How are things with . . ." I can never remember her boyfriend's name. He's never with her.

"Ashton. Tom and I finally got him to head back to Charleston last week. You're looking at a single woman now."

"*What?*" I ask. "How did you manage that? Wasn't he kind of possessive?"

She smiles shyly. "Tom. One night, Ashton hit the bottle a little too hard one night and let loose. Tom saw the bruise on me and . . . well, the rest is history."

My eyes widen at the thought of anyone putting their hands on her. She is such a sweetheart; I can't even begin to imagine. "He hurt yo—"

Mike walks over and puts his hand on my back, leaning in to tell me that they're ready to head out.

I look to Maddie for an answer, but she shakes her head as Tom approaches. "Girls' night soon," she states.

"Deal." I give her one last hug as Mike leads me out to the truck. "Did you know that she's single now?"

"Hmm. No, I didn't. I'm sure Tom's thrilled."

I get into Mike's truck with a lot of assistance, scoot to the center, and wait for him to get settled behind the wheel.

"Tired?"

"Yeah. I seem to always be tired these days."

Mike backs us out of the parking spot, pats my belly, and smiles. "I think tired is a new normal for us. When Bean comes, I doubt we'll get much sleep."

Laying my head on him as we go down the road, I rest

my eyes, enjoying the moment—one I didn't think was possible just months ago.

I'm woken from my nice nap when I feel Mike lift me from the truck. I open my tired eyes and squirm. "Put me down. I can walk."

He smiles and leans in to kiss my forehead and continues walking without saying a thing. Once we're on the porch, he sets me down on my feet and takes out his keys to let us in. Then again, he lifts me as if I weigh nothing and settles me on the couch. "Stay here and find us something to watch."

He hands me the remote and makes his way back out to the truck. Mike makes a good dozen trips in and out of the house before he closes up and walks into the kitchen. I get up from the couch. "I'll be back. I need to get into something more comfortable." I head to my room and get changed. A knee-length nightshirt and matching robe is just what I need. It feels so nice against my skin and light too.

I exit the room and make my way back downstairs and come to the living room where I find that Michael has set up a candlelit dinner for two on the coffee table. Instantly, my eyes fill with tears. "Oh, Michael," I cry. "This is so romantic."

He looks up from where he is bent over the coffee table with a smile and walks my way. When he gets close, he holds out his hand. I accept and follow him to the couch.

"How on earth did you get this done so quickly?"

He chuckles. "I've been planning this for a few days now. Most of it was tucked away and ready to go for when we got home. You getting changed just gave me time to set it up." He kisses the back of my hand and smiles. "What do you think? Care to join me?"

I look him over from head to toe and feel horrible. He's still in his nice jeans and dark blue polo shirt from the baby shower, while I changed into my nightshirt. "I think I'm underdressed."

"Not at all." Michael turns and kicks off his shoes and begins to strip.

I raise my hand to my mouth, trying to cover my giggle, but fail miserably when it turns into a full-on laugh.

He stops when he's down to his green boxer briefs. "Better?"

I try to keep my eyes chest level or above, but this man is a work of art, and my eyes can't help themselves. They roam. "If I weren't already carrying your baby, I'd say this was highly inappropriate."

"If anything, I'd say we've just hit pause for all these months. Nothing inappropriate. I still think of you as my wife, and I'm sure you will be again one day. I see nothing wrong with this. But . . . if it makes you uncomfortable, I can put my pants back on."

He still thinks of me as his wife? I know he's mentioned that he wants to give marriage a go in the future, but he thinks of me like that now? That's crazy, right?

I reach out my hand to stop him. "This is fine, this time. Unless we have rings on our fingers and a certificate in hand, this is as far as it will go." I raise a brow to make sure that he understands what I mean.

"After what I put you through, I have no problem taking things slow." He turns to look at the food on the table and holds out a hand. "Ms. Covington, your dinner awaits."

Candles are all over the table, along with sparkling cider, chocolate-covered strawberries, and what looks like pot roast and veggies—no wonder the house smelled amazing when we got home. I take a seat on the couch and Mike hands me a plate.

"Thank you. This all looks good."

We eat in silence, stealing glances at one another from time to time.

"Do you really see yourself as my husband?" I can't help but ask. Putting it out of my head is not working.

"In a way, I do." He takes our empty plates and puts them on the table, then takes my hand in his, turning so he can look at me. "You are the mother of my child. The woman I am deeply in love with. The only one I ever want to be with. I wouldn't be working so hard to make amends for the past if I didn't see a future with you." He smiles softly. "Kayla, if I could go back in time and change the way I was to you, I would. I hate that you have those memories of me. I know that I can never undo them, but I can show you that I am not that man anymore, and I can promise that I will stay in therapy for the rest of my life if it means that I get this chance with you. You and Bean are my world."

I reach out and move a stray hair that has fallen in his eyes and smile. "I love you, Michael, so much. I appreciate everything that you've done and continue to do."

Michael smiles, then turns and grabs the flutes with

cider and a tray of strawberries. He offers me the first, and when the juice of the strawberry threatens to run down the side of my mouth, he moves in for a kiss. "Delicious," he says as he pulls back.

Forgotten are the strawberries and cider—the only thing on my mind is the man in front of me, who I've never seen look happier than he does right now.

Maybe, just maybe, this time it'll work out.

# Chapter Thirty-Two

I line up ready to walk down the aisle, along with Leah and Janet's daughter Sheila. We look for our partners—or in Sheila's case, her younger brother. Her other brother will be escorting Janet.

When it's my turn, for the entire walk, I can't take my eyes off Uncle Joe. He's beaming with pride. Once we take our spots, I only have eyes for Mike. I love you, I mouth. He does so in return. It has been just over three weeks since the baby shower, and the day after tomorrow is my due date. We've had time to get the nursery done and personalize the house a bit. Not to mention the copious amount of make-out sessions we've had. Those have been some of my favorite moments since being home.

Leah turns and looks at me with a smile on her face. "You doing okay, sis?"

"Yeah," I whisper. "Just a sore back. It's hard carrying around such a big baby all day."

She chuckles, then all eyes turn to Janet. She is beautiful in her half-sleeve, knee-length, white-lace dress. Her hair is down with a simple pink rose to hold it back on one side.

I get a pain in my lower back that nearly takes me to the ground. I try to breathe through it and grit my teeth. I'm sure I've overdone it and need to sit down, and I will soon enough, but I don't want to interrupt their vows. I put my hand on my belly and rub. *Be good for Momma, Bean. We'll rest soon. I promise.*

Mike raises a brow in question. I smile and point at my back. He nods as if he knows. It's been hurting a lot more than normal these last few weeks.

"You may kiss your bride," the minister says.

I look that way and realize I missed them saying their vows, but the smile on Uncle Joe's face says it all. He's a man in love. He takes Janet in his arms and lays one on her that's a little too PG-13 to be inside a church. He dips her back and Tom wolf-whistles, causing me to chuckle. Uncle Joe picks up his bride and struts back down the aisle.

After Mike and I make it out to the corridor, I take a seat, needing to rest my back.

He sits next to me and starts rubbing it in soothing circles. "We can leave right now if you need to. I'm sure Uncle Joe and Janet would understand."

"Michael," I start, but another back spasm hits and I have to move around to try and get comfortable. "That man gave up everything to raise Leah and me. He put off his happiness all these years for us. I think I can give him an hour or two. I'll rest in a couple hours. I'll be fine."

Mike helps me up and we make our way across the street to the dance hall where the reception is being held. I find a table and take a seat, resting with my feet up until the dancing begins.

Uncle Joe and Janet share their first dance.

"Do you think you can do the dances?" Leah asks. "I see you favoring your back."

"I'm gonna try," I reply. When I see the look of worry in Mike's eyes, I take his hand in mine. "I'm fine, I promise. I won't overdo it. I'll rest when I'm not needed."

We're supposed to do a wedding party dance where all of us are on the floor, then both Leah and I will do our own father-daughter dances. I have at minimum two that I need to try and stand for, and it's not like they're fast songs.

The sound of "My Little Girl" by Tim McGraw comes over the speakers. Uncle Joe walks over to me and extends his hand to help me up. I take it and walk out to the center of the dance floor and wrap him in my arms, leaning my head on him as we sway.

"How are you holding up?" Uncle Joe asks.

I pull back and smile at him. "This is your wedding day. You shouldn't be worrying about me."

"Baby doll, I'll always worry about you. That's my job." He leans in and kisses my forehead.

"Thank you for being the best dad a girl could ever ask for." He starts to argue, but I kiss his cheek and carry on. "You and Leah have told me all kinds of stories about Dad, but you're the only one I've ever known. Mike and I have been talking about it a lot lately. Leah is naming the twins after our parents, and we'd like to name ours after my dad." He nods, and I pat his chest. "You, Uncle Joe. You are my dad. Michael and I have spoken and decided on a name." I wipe his eye as a tear slips free. "Your granddaughter's name is Lily Jo Buchannan."

Uncle Joe pulls us to a stop, his hands on my arms as he looks me over. He smiles so brightly that I nearly have to look away. "You're not playing with me, are you?"

I shake my head.

He throws his head back and laughs, then pulls me into him again. "You've just made this day so much better, and I didn't even think that was possible. My God, Kayla, I love you so much."

"I love you too."

Uncle Joe spins me out one last time as the song comes to an end, then bows to me. "It has been my honor to be your dad and now a grandpa to little Lily Jo. Poor baby girl, being named after the likes of me. She's going to be one tough kid. I hope you and Mike are ready."

I nod as Leah walks over for her dance. He kisses the side of my head and lets me go as he wraps his arms around my sister.

I find my way back to Mike, trying like hell to ignore the tightness in my lower back.

"Beautiful, I think it's time to call your doctor. This kind of back pain can't be normal."

"Let me get through this next dance and then you and I can leave. If you want to call her then, I won't argue. I probably should be seen." I sit next to Mike and lean back against him as he begins to rub my back.

"What if you're in labor?"

"If I am, you heard the same as I did. It can take hours, and we don't need to head to the hospitals until the contractions are five minutes apart for a couple hours. I have not had any contractions yet, just back pain."

Mike drops it.

In time, the wedding party is called up for our dance. Thankfully, they decided on a slow dance with the couples due to Leah and me being pregnant. I lean into Mike's embrace and let him hold me up. My lower back and further south begin to tense so hard it has me groaning in pain. I nearly double over—if not for him holding me up, I would have.

This is much more intense.

I really need to get off my feet.

I think this might be a contraction.

"Janet!" Mike hollers as I breathe through the pain.

If looks could kill, he'd be ashes right now. This is their wedding; it should be about them.

We could have snuck out.

She walks over to us as he holds me up, rubbing my back. I stand up a little better once the spasm passes.

She looks me over and furrows her brows. "You're too stubborn for your own good sometimes. How long have you been hurting like this?"

"This just started. But my back has been hurting all day." I smile shyly. "I'm fine. After this dance, I'll let Mike take me to the doctor's."

She shakes her head and looks at Mike. "Call the doctor, now. Tell them Kayla's on her way in. I'm pretty sure she's in active labor."

I want to cry but I keep my mouth shut. I know I won't win this one.

She pulls me from Mike and walks me to a chair to help me stand. The pain has started shooting down my legs now. "Sugar, there's such a thing as back labor. I wish you had told me."

I shake my head as another spasm hits. I lean over more and grumble as my knees nearly give out. "It's your wedding day!" I say through clenched teeth.

"I'd have married Joe in the waiting room of the hospital if I had known. Hon, it's not the fancy place that makes the marriage."

Uncle Joe's words about Lily Jo being tough couldn't be more fitting. As I'm standing here in a room filled with people . . . my water breaks.

"Michael!" Janet shouts.

He comes running over and sees what the fuss is, his eyes going wide.

"It's go time. Get her to the hospital now."

He starts to lift me, and I try to protest, but he's not having any of it. "Someone's going to have to give us a ride. My car's back at Joe's."

I wrap my arms around his neck and settle in.

Tom steps forward. "We've got you." Maddie has already started heading toward the door.

"We'll meet you there," Meg says.

"Us too," Leah chimes in.

Mike follows behind Tom as we make our way out of the reception hall. By the time we make it to his truck, I have to have Mike set me on my feet. The pain is so intense, all I want to do is scream, but I grit my teeth instead.

Mike rubs my back, then leans in to kiss my shoulder. "You've got this, beautiful. You are strong . . . You are beautiful . . . You are deserving. It won't be long and we'll be holding Lily in our arms, teaching her the same."

I nod. "Okay, let's go meet our daughter."

Michael smiles brightly and puts me in the back of the truck, climbing in and pulling me to his chest. He reaches over me as I lie down, feet toward the door, rubbing my belly. It hurts too much to sit upright.

Tom looks over his shoulder and smiles softly. "We're about twenty minutes out, but I'll do my best to cut that short. Just hang in there. Mike, keep her from falling out of the seat."

Another contraction hits hard. I try and breathe through it as best as I can while squeezing Mike's hand. The pain in my back is excruciating at this point.

"You're doing so good," Mike encourages.

Maddie hands him a cloth and Mike wipes my face. I'm sure I'm a mess.

"It's so hot," I complain.

"We'll be there soon," Tom says. "I'll crank up the AC."

A couple minutes pass and I feel us slowing down. "What's going on?" I ask.

"There must be an accident or something. Traffic seems to be coming to a stop. I'll see if I can get off at the next exit and we'll take back roads."

At this point, I don't know if we're going to make it. The contractions are coming on fast and hard. I've heard that labor takes hours, if not days. Unless the back pain from this morning was indeed labor, I've only been in it for less than an hour.

Tom looks over his shoulder at me and smiles softly. "Hang in there, Kay. We'll be there soon."

Ten minutes and another contraction later, we're still at a standstill. Another hits, and I'm so worn out already, I don't know how I'm going to do this. After it passes, I lay my head back on Michael's shoulder and close my eyes.

He rubs circles over my stomach and kisses my head. "You are the strongest woman I know. I love you so much."

I hum, unable to muster the strength to carry on a conversation. I feel Tom change lanes and then pick up speed. I look and see that he's gotten off the interstate. No sooner than we make it to the bottom of the hill does another hit.

"I don't—" I try. The burning is so bad, I cry out. "Owww. Oh my God, I think she's coming!"

Mike maneuvers so that he's holding my head with one hand as he scoots to lift my dress to check. His eyes get big as he looks at me and then at Tom. He swallows hard, and with a slight tremble to his voice, he starts. "You better pull over, man. I see the baby's head." Mike moves back so that he's supporting my back.

"Okay, okay. Maddie, call an ambulance and tell them where we are. Mike, I have a go bag on the floor back there. Get out a blanket, and as soon as we park, you'll need to move."

"Have you done this before?" Maddie asks.

"Yeah, twice," he replies. "Don't worry, I can help until the EMT gets here."

"What?" I cry. I did not picture having her here, on the side of the road. The last person I imagined birthing my daughter was Tom. I look up at Mike as tears roll down my cheeks.

He wipes them and kisses my head. "You are so strong. You can do this."

"I can't," I cry.

"You *can*," he states. He takes my hand in his and kisses it. "You've got this."

I'm so scared.

What if I can't do this?

What if something happens to Bean?

Mike nudges me to look at him. "You've. Got. This."

I nod. At this point, I don't have much of a choice. I have to do this.

Tom pulls us into a gravel turnaround at the end of the road and parks so my side of the truck is facing some trees. Michael hops out and switches places with Maddie. He leans over the front seat while Maddie gets in behind me to help prop me up.

Tom grabs his bag, lays some mat under me, puts on some gloves, then he looks at me and smiles. "I know this has got to be weird for you, but right now, I'm just a first responder, okay? Don't let this—"

He's cut off by me groaning through a very intense contraction. Mike takes my hand in his and I squeeze through it.

Once it passes, Tom lays something over the top of my legs and gets started. "On your next contraction, you need to push." He takes my feet and puts them on either side of the door frame. I swear I want to cry, but the next contraction hits and I give it all I've got.

Within twenty minutes, the EMT is here, and Lily is close. Instead of taking over, they only assist.

Lily Jo Buchannan is born on the side of the road, assisted by her adopted Uncle Tom, Daddy, adopted Auntie Maddie, and an EMT. They lay her on my chest and step back to get the stretcher. Tom stands behind Maddie, holding her against him. Mike leans over the seat, one hand on my cheek, the other touching his daughter's tiny hand. She's the most beautiful baby I've ever seen. How can I love her so much already? There isn't a thing I wouldn't do for her.

# Chapter Thirty-Three

*Five months later*

Mike and I stand in the airport waiting for Megan and Damon. We had to postpone our annual Vegas trip by a few months, but we're still making it. With Lily's birth, then the planning and execution of Damon and Megan's quickie wedding—they got engaged the same night of my shower and decided they didn't want to wait to get married—followed shortly by Leah and Cam's twins coming along, there was no time to leave. Now that Lily is five months old, we're able to slip away. I already miss her like crazy, but she's at home with her Grandpa Joe and

Grandma Janet. I know she'll be well cared for.

"They'll be here," Mike says, pulling me against his chest. He leans in and kisses the back of my head. "They've never missed one before, so I don't see them starting now."

I turn and wrap my arms around the back of his neck and lean in. There are times when I miss having a pregnant belly, but times like this, when I can stand flush against his hard planes, are not those moments.

Last week, Michael and I celebrated seven months of being together, and though I love making out like a lovesick teen, it's starting to drive me crazy. I told him when we started this that we needed to take things slow and that there would be no procreating unless we said vows. He agreed, but living together, raising our daughter, and then finding our way to separate rooms each night is driving me nuts. It's not so much the actual act that I crave as much as falling asleep in his arms and waking up next to him every day.

He leans in and kisses my nose. "I love you, beautiful."

"We're here, we're here!" Meg hollers.

I turn my head enough to see her coming, but before I let go and step back, I lean in and give him a sweet kiss. "I love you too."

I turn just in time to see Megan leave Damon and head

my way. "Hey, chica. You ready for this?"

"As long as it's better than the last one, I'm all for it." My shoulders deflate. "I already miss Lily, though."

"Same," she says. "I might not be her momma, but I miss that kiddo every day she isn't with me."

Meg and Damon are at the house so much that we tried for months to convince them to build a home nearby. I even offered a piece of property to them. They refused, but then last week, they let me know that they closed on a plot across the way from us. They break ground on their home this spring. Megan told Damon that she couldn't picture growing a family while living on such a busy street, no matter how much she loves their home. That next day, he called Tom to get the number of the guy who owned the property.

"Ladies," Mike says. He reaches out his arm toward me. I take his hand and melt into him. "It's time to board."

I furrow my brows. "They haven't called for boarding yet."

"You must have not heard it," he replies.

I link my fingers in his and walk over to the gate, bypassing the line that is starting to form. Mike lets them scan our tickets and we're allowed to board.

"First class?" I question.

Mike smiles. "It's my turn to treat my girl. I have some making up to do. Vegas should be filled with good memories, not bad. Let's consider this a do-over." This man. I swear he's still showing me that what happened last year is not who he really is.

Megan elbows me, smiling. "Looks like it's your turn to get spoiled."

I shrug her off with a smile on my face. While I don't need Michael to spoil me, if he wants a redo of last year, who am I to argue?

He tucks away our carry-ons as I grab the window seat. Meg and D take the seats across from us.

Mike sits down and I wrap my arm around his and cuddle in.

"Sleep well, beautiful. I'll wake you when we get there."

"What makes you think I'm going to sleep?" I tease.

He laughs. "Only about the ninety-eight percent of flights that we've shared where you've fallen asleep."

I lean up and give him a quick kiss. "I guess I'll see you in Vegas then."

Mike chuckles and rubs the back of my head before he looks across the aisle and starts talking to Damon.

"Hey, beautiful," Mike says. "We're here."

I sit up, wiping the spittle from the corner of my mouth and stretch. Mike grabs our bags and leads the way.

Meg takes my hand in hers and hangs back a tad. "We need to talk."

I raise my brow but nod in confirmation that I heard.

Once we're off the plane, I find the closest restroom and pull Megan inside. Thankfully, it's a private bathroom and I don't have to start searching stalls. Megan walks to the sink, and I hop on the counter.

"Okay, spill."

"I'm three weeks late," she whines,

I start to squeal, but she puts her hand to my mouth quickly with big eyes looking back at me. "Don't. You can't say anything! I don't know if I am or not, but I need to find out before Damon starts pouring me drinks."

"Why not just tell him? You know he'll be over the moon with joy."

Megan smirks. "I know he will, but Kay, I don't want to get his hopes up. We're not even trying yet, so if I tell him I might be, he'll make baby talk a part of every conversation. I love the man to death, but I need to know before I tell him anything."

"Okay, I'm going to tell Mike to meet us at baggage claim. We'll stop at the shop on the way, claiming female troubles, and grab a test. If you're that late, we should be able to slip into the bathroom there and take it. You'll know before we leave."

Megan links her arm in mine as I hop down. "Do you think he'll buy it?"

"I know he will."

We step out and make way to the guys.

I lean in and kiss Mike, then whisper, "Meg needs me. Girl problems."

He just nods.

"Meet us at baggage claim? We have to run into the shop really quick."

He looks at me in question. "I'm not leaving you alone in the Vegas airport. We'll wait outside and give you twosome privacy."

We start walking and I give Meg a thumbs-up.

"I can tell D all about Lily saying *da-da* first," Mike teases.

"Really?" I question, shaking my head. I really don't think she has said any real words yet. Baby babble sure, but she isn't saying actual words. Besides, I've been saying *ma-ma* nonstop. When she does finally speak, I'm sure it'll be that.

The convenience store comes into sight, and I leave Mike's side to make my way there. I grab Meg and pull her with me. Damon seems confused, but Mike leads him to the bench nearby. I head directly to the aisle carrying the tests and grab three that mention early testing. Meg pays, then we find the bathroom and make sure the door is locked behind us. Meg takes the little coffee cup she snatched along the way and does her business while I begin reading the instructions. In no time, all three tests are laid out on the counter and all we're waiting on is the timer. She's pacing the room, chewing on her nails.

"What are you more nervous about? It saying yes or no?"

"I'm not sure. I'd love to have a kid with Damon, but we haven't even started trying. What if he gets mad?"
I stop her with my hands on her arms and make her look at me. "Do you honestly think that?"

She looks down at the ground. "Probably not, but I'm freaking out here. I don't know why."

I smile. "Because you might be pregnant. That's a big deal, especially when you're not planning on it."

The timer goes off and her eyes get big.

"Do you want me to look?"

She nods.

I walk over to the counter and take them in my hand.

*Positive.*

*Positive.*

*Positive.*

I smile and look over at Meg. "Honey, you're having a baby."

Tears begin to fall, and she crouches down, hands to her mouth.

I walk over and kneel beside her, hugging her as she lets it out. "Are you okay?"

She nods. "I'm pregnant?"

"Yes, honey. You are."

"I'm having a baby!" she squeals. She stands, and the smile on her face begins to grow. Megan puts a hand to her still-flat stomach and whispers, "I'm having a baby."

I nod with a smile on my face. "You are."

After we share another hug, Megan puts herself back together. We drop the tests into one box and in her bag. She takes one deep breath, and we open the door, determined to make this trip the best yet.

The next morning, Megan and I lie in bed and look at pictures of Lily. Mike got us a room similar to what we had last year. I'm glad he didn't get the same room, but then again, it was hard even coming in here. Since Mike and I aren't sleeping together, Megan volunteered to stay with me in the double bed rather than Mike and me sharing separate beds in the same room. Damon grumbled a lot, but when she said that she needed a girls' night, he relented.

There's a knock at the door and Damon sticks his head in. When he sees that we're decent, he pushes the door open, and he and Mike walks in with trays in hand. Megan and I sit up, making room for them to join us. Damon hands Megan a plate of eggs Benedict and fresh fruit.

I see her hand fly up and I grab the plate from her right before the bedding is thrown back as she runs to the bathroom. Damon is caught off guard, unsure of what just happened.

"Go take care of her," I tell him.

He nods and heads that way.

Mike looks at me in question, but I don't have to say a thing.

"You're pregnant?" Damon shouts. There's a pause, and then he says it once more in a loving manner.

Michael smiles at me, then sits. "I'm still sorry for how things started with us. I wish I had been better from the start."

Setting down Meg's plate, I move to sit in his lap. "This is your do-over. The past is where it needs to stay."
Mike pulls me closer and takes a deep breath. "I love you."

"I love you too."

Michael and I finish eating and then take in a show on the Strip while Damon and Megan stay back at the hotel so she can rest. We meet at a restaurant not far from our hotel for dinner. Meg looks to be doing so much better. She even eats most of her meal. Then we walk back to our shared room to get ready for the night.

We're nearing the fountain when Mike pulls me aside.

He takes my hand in his and looks like he's about ready to pass out.

I put my hand to his cheek, and he melts into my hand for a moment, closing his eyes.

"Are you okay?"

He opens them and nods. "This is the same spot where our lives changed last time we were here."

I nod, not wanting to look around. The last time I did, the romantic setting was everything—the day after, not so much. I'd be lying if I said it didn't still sting.

"This is also the spot that I want to take back as ours. I can see why I thought that this was the perfect place the first time." Michael looks over my shoulder and smiles.

I turn and spot Damon and Megan standing there, looking at us with huge smiles on their faces.

Mike puts a hand on my waist.

I turn back and find him on his knee. Again.

My heart feels like it's beating out of its chest and my knees are weak. I take a calming breath and look down at him. His smile is unsure. I take his hand to assure him that I'm here with him.

"I can stop if it's too much."

"I'm good." For a moment, I started to freak out—over the location, not him asking. But I'm good now.

"Kayla," Mike starts. "I knew getting down on one knee in this location would be a risk, but it's one worth taking. What I did the first time was not fair of me. I took all your firsts from you. That thought still haunts me . . ." He trails off, but then looks up at me and smiles. "This is our do-over—our coming home. During the lowest parts of my life, you were my anchor, the one who taught me that love is not something that hurts, but something that can be beautiful. It fascinates me how far we've come, that you opened yourself up and gave me a second chance." He reaches behind him, pulls out a tiny box, and opens it. I only see Michael. "Through it all, one thing has never changed—you are who I want to spend the rest of my life with. Will you do me the honor of becoming my wife?"

Through a teary smile, I answer. "Yes! *Absolutely*, yes!"

He puts the ring on my finger and stands, leaning in for a kiss.

Michael pulls back and shoots an arm in the air. Head tilted back, he shouts, "She said yes! This amazing woman agreed to be my wife."

I take his collar, pulling him to me. Behind us, they're hooting and hollering as my lips descend on his.

"Tonight," I say as I kiss his jaw. "We marry tonight."

Not wasting another minute, I find his lips with mine.

*Dreams do come true.*

H K Brown's *Coming Home* is book two in the Baycliff Valley Series. Keep following along to find out what's going on between Tom and Maddie. Will they finally let loose and make a go of things or will they move on and find happiness elsewhere?

*Standing Strong*—book three of the Baycliff Valley Series —coming soon.

**Follow me for up-to-date information.**

**Facebook:** authorhkbrown

**Instagram:** authorhkbrown

**TikTok:** hkbrown_author

Make sure to join my mailing list.

Subscribers get to see cover reveals and receive general

information earlier than those who don't.

**www.authorhkbrown.com**